"Mercy, I want you.

"I want to make love to you, Mercy," Sam whispered, following her down, leaning on his side and one arm while the other continued to pleasure her. "Let me make love to you, Mercy, honey...."

"No, I don't think—" She looked around her, away from him. Heavens, it was more of a case of she *couldn't* think, not while his mouth was just two inches from hers and while his stroking was making her tingle all over.

"You don't want me to make love to you out here in the open, under the stars?" he murmured, his breath warm against her ear. "Mercy, I think you're about the loveliest thing I've ever seen in the moonlight—it makes your eyes all silvery and mysterious." He stopped and kissed her lingeringly. "I just can't even *begin* to imagine how pretty the rest of you would look dressed in nothing but moonlight...."

Dear Reader,

Love and loyalty clash in *Devil's Dare* by Laurie Grant, a fast-paced Western about a sweet-talking cowboy and a straitlaced preacher's daughter whom he mistakes for a soiled dove. We hope you enjoy this delightful tale from recent Readers' Choice winner Laurie Grant.

The Gambler's Heart is the third book in Gayle Wilson's Heart Trilogy. This passionate Regency features a war-scarred French gambler who acquires a wife as payment for a debt, and must learn to accept her love for him. We are also pleased to bring you the second book in Susan Paul's medieval Bride Trilogy, *The Heiress Bride*, the lively story of a rogue knight running from his past and a strong-willed noblewoman running from her future.

Elizabeth Lane's *Lydia*, our fourth selection for the month, is the touching story of a former Union spy who moves to Colorado and falls in love with the brother of a man who died as a result of her actions.

Whatever your taste in reading, we hope that Harlequin Historicals will keep you coming back for more. Please keep a lookout for all four titles, available wherever Harlequin books are sold.

Sincerely,

Tracy Farrell
Senior Editor

Please address questions and book requests to:
Harlequin Reader Service
U.S.: 3010 Walden Ave., P.O. Box 1325, Buffalo, NY 14269
Canadian: P.O. Box 609, Fort Erie, Ont. L2A 5X3

Devil's Dare

Laurie Grant

Harlequin Books

TORONTO • NEW YORK • LONDON
AMSTERDAM • PARIS • SYDNEY • HAMBURG
STOCKHOLM • ATHENS • TOKYO • MILAN
MADRID • WARSAW • BUDAPEST • AUCKLAND

ISBN 0-373-28900-6

DEVIL'S DARE

This edition published by arrangement with Harlequin Books S.A.

Printed in U.S.A.

Books by Laurie Grant

Harlequin Historicals

Beloved Deceiver #170
The Raven and the Swan #205
Lord Liar #257
Devil's Dare #300

LAURIE GRANT

combines a career as a trauma center emergency room nurse with that of historical romance author; she says the writing helps keep her sane. Passionately enthusiastic about the history of both England and Texas, she divides her travel time between these two spots. She is married to her own real-life hero, and has two teenage daughters, two dogs and a cat.

If you would like to write the author of *Devil's Dare*, please use the address below:

Laurie Grant
P.O. Box 307274
Gahanna, OH 43230

With grateful thanks to the Abilene Heritage Center for their invaluable assistance in my research, to Rebecca Brandewyne for providing information on the natural features, flora and fauna of the region, and to Ann Bouricius, tireless critique partner and friend.

And, as always, thanks to Michael, who keeps me going with his love and moral support—and who kept me from using the wrong knife.

Chapter One

"Gentlemen, Abilene is a fine town," Wyatt Earp, one of Abilene's premier cardsharps, told them as they sagged against the stock pen that held the three thousand milling, bawling longhorns they'd trailed all the way from Texas. "You may ask why I think so. Well, boys, Abilene is a fine town because there's so much easy money in it, so much sin and so little law. Why, there's twenty saloons, twenty gambling houses and ten dance halls—as well as three restaurants, for when you're all tuckered out from all that carousin' and just want some tasty vittles. Yessir, I believe you boys are gonna have a high time here, a high time indeed."

Sam Houston Devlin began to grin as he pushed back his wide-brimmed hat. After endless weeks on the trail, driving the meanest beeves on four hooves over the plains and through the rivers, enduring storms, stampedes and endless dust, dodging Indians and rustlers, he was more than ready for a little fun. In fact, if he looked back on his twenty-five years, it seemed as if he couldn't remember having fun since he'd left home at eighteen to join the Confederate army.

Following the grim years of war, during which he'd grown to manhood, he'd returned to find the Devlin farm close to ruin. Three dreary years of hard work had followed, until at last he'd realized the only way to recoup their prosperity was by rounding up the hundreds of longhorned cattle, running loose in the brush, and driving them to market in Kansas.

And now he was here at last in Abilene—trail's end. Once he'd paid the men's wages and allowed for expenses, he figured he'd have some thirty-six thousand dollars to take home with him. Seemed like he'd earned a good time before returning home to Texas, and it sounded as if Abilene was ready and willing to oblige him.

"And if you'll join me down at the Alamo Saloon tonight," the cardsharp continued, "I'll see that you have the finest time playin' monte and poker and faro you ever thought of having. And cards, gentlemen, are just the beginning. The liquor flows freely at the Alamo, boys, and the women, well . . . they ain't free, but they're pretty easy."

A collective guffaw greeted his sally. The "Devil's Boys," as Sam's crew liked to call themselves, were even more eager to begin tasting the delights of Abilene than their trail boss, if that was possible.

"We'll be there with bells on," promised one of the drovers, and there was echoed agreement all around him. "And just where *is* this Alamo Saloon, Mr. Earp?"

"Why, the corner of Cedar and Texas streets, the two streets where all the pleasures a cowboy could hope to have are located," Earp answered. "I'll be at my regular table 'bout seven, okay, gents? Meanwhile, be sure not t' miss the promenade."

"Th' promenade?" questioned one of the younger hands, a baby-faced kid they called "Boy" Henderson for his beardless cheeks.

Earp smiled at the youth, then pulled out an ornate gold pocket watch and flipped the case open, studying it. "Fellas, you're in luck. It's just half an hour before the daily ritual unique to this fine town. Every day except Sunday, at nigh onta four o'clock, the sportin girls' of Hattie's Hot-House and Saleratus Sal's Sink of Sin go for a stroll down Texas Street, yonder." Earp pointed to where the facades of buildings could be seen through the dust raised by the milling, bawling longhorns. "If you'll walk on up the street, gentlemen, you'll have plenty of time to select the ideal vantage point, so as not to miss a collection of female pulchritude that will fairly make your mouth water."

"I sure 'nough don't wanta miss any o' that!" Boy Henderson exclaimed, and spun around, bolting in the direction of the promised spectacle. "Come on, fellows!" he called over his shoulder with a beckoning wave.

"Hey, Henderson, don't you think you're forgetting something?" drawled Sam.

The youth looked back, and seeing that none of the other men had moved from where they had been lounging against the stock pens, he halted. "What, Sam?" he asked. None of his crew called him "Mr. Devlin." Sam was not one to stand on ceremony.

"Aren't you gonna draw your pay, Boy?" Sam reminded him with a teasing grin. "Lookin's free, but you got a hundred and twenty dollars comin' to you after all those weeks on the trail, and I don't think that these fancy girls are gonna let you do more than look unless your pockets are full. And you *do* want to do more than look, don't you?"

"Gosh dang, yes!" he replied with so much enthusiasm that the rest of the cowboys snickered, causing Boy to blush.

"Then come on back and stand still while I divide the money you boys have comin'," Sam said, wondering if he'd looked that eager the first time he'd been taken to that brothel in New Orleans before the war. Lord, to be that young and innocent again! Compared to Boy, most days he felt a hundred weary years old. But now that he'd have gold jingling in his pocket again, he meant to see if he could reclaim some of his lost spirits. And perhaps Texas Street had a female or two who could help him try.

The pay was soon dispensed. All but one of the hands took their money with smiles and remarks about wanting to work for Devlin on subsequent drives.

"A hunnerd and twenty dollars don't seem like much fer three months' work and nearly gettin' drowned in the Red River," Tom Culhane mumbled sourly.

"You knew the wage when you signed on, Tom," Sam Devlin said evenly, hoping an ugly fight wasn't going to mar their first night in town. "And danger comes with the work. Hellfire, you probably wouldn't have had any difficulty in the river if you hadn't ridden the horse I told you was a panicky swimmer. As it was, you got a good cowboy drowned." Culhane's lower lip drooped sulkily. It was obvious he didn't like being reminded that the tragic incident at the Red River was essentially his fault.

"You give Jase Lowry a hunnerd an' forty," Tom Culhane retorted.

"Jase Lowry's my point man, my second-in-command," Sam reminded him. "If anything had happened to me, it would have fallen to Jase to get the herd to Abilene and take the profits home to my family. He gets paid more for taking more responsibility." Sam kept his tone neutral.

Tom walked off, grumbling. Sam supposed Tom would either get over his sulk and appear again next spring, looking for work, or he wouldn't. And if he didn't, that was just fine by him. Culhane had shown a tendency to bellyache about every little hitch that came up on the drive, and on a three-month drive, that was a lot of bellyaching he'd just as soon not have listened to.

* * *

"Heavenly days, Mercy, just *look* at them," said Charity with a sigh, her face enraptured at the sight of so many handsome cowboys lining the opposite side of the street.

"Charity Fairweather, I declare, you're such a featherbrain! I should have known better than to bring you out on the street with me any time from spring to fall!" snapped her older sister, Mercy, trying in vain to pull Charity away from her vantage point at the window of Moon's Frontier Store. In the fall and winter Abilene was free of the scourge of Texan invaders. "Come away before one of them sees you!"

"It won't hurt to look," the fifteen-year-old girl insisted stubbornly, smoothing her blond corkscrew curls and pinching her cheeks as she continued to study the lined-up men with their tanned faces, leather chaps and red bandannas.

"Well, looking better be all you're doing," warned Mercy in an exasperated voice. "Charity, aren't you ever worried that you're going to get a reputation for being *fast?*" she hissed. A wary glance over her shoulder confirmed that Mrs. Horace Barnes, the chief of Abilene's gossips, had entered the mercantile and was trying not to look as if she were eavesdropping on the conversation. It was clear as day from her smirking expression, however, that she was.

"Oh, pooh! Anything faster than a turtle is considered fast by Papa's congregation." Charity sniffed. "And you talk just like them. You'd think you were an old maid, instead of just eighteen! Ooh, just look at the tall one over there, the one with the dark mustache! Doesn't he look just like a desperado?" she asked in awed tones.

"He probably is, the rest of the year," Mercy said tartly before repeating, "Come away before he sees you." Charity ignored her, of course. And Mercy found she couldn't help looking through the fly-specked, blurry window in the direction her sister's pointing finger indicated.

The stranger lounged at his ease against a hitching rail, his thumbs hooked through the belt loops of his denims above the black leather chaps. He did indeed look like a dangerous character with the brim of his hat shadowing most of his face. All she could see were high, angular cheekbones and a black, shaggy mustache above an unsmiling mouth.

The cowboy was talking to another man, probably a cardsharp, Mercy guessed after studying the other man's fancy waistcoat and its hanging watch chain. As she watched, something the cardsharp said must have struck the stranger as funny, for suddenly the tightly held mouth relaxed, parting in a grin. He tipped his head back, and she caught a glimpse of eyes crinkled with merriment.

That grin not only transformed the lean, angular features, but produced some startling changes in Mercy, too. All at once she felt warm all over, as if she'd worn black flannel instead of her light, figured calico everyday dress. Her pulse raced.

How ridiculous, she chided herself, to feel so silly about one of those wild hellions from Texas who swept through Abilene from May to September, drinking tanglefoot, shooting up the town and sending respectable citizens diving for cover. "Hurrahing the town," they called it. But now that she'd seen this particular cowboy smile, she knew she'd have to make certain that he and Charity never met. He was just the sort of man who could wreck her sister's tenuous hold on virtue.

Worried, Mercy glanced back at her sister, but with so much walking virility to feast her eyes on, Charity had already been distracted. Her eyes had wandered to a towheaded, somewhat bowlegged cowboy down the street who was tipping his hat to a lady—

Who was no lady, Mercy realized as the first of the working girls strolled past Moon's Frontier Store.

"The shameless hussies!" hissed Abigail Barnes. The big, homely woman had come up soundlessly behind them and was now peering out the window between the sisters' shoulders. "They shouldn't be allowed in the same town as decent women, my Horace always says. Someone should do something!"

The women were indeed a fearsome sight in their gaudy-hued dresses with tight, low-cut bodices and two-foot bustles that caused their skirts to sway gracefully behind them like the wakes of ships. As they descended the plank sidewalk to the street, they raised the edges of their spangled skirts to clear the dust. The action revealed layer upon layer of red petticoats and tasseled boots with a single star at the top of each.

Outside, the cowboys lining the street began cheering raucously and throwing their hats up in the air. The man Mercy had been watching, however, did not join in any of the boisterous behavior; he merely continued eyeing the painted women in a speculative sort of way. What was he thinking? she wondered. Was he selecting the one he wanted to buy for the night? The thought made her vaguely heartsick, though she did not know why.

"Why, they're pretty, in a bold sort of way, aren't they, Mercy?" Charity said, eyeing the town's infamous "soiled doves" with curiosity. "What is that sticking out of the tops of some of their boots?"

"Pearl-handled derringers," Abigail Barnes answered, as if Charity had been speaking to her. "Those Jezebels always carry their pistols in the right boot, and their ill-gotten gains in the left," Abigail Barnes huffed, her breath smelling of stale onions.

"They carry money in their boots? How do they get the money?" Charity asked, her face a study of puzzled interest.

"Never you mind," Mercy said quickly. "Come on, we've got to go." She grabbed her sister's wrist and started pulling her in the direction of the back entrance.

"But *Mercy,* wait, I wasn't ready!" wailed Charity.

Mercy ignored her and kept pulling. She didn't want Abigail Barnes to have time to commence a lecture as to how a fallen woman earned her living. As it was, she'd probably have to contend with the gossipy, shovel-faced woman telling the Ladies' Missionary Society about Charity Fairweather's indecorous interest in saloon girls, which was bound to get back to their father.

She couldn't resist one last look behind, though, at the rangy, dark-featured cowboy across the street. But he was no longer there.

Chapter Two

"A mighty fine supper, girls, mighty fine indeed," the Reverend Jeremiah Fairweather exclaimed in praise. "You know chicken and dumplings are my very favorite—and it's not even Sunday!" he added, patting a nonexistent paunch as he favored Mercy and Charity with a benign smile.

"Thank you, Papa," Charity said, dimpling prettily. "We do like to make you happy."

"God bless you, child, you are such a comfort to me since your mother passed on," Fairweather said, reaching out a bony hand to pat his younger daughter's golden curls.

Mercy, seated opposite, studied her sister with wry amusement. Charity had had little to do with the preparation of dinner beyond keeping her sister company while Mercy had plucked the chicken and cut it up. Then Mercy had rolled out the dumplings, because Charity, whose job that was supposed to be, had been too busy chattering about the charms of the cowboys she had seen lined up on the street. It was just as well, Mercy reflected. Charity was too tenderhearted to wring a chicken's neck effectively, usually resulting in a hen that pecked and struggled pitifully until Mercy finally took over to put it out of its misery. And Charity's dumplings were usually heavy as lead, causing the displeasure of their father to descend on both of them. No, as long as Papa was satisfied with his supper, peace would reign in the Fairweather household, at least for the moment.

"And what did you do today, daughters, other than prepare this fine repast for your poor widowed father, that is?" Jeremiah Fairweather inquired with genial interest. Behind his spectacles, his pale blue eyes regarded them with keen attention.

Here was dangerous ground. Mercy remembered she had not spoken to her sister about avoiding a certain subject. "Well, we had to go to the store, since we were out of flour for the dumplings, and I needed some more thread to mend your shirt," she told her father, then covertly sent a warning look at Charity. *Please, Lord, don't let her bring up the cowboys and get Papa started,* Mercy prayed, gripping the scarred old dining table underneath its much-mended, second-best tablecloth.

Perhaps the Lord was busy just now, for Charity's first words made Mercy's heart sink.

"Oh, Papa, you just can't imagine the sight we saw from the store window," gushed Charity. "The most handsome men I've ever seen, and there must have been twenty of them, all cowboys, all dressed in spurs and chaps and wearing two six-guns apiece and throwing their hats up in the air...."

Honestly, how could her younger sister have lived with her father for fifteen years and not learned what set him off? Was she really oblivious to the sudden chill in the room, and the cold fire that blazed up in their father's eyes?

"Oh? And just what were these *handsome cowboys* throwing their hats in the air *about,* Charity?" Jeremiah Fairweather asked with deceptive calm.

Too late, Charity appeared to see the abyss yawning in front of her. Mercy saw her sister swallow hard and try but fail to meet their father's eyes.

"Oh...nothing...just an excess of good spirits, I guess..." she said, her eyes fixed on a spot on the wall just above their father's thinning, carrot-colored hair. "I mean, well...they've just come in from weeks on the trail, and..."

"Charity Elizabeth Fairweather, you've never been a good prevaricator, and I'd strongly advise you not to start now," her father said in a voice that he had not raised but that somehow seemed to reverberate from all corners of the room. It was the same voice that successfully convicted sinners and usually brought at least one woman to tears every Sunday morning during the services, which they were still holding in their house due to the lack of a proper church building.

"Pre-pre-varicator?" Charity asked. Mercy knew she was playing for time, hoping to find her way out of the maze that was leading straight to their father's wrath, but she didn't hold out too much hope her sister would find it. Charity never could think very quickly—she was too intimidated by the basilisk stare her father was so good at training on her when she erred. Mercy watched, fascinated, as beads of perspiration broke out on her sister's pale brow during the silence.

"You know very well what it means, young lady. It means *liar.* You are lying to me about what those imps of hell, those Texas demons were cheering so heartily about. I would advise you to tell me at once."

Charity swallowed convulsively again, and stared into her lap. A tear, illuminated by the lamplight, shone crystalline as it trickled down her white cheek. "They were—" she began, then stopped as a sob erupted from her instead of more words.

"I'm *waiting,* young lady. They were what?"

Mercy couldn't stand it any longer. "They were cheering at fallen women, Papa. Saloon girls that were parading past them."

Once Mercy had blazed the way for her, Charity seemed impelled to confess the rest. "They wore low-cut dresses, Papa, and boots, with a gun in one and their money in the other. Though I don't really understand how they get the money," she added miserably.

"And just *how* did you learn that these... these *women* had *money* in their boots?" the reverend asked in sepulchral tones. "Did you, perchance, go out on the street and *interview* one of these Jezebels?"

"Oh, no, Papa, Mrs. Barnes told me," Charity hastened to reassure their father, brightening.

Charity had thought she was beginning to climb out of the abyss, but Mercy knew better. If there was anything their father couldn't stand, it was the thought of his small congregation knowing that he or his children were less than perfect. And evidencing curiosity in prostitutes certainly indicated a want of perfection in the Reverend Jeremiah Fairweather's eyes.

The reverend placed the spread fingers of one hand over his bowed head for a moment, as if praying for strength, then lowered them. He gazed at Charity, who stared back, much as a cornered rabbit will stare at the hawk who is about to descend on it. "Daughter, the cowboy, especially that species that ascends to us from Texas, has no regard for law, morals or virtue, defying the first, deriding the second and outraging the third. He has no respect for man, no fear of God, no dread of hell." Mercy recognized the words from a recent sermon, and knew her father was going to wind up to a real diatribe if she didn't do something.

"Papa, there wasn't any harm done," she said hastily. "I got her out of there by the back entrance as soon as I saw the women parading past."

But the Reverend Mr. Fairweather was warming to his subject, and paid her no heed. "My child, in the words of Scripture, 'a whore is a deep ditch, and a strange woman is a narrow pit. She also lieth in wait as for a prey, and increaseth the transgressors among men,' while a virtuous woman, on the other hand, is 'worth more than rubies.' Charity, do you understand what a *whore* is?"

"No, Papa," came the soft answer, the voice still choked with tears.

Mercy quickly lowered her eyes to her lap, afraid their father would somehow discern that she *did* know what the harsh word meant, and would feel the need to go on with his tirade. She'd known ever since she'd overheard the word during their wagon-train trip to Kansas, when some of the bachelors were talking about what they'd do when they next came to a town. She'd gone to her mother, instinctively knowing this wasn't a word she could ask Papa about. Mama had answered her question matter-of-factly, but had gently confirmed her feeling that this wasn't something ladies were supposed to know about. Their mother was dead now, though, the victim of pneumonia during their first winter, when they had lived in a soddy, and she couldn't refer Charity to her to have her questions answered.

"Very well, then we will not say more about them, except to say that they are evil women and evil men, and you are to have nothing to do with them," the reverend said. "If you are so unfortunate as to encounter them on unavoidable trips to town, you are to look the other way. If one of either group should be so bold as to speak to you, you are to ignore them. Is that clear, Charity Elizabeth Fairweather?" Mercy realized with sudden clarity that their father didn't understand her younger sister at all. There was no surer way to fix Charity's interest in a subject than to forbid her to have any interest in that subject. Nothing had really been explained to Charity about *why* the women were bad, and what they did with the cowboys that made them bad, so she would be all the more determined to find out.

She sighed. She'd given her sister an elementary explanation about the birds and the bees a couple of years ago, but now she'd have to go into more detail. She would have to explain the whole matter at night, when they'd gone to bed in the room they shared. *Mama, give me the right words.*

"Dessert, Papa? I made peach pie," she said, relaxing somewhat now that the storm had passed over and neither she nor her sister were too wet.

"In a moment, Mercy. I have not finished," their father said in that precise way of his that told her not to look for any rainbows just yet. "Of course, there must be consequences to every action. Yours, Charity, is that you are to go to your room now and memorize Proverbs chapter thirty-one, verses ten through thirty-one, so that you can recite it at the prayer meeting tonight and so that you will know the qualities of the virtuous woman."

Charity's eyes, a deeper blue than their father's, widened. "But Papa, that's...let's see, twenty-one verses! And the meeting starts in an hour!"

"Then you had better get busy, had you not?" her father responded serenely.

"Yessir," Charity said, her lower lip jutting out, a sure sign, Mercy knew, of incipient rebellion in her sister. But Charity left the table quietly enough and headed down the hall to their bedroom.

Mercy sighed. Charity's punishment was punishment for her, too, for it meant she had the sole responsibility for cleaning up after dinner, washing and drying the dishes. Drat it! She had intended to see that Charity did most of it, since she'd been so little help during the preparation. Mercy had rather wanted to take time to change her dress and comb her hair in case Ned Webster chanced to come.

Ned, the son of the local blacksmith, became all red-faced and tongue-tied whenever he was around her, but she thought he liked her just a little. And though she despaired of Ned's ever framing a whole sentence to her, let alone asking if he could come calling, he was the only boy in town who came to Sunday services on a regular basis—which made him the only boy in Abilene Mercy would be allowed to keep company with. And unless another youth could be persuaded to start attending, God only knew who would be allowed to court Charity.

At about the same time that Charity Fairweather was reciting "the heart of her husband doth safely trust in her" to a properly hushed dozen members of the Abilene First Baptist Church, meeting in the Fairweather parlor, Samuel Houston Devlin was leaving his room in the Drover's Cottage, the hotel set up for the cowboys in off the trail. He had had a bath, a haircut, and a shave, and he felt like a new man. He'd gone to Moon's Frontier Store and bought himself some new clothes, a new pair of denims and a shirt, eschewing the shirts with the fancy celluloid collars and cuffs and derby hats that some of the boys were buying, for such garb would feel foolish. He didn't want to look like some sort of Eastern tinhorn. His only concession to vanity had been a brand-new pair of boots, complete with the lone star and crescent stitched in at the top of each. Yessir, he was ready to find the calico queens of Abilene, as the working girls were sometimes called, or to let them find him.

He headed for the Alamo Saloon. Perhaps he'd have a round or two of poker with that cardsharp first, while he looked over the girls and selected the best one. Now that he was here, he did not feel inclined to automatically accept the first sporting woman who approached him. No, he'd do the picking, and he'd be selective.

In addition, he felt quite sure that Earp thought he could take him for all his money, but blacklegs had thought to swindle the Devil before. The cardsharp hadn't been born that could outbluff Devil Devlin, he thought, breaking into a grin as he sauntered down dusty Cedar Street and into the Alamo Saloon.

Chapter Three

Three hours later Sam Devlin, who was still sitting at Earp's table in the Alamo Saloon, was feeling heartily glad he'd had the forethought to leave most of the money in the safe at the Drover's Cottage. It had been a disastrous mistake to think he could play poker with the likes of this cardsharp *and* pick a woman with whom to spend a few agreeable hours later. Wyatt Earp was a better card player than Sam had ever played with in his life, and had quickly taken possession of the stack of twenty-dollar gold pieces Sam had brought with him.

Several of his crew had joined them at the table, a fact that had pleased him until they'd begun to lose their money. They'd been bragging on their trail boss to Earp, asking the cardsharp how he liked playing cards with "the Devil and his boys." Well, apparently matching wits with the Devil hadn't bothered Earp at all. The Devil's Boys had not only lost the best part of their own money but had seen their trail boss lose his stake, too.

It wasn't that he hated their teasing, or feared that their seeing him lose would mean the loss of his authority—he just purely disliked to have anyone see him get fleeced. Well, vanity never did anyone any good, Sam reasoned, but if he didn't learn which cardsharps to avoid, he'd still be herding cattle up the trail when he was fifty.

The way he had figured it before tonight, there would have to be at least one more drive to get the Devlins financially back on their feet and rebuild the stud. He'd known that this drive would only serve to wipe out their present debt, but if he didn't win back the ten thousand dollars he'd lost it wouldn't even fully accomplish that. He couldn't stand the thought of going back to Texas with much less than what he'd been paid just this afternoon. He was going to have to figure out a way to regain his money.

But not tonight. He knew when he was on a losing streak. "I'm out," he announced, his chair scraping against the plank floor as he rose.

"Hey, what's your hurry, Devil?" the cardsharp asked him lazily, then called for another round.

"I've got no more money to play," Sam said with a shrug, grinning back as if that fact meant less than nothing. "Perhaps tomorrow night." Perhaps tomorrow night, yes, but certainly not with you, he thought, without malice. If Earp was cheating, he hadn't been able to catch him at it. Perhaps he was just good.

"You ain't goin' t' bed, are ya, boss? You ain't got the other thing ya came for!" Cookie Yates protested. "What about that?"

"Yeah, the night's young, don't go yet," Earp agreed, handing him another half-full glass of whiskey. "The music plays all night here at the Alamo, and so do the girls! Thought you said you were interested in a little, ah, female *companionship,*" the cardsharp added with a wink.

"Yeah, could be," Sam admitted, eyes searching the smoky, noisy saloon. At the bar at the south side of the Alamo, a couple of gaudily dressed girls winked at him. He knew the merest nod would have brought either the blonde or the black-haired girl to his side, cooing and eager to please.

"There's a likely-looking pair—Florabelle and Sukey Jane," the cardsharp drawled, following his gaze. "It'd be my pleasure to stake you an eagle—you could probably get both of them for that, if you were so inclined."

"Thanks just the same," Sam said, shaking his head, "but I've got the money. I did have sense enough to keep a few dollars off the table. One girl will be enough, though, I reckon. Two just might kill me, on top of all the tanglefoot I've been drinking."

"Well?" Earp nodded again at the girls lounging at the ornate, brass-trimmed bar, clearly just waiting for his signal.

"I'd take the blonde, boss," Jase Lowry advised him. "Wouldn't you like to see if she's blond *all over?*"

Sam hesitated, though for the life of him he couldn't understand why. Both of the girls were pretty, in a bold, hard sort of way, and their tight dresses and low-cut bodices all but shouted that their bodies would be rewarding to explore. Hellfire, what in blue blazes was he waiting for? In five minutes he could be upstairs wrestling on the sheets with either one of them. But he just couldn't bring himself to move his head or raise his finger to them.

"Then you go ahead and take her, Jase," he murmured, looking back at Earp. "Any others here?"

"Ah-ha! A man of discriminating tastes," the other responded with a grin. "Just look about you, my good man. There's Conchita at the faro table, if you appreciate a little south-of-the-border spice, Kate standing by the roulette wheel if you like 'em freckled, and Jerusha if you prefer a little cream with your coffee," he said, pointing at last to a pretty, doe-eyed mulatto girl. "But say, I just got an idea, if you're interested in a gamble, that is. You could please yourself *and* get double your money back."

"Oh?" Sam slid back onto his chair.

"Devil, I've seen that you're a very selective man," Earp responded, leaning forward. "You came to gamble with the best, didn't you?" He grinned a smug grin.

"For all the good it did me," Sam retorted good-naturedly.

Earp went on. "And you don't tumble for the first likely-looking pair of bobbers. You want a little something extra for your dollars, even in a whore. You like redheads?"

Sam shrugged, wondering where this was leading. Sure, he liked redheads, but no more than any other color of hair on a soiled dove. It didn't matter once she blew out the lamp. Most of it came from a bottle, anyway.

"You like a little challenge, too, I've seen. I doubled the stakes on you and you didn't turn a hair—even when I held the winning hand."

Again Sam nodded.

"All right, here it is—the queen of the Alamo Saloon is one Mercedes LaFleche, a real beauty, with dark red hair and a figure that'll make you pant just to look at it, my friend."

"Mercedes LaFleche, hmm?" He looked around, but he saw no such woman.

"It's a French name," Earp said with a wink.

Sam knew there was about as much chance that this Mercedes was truly French as there was of snow on Galveston Island, but perhaps she was a Cajun from New Orleans. A lot of sporting women in cattle towns came from there.

"The thing is, she's so popular in Abilene, she could charge fifty dollars and still pick and choose who she wants to lie down with, and she'd still make a fortune."

Cookie Yates whistled. "Fifty dollars a night?"

"Nope—that's just for an *hour* with her," Earp said.

"No *señorita* ees worth fifty dollars for an hour!" Manuel Lopez, the wrangler who'd been in charge of Sam's remuda, insisted, but Earp ignored him and went on.

"Far as I know, she hasn't ever given a cowboy a whole night before. Or a cardsharp," he lamented. "No one has yet gotten the pleasure of waking up next to Miss LaFleche in the morning. I'm willing to bet you can't talk her into it for that same fifty dollars, either." Earp lit a cheroot and inhaled deeply.

"Go 'head, Devil, you kin do it!" urged Clancy McDonnell, another of the boys. "The Devil here could charm a snake outa his skin," he boasted to Earp.

Sam considered the challenge, rubbing his unaccustomedly clean-shaven chin. "You've been with her?"

"That I have, on a couple of memorable evenings," Earp admitted. "Believe me, friend, she's worth every red cent of the cash you'll place on her nightstand. She's got tricks that will turn you inside out and leave you begging for more."

"But how do I know you're not in league with the, ah, lady? You two could have set this up ahead of time," Sam noted.

"But I didn't. On that you have my word, Devlin. You gonna take the dare? I'll even give you the fifty—say, as an advance on your winnings."

Sam didn't know why, but he believed the other man. He might be a clever cheat at cards, but he sensed Earp was dealing straight now. "I think I'll go you one better, Earp."

"How's that?" Earp inquired with lazy interest, but his gaze was intent.

"I'll take the same stakes—twenty thousand, twice what you won from me—but I'll have the lady between the sheets within three nights without parting with any of your fifty. She'll be with me all night—and she'll do it for free."

Earp's jaw fell open. "You're loco."

The Devil's Boys hooted and clapped. "That's the spirit, boss!"

"I can't do this," Earp protested. "It'd be like takin' candy from a baby!"

He stared at Sam, but Sam kept his gaze steady. All of a sudden he was bursting with confidence. A clever card-sharp might get the better of him with a marked deck, but with women he knew he had the advantage. He knew the secret—which was that all women, even those who made their livings on their backs, wanted to be treated like ladies.

"So...where is the divine Mercedes?" drawled Sam. Now that he'd figured out a sure bet, he was eager to begin the campaign to win his money back.

"I haven't seen her downstairs for a while. She went upstairs with a cowboy about the time you began losing that last hand," Earp said, then pulled out a pocket watch, which he flicked open with a well-manicured fingernail. "Hmm...by my calculations she oughta be down in about half an hour, unless the cowboy paid double. How about letting me buy you another drink?"

Sam shook his head. "No, thanks. I'll just sit around and keep my boys outta trouble." The whiskey was singing a sweet song inside his head, but he knew better than to drink any more of it. Too much of it, and he'd be just another bleary-eyed, slurred-voice cowboy making importunities to the queen of the calico queens. "But if you'd like me to find another table so you can start a new game..."

Earp shook his head, gracious in victory. "No need for all of you to move. I'm just going to mosey over yonder where those boys're beckoning for me to join them." He indicated a table with a trio of cowboys Sam recognized as some of Lee Hill's hands from San Antone. "But never fear, I'll keep my eye out for Mamselle Mercedes so I can point her out to you."

Earp left, and for a few minutes the Devil's Boys went on drinking, with Sam just watching the stairs.

"Hey, would ya look at what Tom Culhane found, gents?" Jase Lowry said suddenly, pointing toward the entrance.

Six heads swiveled to look up at the swinging doors. Through them sauntered the bowlegged young cowboy who'd groused earlier about his wages, his arm around the waist of a slender, fine-boned blonde who was eyeing him with a mixture of admiration and nervousness.

Spying the table full of familiar faces, Culhane aimed the blonde in their direction, his stumbling gait proclaiming the fact that he'd already been downing a considerable amount of rotgut at another Abilene establishment. "Lookee what I found, boys! A beauty, ain't she? An' guesh what? She sh-said she seen me earlier today an' thought I wuz a han'-some fella an' wanted to meet me! Ain't that a wonderful turn of events, boys?"

Smacking the table and laughing, the Devils' Boys all agreed it was. Jase Lowry rose and pulled out a chair.

"Why don't ya offer the lady a chair, Tom? What's wrong with yore manners?" He bowed with exaggerated care. "Jase Lowry, ma'am, at your service, if this here saddlebum fails t' please ya."

The blonde blinked at the towheaded cowboy she'd come in with, then, blushing, she accepted the chair Jase held for her. "Why, thank you, Mr. Lowry, you're very kind."

Cookie guffawed. "Kind? Jase? Ma'am, he's just hopin' t' cut ya out before Tom here gets his brand on ya!"

Sam's eyes narrowed as he studied the girl sitting by Culhane. She seemed awfully young to be one of Abilene's soiled doves, though the sidelong glance she was currently bestowing on the goggle-eyed Culhane was full of coquetry and much fluttering of her sandy lashes. Her clothing, compared to the flashy, flounced satin dresses of the other whores, was almost demure. She wore an embroidered Mexican peasant blouse, an innocent enough garment—or at least it probably had been until she had pushed it down so that it revealed slender shoulders and the tops of her breasts swelling above her corset—and a somewhat faded black cotton skirt. Jet black earbobs dangled from her ears. Her face was innocent of paint, though.

"Tom, you haven't introduced your lady friend," Sam said, keeping his eyes on her. The blonde giggled at the sight of her companion's crestfallen face.

"Oh, yeah! Sorry, boss!" Culhane said with a grin, as if the scene this afternoon had not taken place. "Gents, this here's Miss Charity Fairweather. Miss Charity, these're the Devil's Boys—my boss, Sam Devlin, Cookie Yates, Manuel Lopez, Clancy McDonnell and Jase, who ya already met."

Miss Charity Fairweather dimpled as she acknowledged everyone's greetings. Then she seemed to start as she saw that Culhane was pouring her a drink of whiskey. As Sam watched, she hesitated, then raised the glass to her lips with a hand that trembled slightly. She sipped, sputtered, giggled, then drank some more.

The boys cheered, and Culhane hugged her with one hand while he whispered in her ear with the other. Then she winked at something Culhane whispered in her ear and was rewarded by an enthusiastic kiss, which she returned with apparent relish.

Well, maybe she was new to the calling, Sam thought, and hadn't been on the job long enough to dress and paint her face like the others. It sure wasn't his job to watch out for the calico queens. Chances were this soiled dove was more than up to coping with the likes of Tom Culhane. Maybe she even left off the paint on purpose, so that her customers would be lulled into thinking her just a whore with the proverbial heart of gold. Meanwhile she'd be picking their pockets, or helping herself to the rest of their money while they dozed.

Yessir, if Tom kept guzzling the Alamo's whiskey at that speed, that was exactly what would happen, and Tom would be grouchy as a gored steer in the morning. But Tom was a man grown, so Sam went back to watching the stairway for the reappearance of Mercedes LaFleche.

Mercy woke with a start in the darkened bedroom, awakened by a sudden sense that something was wrong. It was too quiet. Charity's snoring was a normal nocturnal accompaniment to her dreams, but now all she could hear was the neighing of a horse in a corral down the street. She reached out a hand, and realized the space next to her on the bed was empty.

Had Charity gone to the outhouse? Usually if nature called in the middle of the night, the girls used a chamber pot that was kept underneath the bed, for both of them were afraid of meeting spiders and snakes in the darkness. But perhaps her sister's stomach was upset from something she ate, so that she had felt it necessary to brave the terrors of the path to the outhouse.

Mercy went to the window and opened it, staring out into the moonlit darkness at the darkened shape of the little building between the barn and the house. No candlelight showed through the chinks between the boards. She watched, thinking perhaps the candle had blown out in the soft night breeze, and while she waited she heard the distant sounds of tinkling pianos coming from Texas and Cedar streets. The saloons must be doing a good business, as usual. As she listened, a shot rang out, and then another, followed by some drunken shouting, and all was quiet again.

The sound of gunfire at night from the streets where the saloons were was so usual that it didn't even wake them anymore. She wondered if the darkly handsome cowboy she had seen today was one of the drunken revelers. She hoped not—or at least, if he was, that he wasn't shot in some pointless brawl.

After five minutes she was forced to realize that Charity wasn't in the outhouse. Where could she be? Quietly she found the lucifers in the darkness and lit the candle on the bedside stand. Then, tiptoeing so as not to wake their father, she went down the hall to the parlor.

But Charity wasn't a victim of insomnia, sitting in the parlor, the kitchen, on the porch or even in the barn. She was just . . . gone!

But where? Mercy only had to think for another moment before she remembered the mulishly rebellious expression on her sister's face while Papa had reprimanded her for being so interested in the Texans and the town whores. You had only to tell Charity to forget about a thing to guarantee that that was all she could think about, Mercy reminded herself. Dear Lord, could Charity possibly have been so foolish as to go over to the saloons, in search of her towheaded drover?

With a sinking heart Mercy realized that was just where her foolish sister must have gone.

Her heart pounding, she stole back through the darkened house and into their bedroom. A quick check of the nails on the wall revealed that Charity had taken her Sunday skirt and the Mexican blouse Papa had said was too sheer to wear except at home, as well as her high-buttoned Sunday boots.

Charity had no idea what she was getting into! Mercy had had no chance to have that talk she'd promised herself to have with her younger sister, for Charity had gone up to bed while Mercy was still saying good-night to her father's congregation, and Mercy had found her with her face turned to the wall, apparently asleep. She was going to have to rescue the foolhardy girl from the consequences of her folly, Mercy realized, but to do so would mean braving the vice-ridden dens of depravity herself! And if their father discovered what they'd done, neither one of them would be able to sit down for a week, let alone leave the house. But she couldn't just leave Charity to her fate, as much as the silly girl deserved it.

She stared at the remaining dresses hanging from the nails on the wall. Which of them would look enough like the garb worn by the whores that she wouldn't be stopped at the swinging doors of the saloons, yet not encourage drunken cowboys to treat her as fair game while she searched for her sister?

Chapter Four

In the end Mercy settled upon a dress that had been Mama's, realizing that she had nothing of her own that did not shout the fact that she was the preacher's daughter and had no business in Abilene's saloons. But Mama had been the daughter of a banker, and had possessed a great many dresses for events more worldly than those she would attend after she had made her unlikely match with the Reverend Jeremiah Fairweather. She had saved some of these in the large cedar chest at the foot of Mercy and Charity's bed, thinking the girls might be able to use them someday.

The forest green silk dress had a round neckline that dipped low, and since their mother had been a little smaller in the bust than Mercy was, when Mercy dropped it over her head it revealed a shadowy hint of cleavage. She would have to remember to keep her shawl wrapped around her.

She crept down the short hallway as quietly as she could, freezing momentarily when she forgot which plank in the floor always creaked. But her father's snoring, audible as usual all over the house, continued unabated.

By the light of her candle the grandfather clock in the parlor showed the time to be ten minutes to midnight. Shivering, Mercy patted her hair, which she'd twisted into a knot at the nape of her neck, and gathered the fringed black paisley shawl tightly over her mother's dress. Then, murmuring a prayer that Papa wouldn't hear her and that she'd find Charity before he awoke, she exited the house. She'd try the Alamo Saloon first. It was the biggest, and catered to the Texans. It was the most likely place her sister had gone.

The merriment showed no signs of diminishing as the ornate clock over the door of the Alamo Saloon struck the hour of midnight, but Sam's mood was far from merry. He'd drifted over to the mahogany-and-brass bar and was leaning on it, nursing a beer. So far he'd seen no signs of Miss Mercedes LaFleche, though he'd kept a steady watch on the staircase. Earp had disappeared at some point. The only thing left to do was watch his cowhands get steadily more drunk, and that was getting old quickly. He was wasting his time. Maybe he ought to call it a night and begin his hunt again after a good night's sleep.

Tom Culhane had gone out the back door a few minutes ago with his little blonde, "for a stroll," he'd said, but Sam knew darn well what was on the cowboy's mind. He'd start by kissing Charity Fairweather, then his hands would start to stray.... No doubt by then they'd already be discussing her price. Maybe they'd even consummate the deal right out there in the alley, up against one of the buildings. He'd heard some of the whores had been forced to conduct their business that way the last year before the brothels had been built, and Sam imagined most weren't averse to doing it that way again if their customers were impatient.

Sam only hoped that Tom wasn't going to try to sneak the little blonde into his room at the Drover's Cottage and get them all in trouble. The landlord had already made it quite clear that he didn't hold with such things—the soiled doves were not to roost in his rooms, he'd said.

"New in these parts?" the bartender asked him as he wiped a glass dry behind the bar.

He barely glanced at the man before replying, "Just in town to sell my herd."

"Up from Texas?"

"Yeah." He knew his answer had been curt. It would have been mannerly to extend his hand and give the man his name, but he wasn't feeling very mannerly right now. And anyway, a man never knew when admitting to being a Texan would land him in a ruckus. He'd already run into some hostile Kansans fussing about their own cattle being endangered by tick-infested Texas longhorns bringing the Texas fever. The danger had been exaggerated out of proportion, of course, and it seemed that the Kansans had forgotten about the boom the drovers were bringing to the area.

But the man, who wore a patch over his right eye and had several scars marring the same side of his face, didn't seem hostile. "Deacon Paxton's my name." He wiped his hand dry with the towel he had over his shoulder, then offered it to Sam.

Sam felt vaguely ashamed as he shook the man's hand. There was no need to take his sour, suspicious mood out on the bartender. "Sam Devlin. You say your name is Deacon?" he asked, more to make amends for his earlier abruptness than because he was curious.

The man smiled, his expression lightening the somewhat weary, somber side of his face beneath a silvering thatch of hair. "They like to joke with me because I read the Bible when it's not busy around here. So they call me Deacon."

"You oughta be a preacher—seems like they're scarce around here," Sam commented, nodding toward the street to indicate the whole town.

Deacon Paxton chuckled. "I am—or at least, I was once. There ain't no church built in Abilene yet. There's a Baptist preacher who holds services in his house a couple of streets over, though, so I reckon he sees to folks' souls around here. In addition to informing us that the saloon keepers an' the cowboys an' the gals in th' saloons are bound for perdition, that is."

Sam snorted. "That's just about the whole population of Abilene, isn't it?"

Meeting Deacon and talking about the fire-and-brimstone Baptist preacher had made Sam think about his brother Caleb, who'd been a minister, too. Unlike Sam and the oldest Devlin brother, Garrick, Caleb had been in the Union army, because of his belief that no man should own another—though the Devlins themselves had no slaves. Unlike Sam and Garrick also, Caleb had never returned. Sam barely remembered his older brother's face now, some seven years after they'd said goodbye. Cal had been a gentle man of the cloth, who spoke of God's love rather than his wrath. He wondered what had happened to him. Where was the markerless grave that held his elder brother's body—or had there even been enough of him to bury?

"Say, where in Texas—" the bartender began, then broke off as he saw his customer's attention was distracted.

Sam had just been about to politely excuse himself and go back to the Drover's Cottage when an auburn-haired woman had peered over the curved doors, then let herself in.

Could it be...? It had to be. The woman was lovely, though far younger than Sam had imagined she'd be, small boned and dainty. He couldn't see much of her figure; she kept a shawl clutched tightly about her, but her face would have held his interest in any case—a classic oval with large, deeply green eyes and a mouth that was wider than the rosebud pout favored by the classic beauties of the day, but which looked to him as if it were meant for kissing.

But how had she gotten from upstairs to out in the street? Either Earp was wrong about her going upstairs, or the saloon had a back stairway, which was more likely.

The woman had to squint to see through the haze of smoke that filled the saloon. She looked in all corners of the room, and it was obvious from her frustrated, worried expression that she hadn't found who she was seeking.

He was not the only man who had spied her. A pair of cowboys, slouched over beers near the door, had straightened and were just preparing to rise when Sam stepped forward, cutting them off at the pass. If this was his quarry, he wanted to get to her first.

"You seem to be looking for someone, ma'am...may I be of service?" he said, going to the door and motioning her through.

She stared at him, clearly startled, as if she had not seen him approach.

"Sam Houston Devlin, ma'am." He raised his voice a little to be heard over the piano music, and made a little bow. Gallantry was always a good touch. "May I buy you a drink?"

She glanced at the bar, and at Deacon Paxton standing behind it, then looked quickly back at Sam, shaking her head. "No...I...I *am* looking for someone just now...my sister..."

He was disappointed that she seemed too preoccupied to have noticed his gallantry, but grinned and said, "Well, then, why don't you tell me your name, ma'am, and then tell me your sister's name, and I'll sure help you find her." He gave her his biggest, friendliest smile, the smile that had melted the hearts of the belles back home, and occasionally their resistance.

"M-Mercy," she said, her green eyes round as marbles as she stared up at him as if trying to memorize his features.

Mercy. *Mercedes! Hot damn, she was the one!* He congratulated himself at finding her at last. Earp should have told him she went by a shortened form of her name. Maybe this night wasn't over yet. Maybe—just maybe—he could even win the bet *tonight*. He imagined finding Earp tomorrow and telling him he'd already won the bet. She was still studying him, which meant she apparently found him interesting, and that was a good start.

He winked at her. "Are you begging, or is that your name, darlin'?" he asked her, his drawl caressing and honey sweet.

Mercy stared up at the very man who had been haunting her thoughts most of the day—when she hadn't been worrying about her errant younger sister, at least—the dark-haired, mustachioed Texan she'd glimpsed through the window of the Frontier Store, the one who'd been standing and watching the saloon girls promenade down Texas Street. And now he was standing right next to her, looking down at her!

She'd thought his eyes would be brown, because of his nearly black hair and mustache, but she noted with surprise that they were blue, the deepest, darkest blue she had ever seen. Blue like the ocean's depths, she thought, remembering a colored illustration in her mother's Bible, which had been captioned, "Genesis chapter one, verse two: '...And darkness was upon the face of the deep...'"

His lean face was bronzed by the sun, and his eyes had crinkles around them at the outer corners, lines that meant a man was used to being out in the blistering glare of the sun. When she had first seen him outside he had not been smiling, and his eyes had been narrowed against the sun, like the eyes of a wolf; yet now, in the dimmer lamplight, his eyes were no less predatory than they had looked then. And the smile he had leveled on her, a smile that was making her heart thump against the confines of her corset, made him dangerous indeed.

She felt herself blushing as she realized he was making a play on words with her name. The realization brought her out of the rosy haze his presence had produced.

"Mercy is my *name,* Mr. Devlin," she explained, a trifle sharply, to make it clear she didn't find his double entendre amusing.

"Have *mercy* on me and please, call me Sam," he responded with an easy grin, as if he hadn't noticed her sharpness. "I'm right pleased to make your acquaintance, Miss Mercy. Sure I can't buy you a drink before we look for your sister?"

Oh, dear, this was just the very thing she had feared, some cowboy thinking she was one of the girls who worked here! But it was too bad it had to be *this* man who had acted just like the lecherous demon-Texans her father preached against.

"No, I'm afraid I must find my sister, but thanks all the same. Her name is Charity and she's blond, and about as tall as I am. Have you seen her? It's important that I find her immediately. She...she really shouldn't be here—she's only fifteen, though she looks a little older," she added, frowning, glancing away from his face to look around the smoke-filled saloon again. She didn't see Charity, but there were several other females, a couple of them draped around men playing cards, another sitting in a cowboy's lap as he openly fondled her, still others paired with cowboys dancing recklessly around the room to the tinkling piano music.

The sight made her realize anew how urgent it was to find her sister—before she got herself into trouble. "*Have* you seen her?" she repeated, allowing the impatience to show in her voice. "If she isn't here I'll have to look elsewhere."

His smile had vanished as if it had never been, and he looked suddenly unsettled. "You don't mean Charity Fairweather, do you? Little blonde, about so high?" His hand indicated a height just shorter than Mercy's own five feet five inches.

Mercy gasped. "Yes, but how do you know her last name? Please, do you know where she is? I must find her right away!"

She heard him swear under his breath. "I had a feelin' in my bones she was trouble," he muttered. He took her by the arm—gently enough, but without waiting for her assent. "I think I can find her. Come with me," he commanded grimly, and headed for the door.

In a few rapid strides he had taken her out of the saloon and under the starry midnight sky. But Sam Devlin did not seem inclined to stop and stargaze. He seemed to have caught her sense of urgency, for she had to nearly run to keep up with him as he rounded the corner and went into the alley that ran behind the Alamo. His spurs made a clink-clinking sound as he strode along.

"Mr. Devlin, please!" she said, panting a little. "Where are you taking me?" It was possible he didn't know where Charity was at all, she realized, and was merely luring her out into the dark for his own nefarious purposes....

He paused and looked back. "Sorry," he said, and the moonlight lit up his faint smile. "Forgot you didn't come equipped with long legs, too." He indicated his own, which were very long indeed.

She started as they neared a mass huddled up against the back of the building, a mass that writhed and shifted, panted and moaned. Devlin hesitated and peered at the shape, which seemed oblivious to their presence. "Just a courting couple," he reassured her as he walked her rapidly past it.

Then, when they had reached the far end of the alley, she heard something that sounded like ripping cloth, followed by a squeal of outrage and a ringing slap. Then they heard a girl's voice—a familiar one to Mercy—cry out, "Now, stop that! Stop that right now, you hear me? Gentlemen do not behave that way!"

"Charity?" Mercy started toward the sound, but not before she heard a man laugh and then say in an amused drawl, "Now, honey, jes' *what* gave you the idea I was a *gentleman?* Now, settle down and give me some more o' those sugar-sweet lips, sugar—"

Devlin lunged forward at the man's voice, and a second later Mercy saw him pulling a shorter man out of the shadows. "Let her go, Culhane," he muttered.

"Aw, boss, what d' you mean, interruptin' our spoonin' like that? I was makin' out jes' fine till you came along," whined the cowboy, pushing back a few strands of tousled yellow hair from his forehead.

"It didn't sound like it," Devlin retorted. "Sounded like you weren't pleasin' the lady a'tall. Miss, are you all right?" he called into the deep shadows that still hid the girl.

"I... I th-think so," came a quivery voice.

"Charity!" Mercy cried as the younger girl emerged from the indistinct darkness, clutching the torn ends of her ripped bodice together.

Mercy had only a second to stare at her sister's disheveled hair, swollen lips and frightened face before Charity hurtled into her arms, weeping.

"Hey, what's goin' on here?" the cowboy protested. "Me and the gal, we was jes' havin' some fun, boss, I swear it!"

"Oh, Mercy, thank God! I'm so glad you came!" Charity cried against her. "Mercy, I was so afraid! That man, he was going to—he was gonna—"

"Shh," Mercy soothed her sister. "It's all right, you're safe now. . . ." Over her sobbing sister's head she stared at the two men, wondering what would happen next.

"The girl wasn't what you thought she was, Tom. She's just fifteen. Now get on back to the Drover's Cottage and call it a night," Devlin commanded.

"But boss—"

"You *made a mistake,* Culhane," growled Devlin. "Go on, now. You're disturbin' the ladies."

Culhane started moving, but he fired one last parting shot as he stumbled unsteadily past them. "Huh! She ain't no lady—I guess I know a whore when I see one! She was kissin' me real sweet till you came along. . . ."

"Culhane, *shut up and get out of here!*" Devlin snapped, and applied his boot to the cowboy's backside to add emphasis.

After watching the Texan banish his drover, Mercy busied herself with wrapping her shawl around Charity's shoulders, covering her torn bodice. She shushed her sister's tearful efforts to apologize. There'd be time for that later, but not now, not in front of Sam Houston Devlin, who had now turned back to them and was watching her with hooded, speculative eyes.

"We can't thank you enough, Mr. Devlin," she said, trying not to betray the trembling she badly wanted to give in to herself. Charity might well have been raped if the Texan hadn't found her then. And how *had* he known where to find her? She hoped there'd be time later to discover that, too. But for now all she wanted to do was to escape the Texan's knowing gaze and get home and into bed before Papa noticed they were missing.

"*Sam,* Miss Mercy. The name is Sam, and it was my pleasure to assist you," he added in that rich, Southern drawl that poured like honey over her heart. "Is she—is she all right? I apologize for my drover's crude behavior, ma'am. He's just in off the trail and got a little liquored up tonight. He thought...he thought she was..." He hesitated.

"A whore?" Mercy supplied, inwardly flinching at a word she'd never said out loud before. "No, she's not. She's just a foolish girl who didn't know what she was getting into, I'm afraid. And now," she concluded in brisk tones, "we must say good-night, and thank you again. Charity?" she prompted.

Charity lifted her head from her sister's breast. "Th-thank you, Mr. Devlin...."

They started to walk away, but Sam Devlin started after them. "I'll escort you back to your rooms, Miss Mercy," he informed her. "Wouldn't want you to meet up with any more drunken cowboys on your way."

"That won't be necessary," Mercy said quickly. She sure didn't want to take the chance of having Papa look out the window and see them with a stranger! Why, the clink-clink of his spurs might be just the sort of unfamiliar noise that was liable to wake their father. Then she realized how unfriendly she had sounded, and after Devlin had saved her sister from a fate worse than death, too!

She paused. "That is, I appreciate your offer, Mr. Devlin, but we really don't live far. Please, don't let us trouble you any further...."

She had forgotten about the Southern sense of chivalry. "Oh, it's no trouble, Miss Mercy," he assured her, that impudent grin back on his face.

"No, really, Mr. Devlin—Sam," she amended as she saw he was about to correct her. "I—I really don't want you to. I need to speak to my sister—alone."

"Well, all right," he said reluctantly. "Could I—could I just speak to you a moment, before you go?" He looked at her, then at Charity, and while Mercy was trying to find the words that would send him away, yet not rudely, Charity spoke up.

"I'll just stand over here, Mercy," she said, pointing to a place a little way up the street. "Go ahead and listen to Mr. Devlin—it's the least you can do after what he did for us."

Mercy was too surprised at her sister's sudden return of composure to argue, and stood still as her sister walked out of earshot, yet where she could still easily be seen in the moonlight.

A wandering night breeze kissed Mercy's neck as she turned back to Devlin, and she was suddenly aware of her exposed neckline, now that Charity was wearing the paisley shawl. She sensed the Texan was aware of it, too, though she hadn't actually caught him looking. But he gave her no time to worry about it.

"I'm sorry the evenin' turned out the way it did, Miss Mercy," he said. "I'd like to ask you to supper."

"Oh, you don't have to do that," she said, looking away from the eyes that had gone gleaming black in the darkness. "There's no need for any further ap—"

"I'm not askin' you 'cause I want to apologize for Culhane," he interrupted, smiling faintly down at her. "If you'll remember rightly, I'd just asked you if you wanted a drink when we...when we were interrupted. I was intendin' all along to work up to askin' you to supper," he finished with a boyish grin that made her knees suddenly feel like that jelly she'd made, the batch that had never quite jelled. Like water.

Of course, there was no way she could say yes. Papa would lock her in her bedroom for a month before he'd ever let her spend five minutes in the company of a...a Texas cowboy! To him they were the same as Satan himself.

"Please?" he appealed, actually having the nerve to take her hand and squeeze it a little. "I'd sure like to take you to the hotel and give you a nice supper, if only just to prove all Texans aren't ravening wolves."

It was so near the image Papa had painted of them that she had to laugh. And all at once she realized that she very much *wanted* to go to supper with this Texan with the winning smile and wicked blue eyes. Just once....

"All right, Mr. Devlin—Sam," she heard herself saying. "I'd be pleased to have supper with you."

Chapter Five

Sam was whistling as he strolled over to the Drover's Cottage after watching Mercy and her sister walk away down the street. The night hadn't turned out so badly, after all. He'd met Mercedes LaFleche, the subject of the cardsharp's dare, and he had an appointment to take her to supper tomorrow evening at nine o'clock.

This evening, he corrected himself with a grin, realizing it was after midnight. By the time the clock struck midnight again, he would have had an enjoyable supper with a beautiful woman whose sister he had rescued—a chivalrous act that should weigh heavily in his favor—and if his luck held, by the next morning he just might already have won the wager.

"Mercy, Mercy, have mercy," he mused aloud, grinning all over again as he remembered how her green eyes had flashed sparks at him for making a play on words with her name. *So her real name is Fairweather, hmm? Yet she goes by Mercy, rather than Mercedes....* The sparks—of anger? of challenge?—hadn't dismayed him. Sam liked a woman to have some fire in her nature. It usually made the time in bed a lot more worthwhile, and the morning after a hell of a lot more interesting.

So her sister wasn't a prostitute—yet, he amended. His quick impression of Charity Fairweather, made when she had been sitting at the table with the boys and himself and flirting with all of them, was that the foolish little blonde was the natural harlot, not Mercy. Still, Charity's distress at Culhane's pawing had *seemed* genuine enough. But you could never tell with sporting women. It may have just been a matter of her asking more money than Tom wanted to pay.

What was clear enough to Sam, though, was that Mercy didn't want her sister in the business, and to him that indicated a basic goodness in her that he found very likable. He thought he would enjoy their little supper tomorrow, quite apart from considerations of winning the bet.

He hoped she'd wear that green dress again, or something like it. The neckline of that dress had been just high enough to make her look like a lady, so that he could take her to dinner at Abilene's one respectable hotel, and just low enough to hint at the delights that awaited him later. Farther down, its silken folds had clung lovingly to a slender waistline above enticingly feminine hips. He liked the fact, too, that she didn't seem to paint her face like the other sporting women did; in fact, unless he missed his guess, Mercy's face was completely clear of paint. But then, some women didn't need paint to make them appealing, and perhaps this woman was one of the few who realized that fact. Though not classically beautiful, she was pretty in her own way.

She had told him she would meet him at the hotel. She hadn't wanted him to come and escort her from her rooms above the Alamo, and he wondered why. He didn't think she was worried about him seeing some other well-satisfied customer leaving her. Most saloon girls didn't start working, so to speak, until later in the evening.

Was it possible she was attracted to him, and saw his invitation to dinner as romantic, rather than just business? If so, she might not want to remind him of what she was by having him pick her up at her place of employment. He hoped that was the reason, and his hope had little to do with the money he had a chance to regain by succeeding with the lovely Mercedes.

Mercy waited until they'd walked a block from the Alamo Saloon before rounding on her sister. "How could you? How *could* you, Charity? After all Papa has told us about the things those cowboys get up to! You could have been . . . well, *violated* out there, Charity, did you realize that? How do you like your yellow-headed cowboy now?"

Charity shuddered. "He was horrible, Mercy. He said he just wanted to go for a stroll! His breath stank of whiskey and tobacco, and his teeth were yellow. And his hands—I swear, Mercy, he had more hands than that octopus in our old picture book! And the way he kissed me, Mercy—it started out kinda nice, and then all at once he stuck his *tongue* right in my mouth! It was awful! Mercy, I'm not *ever* g-going near a m-man again!" Her breath caught on a renewed sob.

Mercy put her arm bracingly around her sister's shaking shoulders bracingly, and spoke in softer tones. "Yes, you will, honey. They're not all lecherous beasts like that cowboy. You'll find a good, decent man someday. But in the meantime, we need to have a talk about men. . . ."

"When we get home?"

"No, silly. It's going to be tough enough to get us both back inside without waking Papa, if he's not already awake and waiting up with a switch, that is. No, we'll have that talk soon, I promise, but tonight we need to get some sleep. That ol' rooster's going to crow before you know it."

"I don't think I *could* sleep now," Charity confessed as they walked through the darkened streets of Abilene. Here and there lamplight spilled through a saloon window, illuminating a patch of the hard-packed dirt beneath their feet, enabling them to see and step around piles of horse droppings and, in one case, a snoring cowboy, obviously the worse for wear after an excess of tanglefoot.

Mercy didn't think she could sleep tonight, either. As she lay in bed, she was sure she would be thinking about the darkly handsome Sam Houston Devlin, with those dangerous, deep blue eyes and that predatory smile.

She found it difficult to believe she'd agreed to go to supper with him. A frisson of terrified delight tingled all the way down her spine. She knew instinctively that he was dangerous to her, though she could not define what that meant. And yet, she would not have given up trying to see him tomorrow night for the moon and the stars. But how on earth was she going to be able to manage to do it?

She'd almost lost her nerve when he'd asked to come pick her up. He'd raised an eyebrow curiously when she'd refused, and for a moment she'd been afraid he was going to ask her why not. She couldn't very well tell him that the reason for her reluctance was a fire-breathing papa who'd shoot him on sight rather than let his daughter spend a minute in a Texas cowboy's company.

But thankfully, he'd accepted her request without further comment, and now she just had to figure out a way to get out of the house tomorrow night, dressed appropriately for supper at Abilene's Grand Hotel.

She'd wear Mama's garnet silk dress with the bishop sleeves and the ivory lace trim, she decided, along with Mama's garnet earbobs and black cameo on black velvet ribbon.

"Mercy..." began her sister, breaking into her thoughts.

"What?"

"What did Mr. Devlin say to you? If...if you don't mind my askin', that is."

Mercy said nothing for several paces, so long that Charity finally spoke again. "Did he... did he say he thought I was an idiot? That I deserved what could have happened? He...he has such a fierce look about him, Mercy. You can't tell for sure what he's thinking, can you?"

Her words surprised Mercy. Charity could be such a featherhead so much of the time, and then she'd come up with these perceptions about people that were dead on target.

"No, he wasn't saying anything about you at all, you silly," Mercy said, putting her arm around her sister as they walked on toward their house. "I...I shouldn't even tell you this, Charity, but he was asking me to supper."

Charity stopped stock-still in the road for a minute, her mouth making an O of astonishment. Then a smile began to play about her lips.

"Are you going to go? Do you *want* to go?"

Mercy pretended to be concentrating on making her way past a particularly dark stretch between two buildings. "I shouldn't even consider it for a heartbeat, and you know it, Charity. He's just the sort of man Papa's warned us about. He might be just like that Tom Culhane, in spite of the fact he helped me find you just in the nick of time tonight, and got rid of Culhane when he wanted to be ugly about it."

"But?"

Mercy could hear the grin in her sister's words, even though she couldn't see her face just now.

"But I want to go, *if* there's a way to get out without Papa knowing."

Charity let out a whoop of glee, and hugged her sister. Mercy immediately put a hand over Charity's mouth to smother her outcry. They were passing the house of Horace and Abigail Barnes. The fat would sure be in the fire if that gossipy matron found them out strolling through the streets at a time when respectable ladies were long abed!

"Good for you, Mercy! I'm glad to hear you have some grit, after all! *I'll* help you get out of the house, somehow. We'll think of a way!"

Mercy felt warmed by her sister's approval, and amused by her choice of words. "You didn't think I had any grit? What's that supposed to mean?"

"Nothing bad," Charity assured her sister. "It's just that... well, you've always done what Papa says is right, and you're always so good about taking care of him an' me an' the house. But it seems like you don't ever do anything for *yourself,* Mercy. You don't ever get out of line. I think you should go and have a wonderful time."

"I don't know.... As you say, there's something about this Sam Devlin that's a little, um, *scary*. Something devilish in those eyes, Charity."

"I know." The idea seemed to produce shivers of delight in Charity, rather than the opposite. "He's the trail boss of that outfit Tom Culhane rode in with, you know. They call him 'Devil,' and themselves the 'Devil's Boys.'"

"Oh." All the more reason to think she must have been insane to agree to see him.

"Stop worrying, Mercy—I can practically see what you're thinking," Charity told her. "It's *only* supper. Even if he *does* have any dishonorable notions, he can't exactly carry them out over the supper table, can he?"

"And you thought you were just going for a walk with Tom Culhane, remember?" Mercy retorted.

"Oh, I knew that scalawag wanted to do a little spoonin'," her sister had the grace to admit. "But I didn't think he wouldn't listen when I said no. Devlin isn't Culhane, Mercy. He may look fierce, but I don't believe he'd ever hurt a woman, you know? There's something... something *honorable* about him, deep down."

Mercy devoutly hoped her sister was right.

"Now, what are you planning to wear?" Charity asked, then ran on, "I think..." And suddenly they were both just girls again, discussing the age-old feminine concern.

Deacon Paxton was thoughtful as he wiped up spilled liquor with a damp cloth. That Texan—the trail boss who'd stood talking to him until the girl had come in—there was something familiar about him. Had they met before? In the year since Abilene had gotten the railhead and become the end point on the Chisholm Trail, hundreds of Texans had poured into the town and back out again. Maybe he'd been one he'd met last year, or maybe he just resembled one he'd met. They all started to look alike after a while, he mused—tall, lean, with weathered faces and wary, sun-narrowed eyes. And they sounded alike, too, men of few words, generally—though Devlin had been friendly enough once he'd seen Deacon was inclined to be likewise. But he hadn't been inclined to say much about himself.

He wondered what the Reverend Jeremiah Fairweather's daughters had been doing in here tonight. The blond one, the one they called Charity, was clearly headed for trouble. Should he tell the preacher about seeing her in here tonight, sitting with the cowboys?

He thought about the time he'd asked the preacher if he could attend his Sunday services, and the Reverend Mr. Fairweather had told him he was welcome—in fact, he'd consider making him a deacon in fact as well as name, soon as he quit his job working in the Alamo. Deacon was in Satan's employ, didn't Deacon know that?

Recollecting that conversation, Deacon didn't think he'd be talking to the preacher about his blond daughter. Or the one with the dark red hair, either, come to think of it. He'd been even more surprised to see Mercy Fairweather show up, and then leave with the Texas trail boss, but she'd looked worried. He supposed she'd been searching for her scapegrace sister, and from his vantage point at the bar it looked as if Devlin had offered to help her find Charity.

But Deacon had also seen the way Sam Devlin had been looking at the preacher's older daughter before he'd led her out of the Alamo. It was the look of a predator who'd spotted his prey.

Deacon wondered if the Texan knew that his quarry was the daughter of the only preacher in this wild cow town—and if he knew, if he actually gave a damn. But it was none of his business, Deacon decided—unless he actually saw Devlin acting in a shady way.

"Have a good night, Deacon?" a woman's husky voice asked from the stairs that led right past the bar.

Mercedes LaFleche stood there, lighting a cheroot. Once she was sure of at least one male watching her entrance into the nearly empty main room of the saloon, she descended the final three stairs.

"Yes, Miss LaFleche, how about you?" he asked politely. He liked the woman well enough—Mercedes LaFleche was an amiable person, especially when her customers had paid well.

"Good enough. I haven't wasted my time, I guess." She looked around the room, gauging the remaining customers, and turned back to Deacon, obviously deciding that none of the die-hard drinkers was worth her time and attention. "Give me a beer, Deacon, would you?"

"Sure 'nough, Miss Mercedes. Say, did Wyatt see you? He told me there was a Texan in here hoping to meet you, a drover."

"Hey, what's this 'Miss Mercedes' stuff? I've told you often enough it's just 'Mercedes,' haven't I?" the woman said with a lazy smile, which showed the dimple in one rouged cheek. "Naw, I didn't see Wyatt any time I was downstairs, which wasn't often, if you know what I mean. So some Texas drover wanted to meet me, hmm? How unusual," Mercedes said with a wry quirk to her mouth that robbed her sarcasm of any sting.

"He seemed like a real pleasant fella, Miss Mercedes," Deacon insisted, handing the prostitute her beer and wondering why he bothered to defend the drover to her. "I believe he said his handle was Sam Devlin."

"I'm sure he was a nice fella, Deacon," Mercedes said, patting the bartender's hand. "You've never steered me wrong yet. Well, if I see this Devlin, I'll smile at him real pretty, and listen to what he has to say—*if* he hasn't lost all his money to Wyatt by then, that is."

Chapter Six

Sam woke late the next morning with an enormous sense of well-being. In fact, he felt like a pup with two tails. Tonight was going to go well, he was sure of it. The only difficulty would be in waiting for evening to arrive.

Well, in a cow town like Abilene whose saloons were open twenty-four hours a day, there ought to be plenty he could keep busy with until evening, he reasoned as he rose and dressed and went downstairs. He'd start with breakfast. It would be good to eat his eggs and bacon sitting at a real table, instead of hunkered down by a campfire with hundreds of longhorns lowing nearby. Then he'd check on Buck, his horse, at the Twin Barns, the livery stable beyond the railroad tracks. The buckskin gelding was probably eating his fool head off, but Sam wanted to make sure the liveryman wasn't neglecting the cow pony that had brought Sam so far from Texas.

Buck was fine, he discovered, and whinnied a greeting when he saw his master coming. Sam scratched underneath the gelding's jaw, a favorite place, and fed him the apple he'd talked the Drover's Cottage cook out of.

The horse in the stall next to Buck caught Sam's attention. The tall black stallion was an unusually fine beast to be found in a livery. Thoroughbred, Sam mused, admiring the stallion who gazed back alertly at him, his ears pricked forward. Someone in Abilene must be boarding the beast here, for the black was certainly not the kind of nag a livery would rent out.

He sure reminded Sam of Goliad, the horse Caleb had ridden away from the Devlin farm when he went to join the Union army. Thinking of Goliad, and the kind of horses that had once filled the Devlin stables, made Sam nostalgic. He was going to fill those barns up again with good horseflesh, he vowed as he left the livery, if it took a dozen trail drives to finance it!

It was still only eleven-thirty. Now what was he going to do?

He was going to stay away from the Alamo, that was certain—not because he thought he'd see Mercedes working this early, but to avoid further poker games with Earp. As likable as the cardsharp was, he was determined not to lose any more money to him.

About noon, therefore, he was firmly ensconced in a rawhide-backed chair in the Longhorn Saloon, holding three aces and a king. Boy Henderson, who had been regaling them with a tale about losing his virginity in the arms of a sloe-eyed harlot the night before, had just stepped out back to relieve himself when Tom Culhane ambled in, saw Sam and scowled.

"Morning, Tom," Jase Lowry said in greeting. "Pull up a chair and set a spell, and watch me lose some more money to Dev here."

"I ain't intr'sted in sittin' nowhere with that sumbitch spoilsport," snarled Culhane, glaring at Sam with bloodshot eyes.

Sam sighed. If that cowboy wasn't careful, he was going to ruin a perfectly good morning—make that afternoon, he thought, noting that it was fifteen minutes past twelve on the clock.

"Aw, come on and sit down, Tom," he said, motioning to a chair opposite him. "Hellfire, I'll even buy you a drink to prove there's no hard feelin's. That's why you're such a sorehead this mornin', you know—you need a hair of the dog that bit you."

"*You* may not have hard feelings, you sumbitch, but *I* do," sneered Culhane, pointing a finger at Sam. "You thought you wuz some high-an'-mighty knight in shinin' armor last night, didn't you? Showin' off for the filly you found—an' at my expense! I hope she gave you some disease that makes your pecker rot off."

Sam was determined not to let Culhane rile him, though it was clear the cowboy was spoiling for a fight. "Aw, Culhane, what was I supposed to do? Miss Mercedes told me her sister wasn't in the business. Granted, sashayin' around cowboys like that, it won't be long, but I had to let you know you'd made a mistake, didn't I?"

Sam's reasonableness apparently only enraged Culhane further. "What you wuz supposed t' do, Devlin, was *mind yer own goddamn business!*" shouted Culhane. "You ain't my boss no more! You don't tell me what t' do!"

"C'mon, Culhane. Don't be yellin' like that," pleaded Jase. "I got a headache. B'sides, ya might wanta work for Dev again next spring."

"I wouldn't work for that stupid sidewinder if he wuz the las' trail boss in Texas!" Culhane shouted back, but his eyes remained on Sam. His hands dropped, hovering near the Colts strapped at his hips.

Sam noted the fact. Yep, the pleasant afternoon was definitely about to get ruined. He was armed, too, of course—there was as yet no real law in the wild cow town, so a man had to be prepared to defend himself. But he had no intention of drawing down on the young cowboy. He rose to his feet, slowly and deliberately. "You don't want to do this, Culhane," he advised.

The saloon became very quiet as cowboys nearby took note of the explosive situation. Those nearest Sam's table edged away. A drummer who had come in to wet his whistle backed out the doors, keeping a nervous eye on the two Texans.

Culhane went right on as if he hadn't spoken. "Fact, when I get done with him, ain't none o' you saddlebums gonna work for him. Whenever you're ready, Devlin," he said with a meaningful glance at Sam's pistols.

"Tom! *What are you doin'?*" shouted Boy Henderson from the back of the saloon. He had come back just in time to see Culhane fixing to draw on the boss.

Involuntarily, Culhane glanced in the direction of the boy's voice, and Sam took instant advantage of it, launching himself at Culhane with doubled-up fists. A moment later Culhane was out cold on the saloon floor, and the patrons of the Longhorn were going back to their whiskey and cards.

"We'll get him back to his room, Dev," Jase Lowry said, gesturing for Boy and Cookie to join him, "so's he can wake up peaceable. I'll try an' talk some sense inta him when he comes to."

Sam was just finishing a mental thanksgiving that he'd been able to avoid using his gun on his own drover. "Much obliged, Jase. I'm not so sure anyone *can* talk sense into that mule-headed fool, though," Sam said with a heavy sigh. He'd made an enemy, and now he was going to have to watch his back.

Jase nodded his agreement. "I can try. But I know what ya mean, Dev. I can explain it to him, but I can't understand it for him."

As it happened, all the schemes Mercy and Charity had concocted turned out to be unnecessary. At about four o'clock in the afternoon, when Mercy was just coming in from the barn after having managed to stash her chosen ensemble for the evening there, she noticed George Abels's buckboard parked in front of the house.

Going inside, she found the middle-aged farmer in the parlor with her father and Charity, telling them that his elderly father-in-law, who lived with them and who had been declining for months, was saying he was going to die again. He wondered if the reverend would come out, and sit up with him for a while, and quiet his doubts about the hereafter.

Mercy did her best to smother a smile. This had happened so many times before that it had become something of a joke between the girls, for their father would go out to the soddy out by the Smoky River, spend all night praying with the cantankerous old man, return home exhausted but triumphant that he had helped save the old, nearly deaf reprobate's soul, only to have the process repeated in a few months. Mercy suspected the old man used his imminent death as an attention-getting device, or a means of quieting his daughter's numerous brood when he'd had too much of their noise. Their father never failed to go, however, for old Ike Turnbull was nearing eighty and each time might be the real thing. No, their papa never failed to go; a pastor must tend his flock.

The Reverend Mr. Fairweather said he would go again this time, of course.

"Oh, bless ya, Reverend. I... I think this time he means it," Abels said, just as he said every time. "He's been lookin' might poorly for some time now, laws, yes."

When they had first moved to Abilene, the reverend would bring Mercy and Charity with him on these calls, volunteering them to help with the farmer's twelve children, so that the farmer's wife could be with her father, but after the first couple of times he had told his daughters it wasn't necessary. Perhaps he suspected the old man was hoaxing him, or perhaps he realized that the older children were perfectly up to watching the younger ones, but in any case Mercy and Charity were relieved not to have to go.

She offered one more time, however, just in case God had decided He had favored her enough by allowing Charity and herself to sneak back into the house undetected last night and was not inclined to bless her any further by permitting the secret supper with Devlin this evening.

"Mr. Abels, would you like Charity and me to come out and watch the children, so your wife can sit by her father's sick bed?" Give me a sign, she prayed. *If you don't want me to see Sam Devlin tonight, let Mr. Abels take me up on my offer.* Then she held her breath. Her heart thumped painfully in her chest, imagining Sam Devlin waiting in vain for her in front of the Abilene Grand Hotel.

The reverend beamed proudly, not noticing Charity's shocked, dismayed face, or her attempts to get her sister's attention.

"Oh, bless ya fer offerin', Miss Mercy, but that won't be necessary," Abels replied. "The house is plumb fulla relatives come over from across the Smoky River. They think this might be the end, too, so there's plenty t' help. No, I won't take you girls away from the house, but your papa should be mighty proud of you girls, mighty proud indeed. Laws, yes. You're good girls."

"Thank you, George. Yes, I know I'm blessed in my daughters," said the reverend, rising from his seat. "They've been such a comfort to me since their sainted mother went to her reward. And now, if you'll excuse me, I'll just get my Bible from my bedroom before we go."

Mercy let Charity handle the small talk while they waited for their father to return. She was too full of relief, and a giddy excitement about how easy it was going to be, to speak. Fortunately Charity handled the task well, inquiring about Abels's crops and chattering artlessly about the lack of rain.

Moments later their father had departed in the buckboard with Abels, admonishing the girls, "Don't wait up—it might be morning before I'm back, you know."

The sisters knew, all right.

He was standing on the planking in front of the Abilene Grand Hotel when she came around the corner, leaning against one of the columns that supported the establishment's overhanging roof. She knew he had spotted her and was watching her approach, and the knowledge made her pulse quicken.

Was she doing the right thing? She'd been so sure, when she'd left the house, buoyed by Charity's encouragement. There was no way Charity would have allowed her to back out of going to supper, in fact. She kept reminding Mercy that she owed Devlin that much, at least, for coming to her sister's aid yesterday.

But now she felt very uncertain as she saw Devlin straighten and push himself away from the post, stepping down off the planking to extend his hand to her.

He looked her up and down. "Miss Mercy, you're looking pretty as a field of bluebonnets," he said.

She found it a strange compliment, seeing as how she was clad in garnet silk, not blue, but she figured that must be high praise to a Texan. They were so proud of their oversize state to the south, with all of its unique features. And then his hand touched hers and their eyes met and she almost forgot how to breathe.

His hands were work-worn and callused, but they were warm, and the blood flowing through them called to hers. As Mercy stepped up onto the planking from the dirt of the street, holding his hand as if it were a lifeline, his other hand left his side and she saw that he was holding a small bouquet of red roses.

"For you, Miss Mercy," he said with a devastating grin. "I had no idea they'd go so well with your dress, too."

"Too?" she repeated in confusion, her eyes unable to escape his compelling dark blue gaze. She gathered her white lacy shawl more closely around her.

His eyes lowered a few inches. "I was thinking of your lips," he confessed, handing her the bouquet. "They look soft as these petals," he said, stroking the edge of one bloom in a circular motion with his thumb.

Mercy felt that caressing thumb as surely as if he had been touching her lips. Involuntarily she licked them, tasting the carmine salve Charity had made her rub on.

She took the bouquet. "You're...you're looking very fine yourself, Mr.—uh, Sam," she said, remembering last night's command to call him by his Christian name.

It was an understatement. He wore black trousers and a frock coat with a dazzlingly white shirt and a black string tie. Last night she had noted that he had had his hair trimmed so that it just brushed his collar; since then, he had apparently trimmed, ever so slightly, the mustache that made him look so ferocious. He smelled of bay rum. "Shall we go in? I've got a table waiting," he said, and ushered her inside.

A waiter motioned them over to one of the tables away from the window, for which Mercy was grateful, for sitting by the window would increase the chances that someone passing by would see her in there and mention it to her father. She knew from the way that the waiter had eyed her oddly as he handed her a menu that he had recognized her as the preacher's daughter, but he wasn't one of the few men who belonged to their congregation, so it didn't matter. She hoped he wouldn't refer to her father in front of Devlin, though—she knew he didn't know her father was a preacher, and she was afraid he might start behaving differently with her if he knew. Mercy just wanted Sam Devlin to be himself.

Sam *had* noticed the way the waiter had been looking at her, but he'd misinterpreted it. He'd stiffened, thinking the man had recognized his supper companion as Mercedes LaFleche, the sporting woman, and was considering informing him that the Grand Hotel dining room did not serve women "of her caliber," or some such snobbish euphemism. That would make it awkward as hell for Sam, for then he would want to knock the waiter down, which certainly wouldn't add a romantic touch to their evening. Mercedes LaFleche probably saw brawling cowboys every night she worked, and was entitled to something a little different when she was taken away from the Alamo Saloon.

But the waiter said nothing, and left them to peruse the grease-spotted menus.

He made his decision quickly, then studied her surreptitiously over the menu. He appreciated the fact that she had worn something tasteful and elegant, rather than the gaudy, multiruffled and flounced gowns a woman of her profession often wore. She apparently disliked flashy gewgaws, too, for the simple red earbobs and a cameo on a black velvet ribbon merely called attention to the slender curve of her white neck, rather than to themselves.

What a different sort of woman she was from the usual run of females who made their living catering to the baser needs of men. She was fine-boned and small, not exactly beautiful—her mouth was too wide for perfect beauty—but she had a quality better than that for which he had no name. Her speech was not "refined," exactly, but certainly free from the coarse phrases most sporting women used. And she still had the ability to blush. He found that fact incredible, after all she must have seen in her career. No wonder she was such a favorite that she could pick and choose her customers.

There was a blush blooming on her cheeks now, as if she was not unaware of his scrutiny. "Hmm, what looks good to you, Sam?" she asked him.

You do, he thought, *but I'll have to wait till later to see about that.* "I don't know—what do *you* recommend?"

An anxious frown creased her forehead, and she rescanned the menu. "Umm, I hear the steaks are good," she offered.

"You *hear?* Honey, hasn't anyone ever taken you to supper here?" he said, before he could think.

She shook her head, her eyes still fastened on the menu. "No," she answered in a small voice. "P—" she began, then stopped. "No," she repeated. "You're the first."

What had she been about to say before she stopped herself? He found it amazing that she had never been here. Maybe the hotel was very recently opened. After all, Abilene had only consisted of a few log cabins before the railroad's coming brought on the cattle boom only last year. Or perhaps she thought it made a man feel special to have been the first to take her somewhere nice? No, she'd have to be an awfully good actress if the latter was the case—she seemed sincere about what she was saying.

"Well, then—we'll do our best to make it a memorable occasion, won't we?" he said with a wink, and was touched to see her blush again. Maybe she *did* find him appealing. "I don't think I'll have the steak, though—I just spent three months eating beef any possible way it could be fixed. We had beef morning, noon and night on the trail. No, I think I'll have the fried chicken for a change," he concluded, just as the waiter returned to their table.

"Oh," she said, "how silly of me. Of course you don't want steak. I…I think I'll have the steak, though, if that's all right," she said, her eyes glued to the menu. "We—I—don't eat it too often."

He was surprised by her meekness. "Honey, you can have anything you want to eat—you can have the whole dang menu if you want it."

Did he imagine it, or did the waiter frown at him for the endearment that had slipped out? The old sourpuss! What was he afraid of... that next Sam would start making love to Mercedes right at their table? But the waiter scuttled off and they were alone, so that Sam was free to enjoy the color that had invaded Mercedes's face again—all because he had called her *honey?*

For a moment there was silence, and then she said, "So—you're up from Texas. Where, exactly? Do you have a family down there?"

He wondered if she was really asking if he was married, and if he had been, if that would make a difference to a woman of her calling? Probably not, he reasoned. Women like that were used to servicing a man's needs away from home, knowing that it had nothing to do with the good women they were married to.

"I'm from Brazos County—good blackland prairie country. My father came from Ireland with the clothes on his back and a fine stallion, and started a horse farm there. It was prospering by the time he died. That was before the war, though. The Confederate army requisitioned all our horses, the ones that the Devlin boys didn't ride to war, anyway. Now the Devlins—or what's left of us, anyway—are trying to rebuild the stud, but it takes cash. So I'm here in Abilene to sell the herd we rounded up in south Texas. They're runnin' loose down there, free for the takin.'"

"'What's left of us'?" she echoed. "Did you lose family... in the war?"

He nodded. "My mother almost died of grief. My brother Caleb, the middle boy, never came home, and neither did my sister Annie's husband—but at least we got a letter from his captain telling us where *he* fell. Garrick, my oldest brother, might as well have died. They cut his leg off after it was shattered by a minié ball, and now he just sits around the house and feels sorry for himself. I guess I would, too," he added, feeling guilty for criticizing the brother he'd idolized when they'd been growing up together. "There isn't much he can do around the farm."

She reached out a hand and touched his wrist. "No, you wouldn't," she said with sudden certainty. At his surprised look, she added, "I know, I haven't known you long enough to say that, but I just know you wouldn't. You'd find a way to do what had to be done. Did your brothers have wives?"

He allowed himself a bitter laugh. "Garrick's wife ran off the morning after he came home. Couldn't face the sight of him, I reckon. Cal hadn't married yet—fortunately, as it turned out—though every mama in the county wanted her daughter to marry the parson."

"Your brother was a preacher?"

He nodded, thinking how easy she was to talk to. "Yeah, but not the hellfire-an'-brimstone kind. He said you couldn't teach people about God's love that way. He went and fought for the Union army because of his beliefs. Shocked a lot of folks in Brazos County."

"How did your family feel? Was your father angry?" she asked.

"He was dead by then. Garrick, though, was furious. He thought my brother had shamed the Devlins, even though he knew how Cal felt. The Devlins didn't own any slaves—Papa didn't hold with it, either, you see—but Garrick felt a Southerner ought to support his state."

"And you?"

"I wasn't real happy about Cal's choice, either, but I was a green kid then, all excited about what I believed was the glory of war," he said grimly. "But he was my brother, and I loved him. Before he rode away to join the Yankees, I told him I just wanted him to come home safe."

She looked thoughtful. "My father's a preacher, too. Except he's that other kind you mentioned."

Now he'd put his foot in it. "Oh, say, Miss Mercy, I didn't mean any offense. . . ."

"None taken," she said quickly. "I was just wishing Papa was more like your brother was. I think it works better, too."

Her face looked wistful. He wondered what had caused a preacher's daughter to earn her living whoring in a cattle town? Had her father been so harsh that he had driven her away for some trifling offense? Perhaps he'd caught her out in the haystack with some hayseed swain?

Then their meals came, and he ceased wondering about her for a while.

Chapter Seven

"He's havin' dinner with her right this very minute," Cookie Yates announced triumphantly and without preamble as he stood over Wyatt Earp, seated at his usual table in the Alamo Saloon with three other players, one of whom was Tom Culhane. Cookie was relieved to see that Culhane looked a little more amiable than he had earlier in the day. Maybe he had just had a sore head earlier.

"What're you talkin' about?" Wyatt Earp growled. He didn't much cotton to having his game interrupted, especially when he held the winning hand. Giving the other players too much time to think could cause Lady Luck to smile on someone else.

"Devil—Sam Devlin, my trail boss. He and the sportin' woman you made the bet about was just headin' into the Grand Hotel's dinin' room when I passed by. Sure looked like they was sweet on one another already," Cookie said with a grin. "Looks like you're gonna lose your money, Earp. Sure hope you can afford it."

"Well, lookin' sweet doesn't mean much from a sportin' woman," Earp replied, a cynical smile on his face. "You don't know the breed if you think that means she's gonna give it away—hey, wait a minute, *who* did you say your trail boss was with?" he asked, his eyes on the man and woman descending the stairway as he spoke.

"That Mercedes gal you made the bet about," Cookie repeated. "You know, that sportin' woman you said was so choosy? The one Dev bet you he could poke without payin'? It was her, all right, saw that red hair in the lamplight at the entrance."

"And when was that?" Earp asked, smirking as he motioned the woman over to their table. She patted the satisfied-looking cowboy she'd been with on the shoulder before separating from him and coming in Earp's direction.

"Why, just a coupla minutes ago," said Cookie. "I figure about now they're lookin' deeply into one another's eyes...give my boss an hour and he'll have her layin' down for him, all right. She'll beg him to," Cookie bragged. "The gals in Fort Worth couldn't get enough o' him when we passed through there. Iffen he tells you he can have her for free, you'd best believe it."

"Oh, I'm not arguin' his ability to have *a* woman without payin'," Earp replied, "just the particular woman we were speakin' of. Boys, I'd like you to meet Miss Mercedes LaFleche," he said, rising and holding out his hand to the sultry-looking redhead in a tight gown of turquoise satin, who bestowed a smile on the whole table.

Cookie stared at the woman as if she were a ghost. "But..." he began, pointing at the rich, deep red of her curly hair.

"Is this the gentleman you wanted me to meet, Wyatt?" she asked, eyeing the gray-haired, whiskery Cookie a little doubtfully.

Wyatt was grinning openly now. "No, my dear, it isn't. But tell me something, Mercedes, honey. Were you just over at the Grand Hotel a couple of minutes ago, meetin' a Texan for dinner there?"

She looked at the cardsharp as if he had clearly lost his mind. "Wyatt, you just saw me walk down those stairs from my room, I know you did. You saw the cowboy with me. He was a Texan, all right, most of 'em are, but I didn't meet him at the Grand Hotel. He bought me a drink right here in the Alamo before we . . . went upstairs for a while," she said with a meaningful wink.

Wyatt turned back to Cookie Yates. "Seems like your boss was takin' some other woman in to dinner, doesn't it? Could be he found another gal to charm. Maybe he lost interest in the dare, if he found some gal who's more of a sure thing."

"But . . . but she had red hair just like this one," protested Cookie.

"Is that a fact?" drawled Earp, putting his arm around Mercedes LaFleche, who seemed to enjoy the caress. "Mercedes, you know any other woman in Abilene with red hair that's as pretty as you?"

Mercedes preened. "Why, Wyatt, you always said I had no equal! But there isn't *any* other woman in Abilene with red hair that I know of, anyway—and I know all the sportin' women *and* the 'virtuous ladies,' too, even if that bunch do cut me dead when we pass on the street," she said with a little laugh. "Unless you mean the preacher's daughter, now . . . her hair's sorta the color o' mine, just a little darker red. But I don't think she'd be out with some cowboy," she added. "Her father watches over her like a miser watches his money. And she's kinda, well . . . *innocent* lookin', compared t' me." She gestured at the tight-fitting, eye-catching satin dress she wore.

Wyatt hooted and smacked the table. "Cookie, is it possible your boss is out wining and dining the preacher's daughter, thinking she's a sporting woman?"

Cookie looked distinctly uncomfortable as he considered the possibility. He glared at Tom Culhane, who obviously found the idea as hilarious as Earp did.

"Aw, stop lookin' like you was suckin' a lemon, Cookie," Culhane said when he could stop guffawing. "I think it'd serve th' Devil right if he thinks he's courtin' a whore and finds out she's some prissy little preacher's daughter instead!"

At the moment, however, Mercy was feeling far from prissy. She'd taken a cautious first sip of the wine that their stuffy-acting waiter had brought, not wanting to confess it was the first she had ever drunk. Even when celebrating Communion, Papa served grape juice instead of wine. She found the fermented version very good, too, and as a consequence had been sipping it slowly but steadily as Sam Devlin regaled her with tales of the trail drive.

"No, it doesn't take much to set off a stampede," Sam was saying in response to a question she had asked. "At night we took turns singin' to the herd, soft and low. Some men sang songs from the war, some sang hymns, some even sang nursery rhymes." His blue eyes were distant and unfocused, as if he was remembering. "It didn't matter much what we sang, as long as it sounded soothing to the beeves. But somethin' as sudden as a flash of lightning, or as simple as the snapping of a stick—or sometimes nothin' at all—could set those longhorns loco, and in a flash they'd be up and runnin', with all of us gallopin' hell-for-leather after them an' tryin' to turn them. God help any poor cowboy who wasn't on his horse when they decided to turn in his direction. We lost a good hand that way, just after we crossed the Red River," he said, his expression somber.

Sam hadn't been bragging, just telling her matter-of-factly what a trail drive was like, but she marveled nonetheless. He painted such a clear picture of it. When Sam talked of his days on the Chisholm Trail, Mercy could almost see the choking cloud of dust—she could hear the constant lowing of the cattle and the thunder of their hooves over rocky ground. She could smell the savory odors of wood smoke and beef stew at the nightly campfires. She could feel the incredible heat that could be generated by a stampeding herd.

What a brave man he was—what brave men all of them were, these Texans who brought the hundreds of stubborn horned beasts a thousand miles from where they ran free among the mesquite in south Texas, crossing swirling rivers, enduring all kinds of weather, danger from hostile Indians and murderous rustlers, disease and the ever-present threat of stampede. No ordinary man—no man she'd ever met until now, anyway—was capable of surviving all that.

No wonder the cowboys were so ready to have a little fun, to... *to raise a little hell,* Mercy thought, surprising herself by even thinking about that word that Papa reserved for discussions of the hereafter. She noticed Sam had used it, too—"hell-for-leather"—quite unconsciously, not apologizing up and down because he had used *that word* in the presence of a lady. She found she didn't mind. She didn't mind anything, as long as he would keep on talking. That rich drawl was so easy on the ears, so warming....

Or was it the unaccustomed wine? By the time the waiter brought her steak and Sam's chicken, Mercy was feeling so warm that she wished she had a fan, perhaps one of those black ostrich-feather ones that she and Charity had seen in the *Godey's lady's book.* It would be nice to be fluttering her fan, and flirting over the top of it with the handsome male across the table from her.

"I hear they call you Devil," she said, feeling very worldly-wise and sophisticated as she said it.

His irresistible smile turned into a chuckle. "Aw, that's just some funnin' the boys do with my name. They just like callin' themselves the Devil's Boys."

"I'm sure you're being much too modest," she said, and winked—and then wondered why she had dared to do such a thing in the company of such a man! It *must* be the wine.... Perhaps she had better not drink any more of it, she thought as she took another sip to cover her confusion.

"Well, I do believe the saloon keepers in Fort Worth will be happy if I never darken their doors again," he said, hiding his face in his hands in mock ruefulness. His action caused her to notice the tiny nicks and bruises about his knuckles.

"Sam, your hands—they're all cut up! What happened to you?"

He looked surprised, and inspected the backs of his hands in the lamplight. "Well, I'll be a son of a gun. I hadn't noticed. It's nothing, Miss Mercy. Just had to educate one of my cowboys this morning about proper behavior in a saloon. He had a sore head from drinkin' tanglefoot the night before, and it made him mean, that's all."

"Culhane?" she guessed.

He nodded. "Yep. He doesn't like bein' told what t' do. I guess I won't be hirin' him next spring, even supposin' he wants to work for me, which he probably won't. Don't look so worried, Miss Mercy," he added. "He was just lookin' for a fight, but I knocked him out before he could land a blow."

She hadn't realized her anxious thoughts had reached her face, but the thought that she and Charity had somehow caused a quarrel between Sam and one of his men made her uneasy.

"Don't pay that bowlegged cowboy any mind," Sam said, reaching out and touching her hand as it lay on the table. "With all the mischief he can get into in a town like Abilene, he'll soon forget all about it. Let's talk about something else. We've talked about me—what about you? I know your father's a preacher…but where are you from? A lot of the girls here seem to hail from St. Louis, or New Orleans."

She giggled just a little before answering. Abilene did have a lot of girls who'd come here in the past year from those big cities—but they were the girls who worked in the saloons and brothels, not preachers' daughters. Sam Devlin had not been talking to a very genteel sort of female—except for her and her sister, that is! But cowboys would be cowboys, and after all, it was her he had asked out to supper, not one of *them*.

"No, we came to Kansas from Ohio, actually—Cincinnati, to be exact," she told him.

"'We'? You mean you and your sister?"

Mercy nodded. "And Mama and Papa. Mama died, though, the first winter in Kansas." She saw him frown slightly.

"Your papa still alive?"

She nodded again. She wished she knew how he felt about the fact that her father was a preacher. Did it make him uncomfortable that she was a preacher's daughter? Most men in town treated her with a sort of wary respect, as if the fact that her father was a man of the cloth somehow made her unapproachable. Or had she made him sad by reminding him of his brother who had been lost during the war?

Sam wasn't thinking about Cal at all. Looking at her closely, he realized she couldn't be much older than eighteen.... How long ago had she been estranged from her father? He must live in another Kansas town, Sam reasoned; surely a preacher would not tolerate his daughter practicing the oldest profession in the same town in which he preached the Gospel.

How happy his own growing-up years, before the war, had been in contrast to Mercy's. He wanted to make it all up to her somehow.

The wine had clearly relaxed her, he'd been glad to see. Sam hadn't thought a woman like Mercedes LaFleche, used to dealing with men, would be nervous, but now, slightly flushed from the burgundy's effects, she seemed much more at ease. He'd enjoyed watching the innocent gusto with which Mercy had attacked her steak, too. Sam liked that—he had no patience with a female who just pushed her food around on the plate, either because she'd been taught it was the genteel way to behave or because she wore her corset too tight. He wondered if Mercy wore a corset at all. He hadn't gotten to touch her yet, so he didn't know if that tiny waist above the flare of her hips was the result of nature or stays.

Which reminded Sam of his ultimate goal for the evening.

"Miss Mercy," he began, "that waiter will be back before long to ask us about dessert. It seems a shame to end the evening so soon, don't you think? Now, we could have a piece of pie or cake here at the hotel if you'd like, but I was thinkin' it might be nice to take our dessert with us, and go for a little drive. What would you think about that?"

Mercy looked doubtful. "Go for a drive? Around Abilene?"

He laughed. "There isn't much to see here, and that'd only take five minutes. No, I meant for us to go out on the prairie. There's supposed to be a full moon tonight—I thought it might be right pleasant to make a little picnic with dessert and champagne. That way we could talk some more, and I could get to know you better. I...I'd like to get to know you better, Miss Mercy."

She just stared at him for a moment, and then her green eyes rounded and her lips curved into a smile.

"Why, I think that would be very nice, Sam," she said.

He felt himself grinning, but she couldn't know the feeling of jubilation that washed through him then as she agreed to his carefully thought-out plan to further the romantic mood of their evening together. The surprised pleasure in those big green eyes told him he'd probably been the first cowboy ever to try to mix an element of courting into her dealings with a man. His instincts had been right on target.

He signaled the waiter, who came back to them, looking expectant.

"Will there be anything else?"

He nodded. "I made some arrangements earlier in the day to have a chocolate cake and some champagne waitin' for us to take with us. I'd be obliged if you'd bring that out with the bill?"

The waiter looked nonplussed. "Oh . . . I was wondering who that was for. Uh, sure," he mumbled, then stalked back to the kitchen after giving Mercy another one of those odd looks that made Sam want to punch him. Fortunately, though, Mercy hadn't seen it, for she was still gazing at him as if he'd hung the stars.

Moments later the waiter returned, bringing the champagne bobbing in a bucket filled with—wonder of wonders—real ice! And, neatly boxed, the chocolate cake.

Sam thanked the waiter and tipped him generously in spite of his disapproving face, trying to appear as if this was the sort of thing he did every day, and ushered Mercy out the back entrance. There, waiting, was a horse, hitched to a shay and being held by the livery's little Negro boy.

Mercy clapped her hands over her mouth and laughed. "Why. . . you had it all arranged, didn't you, Sam Devlin? What if I'd said no to your little picnic?"

Chapter Eight

He smiled, a little-boy-caught-in-the-cookie-jar smile, that washed over Mercy like a warm summer breeze. "Well, I guess if you'd said no, I'd be out the cost of the hire, and I'd be one disappointed man. But you aren't saying no, are you, Miss Mercy?"

Mercy knew she should refuse. She'd had supper with him; that had satisfied her obligation to him for helping Charity out of her fix. If she declined politely, Sam Devlin might be disappointed, all right, but he wouldn't be offended. If she ended the evening now, she could get home easily before her father did, and he'd never be the wiser. That was all she wanted, wasn't it?

No, her heart argued. She wanted more, much more. Whether she went for the ride or not, after tonight it was likely she would never see Sam Devlin again. He was going to be gone in a couple of days, he'd told her, heading back to Texas with whichever ones of his outfit wanted to leave at the same time as he did. He'd just stayed in Abilene this long, he'd told her, to enjoy himself a little and to rest up for the long journey home.

No, she'd never see him again after tonight, but the night didn't have to end just yet, did it? It was only about ten o'clock, later than she'd ever been out, certainly, but early, *too* early to end this magic time with the tall, handsome Texan who stood waiting for her answer.

A cooler part of her brain warned her to look for the devil dancing in Sam Devlin's eyes. His boys didn't call him "the Devil" for nothing, despite his easy disclaimer.

If you go, nothing will ever be the same again. Where had that thought come from? Had she been listening to her father's fiery denunciations of the invading horde of demon Texans too long? Something had *already* changed forever—it had been the first time in her eighteen years that she had had an evening out with a man. Lots of other Kansas girls were married and had babies by now! She'd never given her father a moment's worry, and had kept his house spotless and her sister out of as much trouble as she could. Surely she deserved one memorable evening! And if Sam Devlin kissed her, some time during that ride out over the prairie, would that be such a sin?

And what makes you think a man like Sam Devlin will stop at a kiss? the voice persisted.

And what makes you think I want him to? another voice within retorted, astonishing her. She stared back into those eyes that were warmer than she'd ever thought blue eyes could be. There was honesty there. He'd helped her save her sister when it meant going against one of his own men, when it would have been easier to just ignore her plight. But he'd done what was right. Whatever happened during this outing, a man like that would never hurt her.

"Yes, Sam, I think it'd be lovely to go for a ride with you," she said.

He handed her up into the vehicle, settled himself beside her, then reached down for the reins from the little Negro boy. "Thanks," he called, tossing the little boy a quarter. The boy caught it expertly, his white teeth gleaming in the shadows, and then Sam gathered up the reins, clucked to the bay and they were off at a trot.

The carriage's folding hood was down, a fact that made Mercy a little nervous, for what if someone should see her riding out of town with Sam? But it was a pleasant summer night, with just a faint breeze stirring now and then, and she had her shawl. So she couldn't imagine what her excuse for asking that he put up the hood would be, and she said nothing.

She needn't have worried. Just like the night before, only cowboys were out on the streets of Abilene at this hour, and most of them were only intent on leaving one saloon and going into another. They paid the shay and its occupants no heed.

Mercy was pleased to see that Sam headed west out of town, rather than south, the direction her papa and George Abels had gone. It took only a few minutes before they were leaving the lights and the tinkling piano music of Texas and Cedar streets behind. Soon there was no sound but the clip-clop of the bay's hooves and the singing of the wind in her ears. She could feel the warmth of Sam's powerful thigh at her left. It seemed to radiate right through her skirts and petticoats, and though the breeze caused her to gather the shawl more closely around her, her legs felt warm from his proximity.

And then, as they got farther out onto the prairie, she saw little dots of flickering light, perhaps four or five of them scattered over the prairie. The moonlight revealed masses of dark, shadowy shapes a few yards to one side of the nearest of the lights.

"Sam, what are those lights?"

"Drovers' campfires," he said. "Those are herds that haven't been sold yet." Then the breeze brought her not only whiffs of the cattle smell but fragments of sound, the soft, occasional lowing of a steer, a few bars of a night-herding cowboy's song. It was a peaceful scene, and hard for her to imagine the quick transformation into chaos that could happen in a stampede.

"Are we... are we in any danger, so near to them?"

He smiled at her in the darkness. "Sorry, I didn't mean to scare you with all that talk about stampedin' beeves. Don't you worry, Miss Mercy. It'd take a lot to get those critters runnin' on a nice night like this. We're going to go out a little farther before we stop for our picnic, though."

They drove on for perhaps another half hour. The prairie grass, lit by the moonlight, swayed in hypnotic ripples, reminding Mercy of the waves she'd seen on Lake Erie as a child, when her father had taken the family on a rare pleasure trip. Here and there on the almost treeless prairie they passed a sodbuster's sod house, surrounded by rustling fields of corn, and attended by a farm dog who protested their passing with a few deep-throated barks.

Then, on a little knoll, they saw another soddy. Even from yards away it appeared deserted; the moonlight revealed no door covering the entrance, and there was no glass or oiled cloth over the lone window. The sound of bullfrogs croaking their evening song and the splash of one into water revealed the presence of a creek or pond below the back of the soddy.

"There doesn't seem to be anyone living here to bother—why don't we stop here?" Sam suggested.

"All right," she agreed, liking the way the moonlight illuminated the knoll. "But let's have our picnic outside, on that little rise, all right? I don't want to go in that soddy. It looks like it's been vacant long enough that there are probably all kinds of spiders and snakes nesting in there, not to mention mice," she said with a shudder.

He laughed. "I don't much like the idea of sharin' this cake with spiders an' snakes an' mice, myself," he agreed, and set the brake, tying the horse to a short, spindly sapling that someone had obviously tried to transplant to the prairie in hopes of one day having a shade tree near the house. Then he reached up a hand and helped her down before reaching in for the cake, the bucket of champagne and a folded-up old quilt.

They found a level stretch of ground that seemed free of rocks and she helped him spread out the quilt. Then, while she cut the cake with the knife that the Grand Hotel had thoughtfully sent along, and set out the glasses and napkins, Sam drew the bottle of champagne out of its bath of melted ice.

Mercy watched from beneath her lashes as the Texan peered at the bottle, pushing experimentally at the cork with his thumbs.

"How in the heck do you open this?" Mercy heard him mutter, and she watched as he kept trying in vain to budge the stubborn cork. She thought she heard him mutter a cussword under his breath, and smiled in the darkness at his frustration.

He eyed her ruefully. "I surely do hate to look like an ignorant yahoo from Texas, Miss Mercy, but I'll have to admit that champagne isn't in my usual line of drink. I'm sure you're a lot more used to it than I am. If you have any ideas, don't think I'm too proud to hear them. Sing right out."

She shrugged. Now why would he think that a preacher's daughter from Cincinnati would have more experience with a bottle of champagne than a trail boss would?

"All right, then, I'm going to have to get serious," he told her.

Did he mean to break the bottle neck? Mercy watched as he pulled a wicked-looking knife out of his boot and began to try to pry between the cork and the glass neck.

The result, a moment later, was a pop that startled both of them, causing each to fall backward onto the quilt, with

Sam struggling to right the bottle that had bubbly foam pouring over the top.

"What in the Sam Hill—?"

Once Mercy had decided she had not been shot, she grabbed the glasses and stuck out one, then the other, so he could pour the bubbly wine into each. Both of them were laughing at the foolish picture they must have presented when the cork popped, diving for cover as if the peaceful moonlit prairie were under attack.

Sam watched as Mercy sipped the sparkling wine, laughing delightedly as she tasted the bubbles.

"Mmm, it tickles!" she announced, wrinkling her nose, but she looked as if she liked the sensation.

Well, what do you know? Unless he missed his guess, this was the first time Miss Mercedes LaFleche had tasted champagne, Sam thought, surprised. He wouldn't have thought so. He thought sporting women drank champagne, if not often, then at least as often as they had a high-rolling customer they could cajole into buying it for them. Well, it couldn't hurt that he would be the first to have introduced her to the pleasure, he thought, enchanted by the picture she presented with the silvery light playing over her curls. The breeze had teased many strands loose from the elegant knot at the back of her head, but the result made her look approachable rather than disheveled. Besides, he intended to find the pins that held the rest of her hair and see it all loose around her shoulders, and coiled in his hands, before too much longer. Nothing that had happened so far made it look as if she would protest if he went way beyond that—or that she would ask for money in exchange for what he wanted to happen underneath that big Kansas moon.

"Sam, try it," she urged. "Have you ever had champagne before?"

He sipped, feeling the bite of the bubbles, and thought back. "It's been a good while, as I recollect," he told her. "It was before the war and before my father—we called him 'Da' in the Irish way—died. His prize stud had just won a race down in Austin, and he brought a bottle home to celebrate. We cooled it off in the creek while Mama cooked up a great supper, and then Da uncorked it. Now that I think about it, when he popped that cork my brothers and sisters and I jumped under the table."

Their eyes met in the silvery shadows as each of them took another sip. "And how about some of that chocolate cake, Miss Mercy?"

"I really do think it's time you called me just *Mercy,* don't you?" she asked him, smiling with her eyes as she handed him the cake on a napkin.

"It'd be my pleasure, *Mercy,*" he agreed, biting into the cake. "Aren't you going to have some cake? Don't tell me you don't care for chocolate?"

"Of course I do! And I'm going to—" she began.

"Then here, let me feed it to you," he coaxed, holding out a piece between thumb and forefinger. He wasn't sure if she would let him, but after looking at him warily like a fawn he had once taught to take corn from his hand, Mercy did take it, her lips and teeth doing funny things to his insides as they brushed his fingers and took the morsel.

She sat back, her eyes wide, as if she was astonished at her own daring.

Mercy, Mercy. Didn't anyone ever play little love games with you before? Before they... His mind suddenly didn't want to complete the thought, didn't want to interfere with the spell the moonlight was casting over them.

Then, with a small, secret smile, she leaned over and pinched off a hunk of the cake and, kneeling, held it out to him. "Your turn."

Oh, Mercy. Surely Eve in the Garden of Eden hadn't looked any more tempting than the woman before him, her lips curved in an inviting smile, the shadowy cleft between her breasts silvered in prominence.

He leaned forward, too, and took the cake with his lips, and when she would have withdrawn her fingers, said, "No, wait," before taking them gently with his hand and guiding them into his mouth again, where he sucked gently on them until her eyes were big as the moon overhead.

"Sam!" he heard her protest softly. "*What* do you think you're doing?"

He laughed softly. "Gettin' all the frostin' off, honey."

She blinked as he wondered if she found what he'd done as arousing as it had been for him. Lord, he was hard and ready, and all he wanted to do was sweep the cake and the bottle and the glasses out of the way and lay her back on that old quilt. But he wanted it to be more than that, better than that.

Then she pinched off another hunk of cake—a bigger one this time, and she took no care to keep her fingers out of the frosting—and held it out to him, murmuring, "Then by all means, Sam, have some more."

Oh, yes, she'd found it arousing. Her eyes glittered with the reflected silvery light, and her little pink tongue stole out and licked her lip as she felt his mouth close around her fingers once more. And then, as Sam began to suck and caress her fingertips with his tongue, her eyes closed and her head fell back. Her lips parted. She seemed to be having trouble getting her breath.

"Oh! Oh, my," she breathed as she at last gently withdrew her fingers. Her hand was trembling, and she stared at Sam.

He wasn't conscious of closing the distance between them, but a moment later he was kneeling in front of her, pulling her up against him, and his mouth was descending onto hers.

Lord, her lips were sweet, and it was more than the sweetness of the chocolate he tasted there, and what he was feeling was more than the heady buzz of the champagne he'd drunk. For the woman in his arms kissed as if she had never kissed before, as if this were all new to her, and wonderful beyond belief, and he found that unbelievably exciting. He felt her body instinctively arch toward his, and his body was there waiting for her, aching for her, as he felt her arms go around his neck and the delicious pressure of her small breasts against his chest.

He groaned from the sheer pleasure of it, and cupped her face in his hands, increasing the pressure against her mouth until her lips parted between his.

Then, as his tongue swept inside, he felt her give a little start—of surprise?—and begin to pull back. He loosened his hold on her, but kept kissing her, gently and insistently, until he heard her give a soft moan and open her mouth to him again.

Chapter Nine

"Papa, you...you're back already?" Charity said as she stood in front of the closed door of the bedroom, the blanket clutched around her, covering her nightgown. Jeremiah Fairweather set his Bible down in the darkness, then lit the lamp on the table and met his younger daughter's gaze in the sudden flare of golden light.

"Yes, Charity. Mr. Turnbull made a good end, having repented all his sins. He breathed his last an hour ago, and now sleeps in Abraham's bosom. George Abels loaned me a horse so that I could come home."

"He died? Ike Turnbull actually died?" she asked incredulously. "Uh, I mean, how sad for his family."

"'It is appointed unto man once to die,'" the reverend intoned. "Yes, this time Ike Turnbull really did pass on. He is now walking the streets of gold in that heavenly Jerusalem."

I thought you said he was sleeping in Abraham's bosom, Charity thought irreverently. The only important thing was that Papa was back—and Mercy was not. It was imperative that their father not find out that one of his daughters—the sensible, well-behaved one—was missing.

"I—I'll just go back to bed, Papa," she said, turning back to the door and pushing it open just far enough to get in without revealing Mercy's absence.

"Your sister asleep?" he said, freezing Charity in her tracks.

"Y-yes, I think so," she said, dropping her voice to a whisper, as if trying not to wake Mercy. "Are you going to go to bed soon, Papa? You must be tired," she coaxed.

Fairweather nodded wearily. "In a few minutes. I thought I'd just ponder the Scriptures for a few moments. I'll have to be conducting Mr. Turnbull's funeral the day after tomorrow—I think I'll just meditate on what the Good Book has to say about Eternity."

Charity sighed and sent up a little prayer that Papa would not still be up "pondering" when Mercy finally did steal into their bedroom via the window. There was nothing wrong with Papa's ears, and he was liable to hear her.

She looked at the grandfather clock in the flickering light. Ten minutes to midnight. *Oh, Mercy, where are you, and what are you doing?*

The only time Mercy had ever been kissed before was once back in Cincinnati when one of her cousins had stolen a kiss under the mistletoe. Nevertheless, Mercy knew she was now being kissed by a man who was an expert, and for a moment she delighted in the sensations engendered by the first slow, drugging caresses of his lips on hers. She had imagined his mustache would be bristly and stiff, but instead it was silky against her skin, and... exciting.

Then, after a few moments, she registered the shock of his tongue actually invading her mouth. *Heavens, what is he doing?* Was that a *kiss?* It was more like... like a *possessing!*

She felt him relax his arms around her, but as his kiss gentled again, nibbling at the fullness of her lips, she began to miss the sensation of his tongue exploring the recesses of her mouth and shyly, tentatively parted her lips again, her own tongue seeking his. Instantly he rewarded her, deepening his kiss, until her pulse was pounding in her ears and air seemed hard to come by.

His hands had left her face; one was splayed over the back of her head, and now the other had crept between them and was cupping her breast, feeling its weight while his thumb did delicious things to her nipple, his slow, circular motions making her tingle and ache. Mercy gasped at the strange and unfamiliar sensations rocketing through her like fireworks on Independence Day. She felt them drifting backward, was aware of Sam pushing away the box that held the remains of the cake....

"Sam..." she said, opening her mouth to protest. Dimly she registered the fact that things had gone far beyond the little bit of kissing she had thought she and Sam Devlin might be doing. She wasn't drunk; she had barely consumed two fingers' width of the champagne, but something about its dizzying influence, and the insistent skill of his kisses and his hands, had combined to create a hunger in her to experience more, to go on *feeling*—each new caress, each new variety of kiss. She wanted to give something back to him, to repay him for the delicious tingling the hand stroking her breast was causing in the region between her legs.

How on earth could such distant areas of her body be connected by the touch of his hands on one of them? How on earth...and yet earth surely had nothing to do with this *heavenly* feeling....

The hard ground beneath her back felt real enough, though. "Sam, I—" *I shouldn't. I can't. We have to stop now.*

"Mercy, I want you. I want to make love to you, Mercy," he whispered, following her down, leaning on his side and one arm while the other continued to pleasure her. "Let me make love to you, Mercy, honey...."

"No, I don't think—" She looked around her, away from him. Heavens, it was more of a case of she *couldn't* think, not while his mouth was just two inches from hers and while his stroking was making her tingle all over.

"You don't want me to make love to you out here in the open, under the stars?" he murmured, his breath warm against her ear. "Mercy, I think you're 'bout the loveliest thing I've ever seen in the moonlight—it makes your eyes all silvery an' mysterious." He stopped and kissed her, lingeringly. "I just can't even *begin* to imagine how pretty the rest of you would look dressed in nothin' but moonlight. But if you want, honey, we'll go back to your room in town...."

Dressed in nothing but moonlight... The image was so startling that she misunderstood the last part of what he said, and thought he was offering to stop caressing her with his hands and his mouth and take her home. "No, I don't want to go. It's just that..." But she couldn't quite find the words to tell him that he couldn't continue what he was doing, for she liked it far too much.

He was smiling down at her. "I'm glad you don't want to go," he breathed before claiming her mouth again in a kiss that left her gasping and breathless, as his hand began to slowly undo the buttons that marched down the front of her dress. Simultaneously his leg, which had been pressing casually against her thigh, began to insinuate itself between her legs, which she found disturbing—why did its pressure make her want to part her legs the wider, and move against it? But she didn't have time to wonder about that, for by now he had unbuttoned her dress to the waist and was kissing the tops of her breasts that swelled over the top of her corset. The sensation of his maddeningly silky mustache across her sensitive skin made her breathing a ragged counterpoint as her hands clenched and unclenched against his shoulders.

"Sam..." She had to stop him, she had to, for he was now unfastening the front of the corset and pushing down her chemise. But then he lowered his head and his mouth closed over her nipple.... The hands Mercy had raised to push him away instead found themselves tangled in his thick, dark hair as she arched against the feeling of his hot tongue circling the tightening bud.

She was on fire, and only Sam could put out the flames. But apparently he only intended to stoke them higher, and had taken her murmuring of his name as encouragement to do just that.

"Yes, honey. Don't you worry, Mercy, I'm going to give you what we both want...what we both *need,*" he whispered hoarsely as his hand began to inch up the hem of her dress. "I'm going to love you like you've never been loved, Mercy...."

She heard the rustle of her petticoats and felt the night air stealing across her bared leg as the silk was pushed higher and higher, but then his hand followed each inch of exposure, stroking, warming.

I'm going to love you, he had said. That seemed to imply a future to her, permanence. She already loved him, she realized through the haze of passion clouding her brain, and had ever since she had glimpsed him standing across the street through the fly-specked window of Moon's Frontier Store.

They would be married—somehow they would find a way to overcome her father's objections, and then she would have no difficulty in loving him forever, she was sure of that, just as he was promising to love her. *"Like you've never been loved,"* he had said. Did he think she had had numerous boys courting her? She wanted to assure Sam that no one *had* ever loved her before, unless one counted the sort of love her mother and her sister and, yes, even her stern and strict father had given her....

And then his hand had reached her thigh, and was reaching inside her pantalets and touching her intimately. Alarmed at the totally foreign feeling, she jerked in his arms, struggling against him, but her outcry was muffled against his neck and shoulders.

Unaware of her fear, Sam groaned, his breathing ragged. "Oh, Mercy, honey, you feel so good...."

She trembled at the strange but wonderful feeling of him touching her where she had never even dared to touch herself, afraid of the growing power of the desire that was building within her and threatening to burn them both to ashes. It had already seared away most of her fear, and now she was clutching at him, whimpering, as his touch spread the flame through every vein, every nerve.

"Please, Sam..." she moaned, and yet she did not know what she begged for.

He did, though, and he moved over her more completely, to give it to her. Still fully clothed, he thrust against her, and she could feel him, hard and swollen against the juncture of her legs.

"Oh, Mercy, have mercy," he whispered hoarsely. "I can't wait anymore. I promise we'll take it slow the next time, all right?"

Not really sure of what he was asking her to agree to, but trusting that whatever it was it would ease the white-hot longing within her, she nodded wordlessly up to him in the moonlight.

He kissed her, quick and hard, before moving off her, his hand going to the buttons of his fly, opening them with a fevered impatience. She could see little of his body in the shadowy light, but the moonlight caught the hot gleam of his eyes and she focused on that. It seemed to take forever, and yet it was only seconds before he was lowering himself onto her again, blotting out the moon, his fingers finding her again, stroking her, and then guiding himself to her.

"*Now,* honey..." All at once he was pushing inside her, burying himself in her, and Mercy felt a tearing within. She cried out.

But it seemed he couldn't hear her, for he was already convulsing over her, plunging into her again and again as if he couldn't get enough, his breathing hoarse and harsh. Endless seconds later he collapsed on top of her with a sigh.

And then, suddenly it was as if he'd just now heard her outcry and realized what it had meant when he'd penetrated her virginity moments ago—or maybe it was the way she was now trembling beneath him.

He froze over her, inside her.

"Hellfire, girl—what's going on here? *Who are you?*"

Mercy was awash in the pain arising from the area between her legs where they were joined together, and his angry, growled words made no sense to her. "What? What do you mean, Sam? I'm Mercy," she managed to blurt out, staring up at him, bewildered.

He rolled off her, then reached a hand down and touched the tender outside skin around where he had so recently invaded. He raised his fingers to the moonlight, and they could both see the dark stain on his fingers. Blood.

He swore and struck the ground with his fist. "I'm going to ask you again, girl, and this time you'd better tell me the truth. I wasn't expecting a...a virgin. *Who are you? Who put you up to this?*"

She didn't know what had gone wrong, but she bitterly resented his furious tone when she was already frightened by the pain he had caused her. She pushed herself up on her elbows, wincing at the ache within.

"My name is Mercy Louisa Fairweather—though I would think you'd have known that, since you know my sister's name is Charity Fairweather," she hissed. "Why, just who was I *supposed* to be? And what do you mean, who put me up to this?"

He turned to look at her. "You don't go by Mercedes LaFleche also? You aren't... a whore?"

"A *whore?* Why, how dare you, you—you..." Words failed her as her fury rose to match his, and so she raised her arm to slap him instead.

He caught her wrist in a grip of steel, and grabbed the other one, too, so that she could do nothing but face him. "What the hell were you doing out here with me, Miss Mercy Louisa Fairweather? *Did Wyatt Earp put you up to this?*" he demanded.

"Why do you think anyone would 'put me up to' anything?" she said, fighting the tears that threatened to spill over. "I don't even know any Wyatt Earp! I agreed to go to supper with you because I was grateful that you helped my sister out of a fix, that's all!" The magical moonlit night had turned into a nightmare. What was he accusing her of?

Sam, meanwhile, had turned her loose and was lying on his back, staring at the moon.

"I asked you a question, mister," she reminded the silent figure.

"Never mind. It doesn't mean anything now," he said. "So you really are a preacher's daughter?" he asked inconsequentially, turning his head to look at her.

"Yes," she said, dabbing at a tear that had escaped down her cheek. She didn't want him to see her cry, but it was already too late.

"And you live with him right here in Abilene, right?" he asked, staring fixedly at the moon as if he already knew the answer.

"That's right. Why are you asking these things?"

He shrugged. "So I can find out just how much of a damned fool I've been, I guess."

She was silent for a moment, taking it all in. "So you thought I was a whore who went by Mercedes LaFleche? Why?"

"Look, you both have red hair, all right? And when you said your name was Mercy, I thought it was just short for Mercedes...." Aware of just how lame his excuse sounded, his voice trailed off. "Like I said, I'm a damned fool."

"So you thought I was a whore."

"You shouldn't even be saying that word, M-Miss Fairweather," he said, miserably conscious that he was being ridiculous.

She gave a short, bitter laugh. "Would you prefer I called her a sporting woman? And calling me Miss Fairweather *now* is more than a little silly under the circumstances, don't you think? Just keep calling me Mercy, if you please, now that we *know* each other *so well!*" she said with a meaningful glance at the pants he was refastening with fumbling haste. She'd already pushed down her skirts and refastened her corset and bodice.

He wished Mercy would *have* a little mercy on him, though he knew he didn't deserve any. But it was already impossible for her to despise him any more than he despised himself.

"You thought I was a sporting woman, and so you took me out for a nice dinner, and then you brought me out here so I could repay you by doing what sporting women do, is that it?" she went on relentlessly.

How could he tell her she was right, and yet, oh, so wrong at the same time? Was it too late now to try to explain that over the course of the evening he had gradually forgotten the dare and her supposed profession and had begun to see Mercedes—Mercy—as a rare, special woman in her own right, and not just a handy female available to slake his lust upon? That he'd been conscious of feeling—something, what, he didn't know—very different for the woman he'd taken on a moonlight prairie picnic, something *he* hadn't even begun to understand yet?

"Yes, that's how it *began,*" he said, sitting up and facing her. "I won't lie to you, Mercy. Like the rest of my outfit, I've been on the trail for months without a woman—" He stopped as he saw her mouth twist with scorn. Of course, he couldn't expect her to understand a man's needs. She was just a girl!

Was, he reminded himself, being the important word. She'd left girlhood behind rather suddenly and painfully, thanks to his unknowingly heedless initiation. The first time was uncomfortable enough for a virgin, even with a careful, considerate lover, but the way he had plunged right on in!

"Look, never mind all that," he said as she opened her mouth to say something. "Mistaken identity be damned, there's no excuse for what I did."

She nodded, then averted her face, as if he hadn't already seen the tears silvering down her cheeks. "Well, there's nothing you can do about it now. I... I want to go back to Abilene, Sam. Can we... can we leave now?"

He stood looking at his boots, his lips alternately pursing and flattening as if he were trying to decide what to say. Then he raised his eyes to hers, and his gaze seemed to lighten the longer he looked at her. Finally a half smile began to play about his lips, but still he said nothing.

Mercy was just about to repeat her question when he said, "There *is* something I can do. I'm going to marry you, Mercy."

Chapter Ten

Mercy looked at him as if he'd gone loco.

"Marry me? Thank you very much for offering to do the chivalrous thing, Sam Devlin, but that *won't* be necessary. No, just take me back to town, and if I can just get into the house without Papa hearing me, no one will ever... k-know," she said, but her breath caught on a sob.

He would have reached out a hand to comfort her, but Mercy wrenched away from him. "Don't you touch me!"

He let his arm drop. The thought that Mercy would suddenly act the "violated virgin" made him furious. He was willing to take the lion's share of the blame for what had happened, but not all of it.

"Now wait just a dadblamed minute, Miss Mercy Louisa Fairweather," he said. "Five minutes ago you were kissin' me back, and sighin', and beggin' me to keep doin' what I was doin'. Now, I've got ears, honey, and I would have heard if you said no to any of that. You sure as hell didn't say no when I was unbuttoning your dress and pushing up your skirts. *Are you tryin' to tell me you didn't know what was gonna happen when I unfastened my pants, Mercy?*" He was practically shouting by the end of his indignant outburst.

She hung her head, and her hands clenched together. "N-no," she admitted in a small voice. Then she looked up, and he could see the tears welling up in her eyes again. "I...I knew we were going to do...what I thought I wouldn't be doing...until I had a husband. But I thought you *loved* me, Sam!" she said, a sob catching in her throat. "I thought...well, never mind what I thought—it was stupid! And then, all of a sudden, you were so angry...and I found out you had been *thinking I was a whore!*"

"Your father doesn't even know you are out with me, does he?" he asked grimly.

"No, of course not," she said, getting to her feet and taking a few steps away from him before reaching back to dust off the back of her skirt. "He thinks Texans all have horns and tails and cloven hooves. I—I guess he was right."

He stood, too. "Look, Mercy, I said I'd marry you, and I'm going to. And if you still want to think of me as the devil who stole your maidenhood, I guess that's your right. Can't say as I blame you, now that I've heard your side of it. But—"

She whirled back around. "But nothing. Just take me back and ride on out of here tomorrow or the next day, just like you would if I really was that Mercedes LaFleche woman!"

"Look, you can't really expect to go back to just keeping house for your father as if nothin' happened, you know," he noted doggedly.

"Oh, can't I? Watch me!" she retorted. "Or are you saying you feel compelled to tell everyone I'm ruined goods now?" Her tone was defiant, but her frightened eyes begged him to tell her this was not the truth.

His fists clenched at his sides. "No, of course not, Mercy. But have you forgotten the consequences that could arise from what just happened?"

She looked at him blankly. "I told you, Sam, all I have to do is manage to sneak into the house without Papa hearing me, or anyone else. Charity knows where I am, and she's left our bedroom window open."

Inwardly he cursed the times, which decreed that good girls should grow up ignorant as newborn babies of how those babies were made.

He was going to have to say it. "I mean about what could happen nine months from *now,* Mercy. I...I..." He forced himself to go on, to get it over with. "I lost control, Mercy, before I realized you couldn't possibly be Mercedes because you were a virgin. There could be a baby."

Her mouth made an O of silent, horrified understanding, and then her spread fingers covered her face.

"There's no way of knowing... *now,* is there?"

Hellfire, had her mother told her nothing before she died? "No. I...think you have to miss your...monthlies...a time or maybe even two... before you're sure. And sometimes women get sick in the mornings, also, when they're in the family way."

"I... I see."

"But it doesn't make any difference, as far as my wantin' to marry you, Mercy," he insisted. "I'd want to marry you even if I didn't know there was a baby coming."

Her head came up at that. "You...you can't mean that. You don't have to spare my feelings, Sam."

"I'm not, I swear it," he insisted. "Mercy, I know it'll be hard for you to believe this, but I... when we were sitting there eating supper together, I was wishin' you weren't who I thought you were. I was wishin' you were just some girl back home I was courtin'. But then when we kissed, and I began to touch you, and you seemed to enjoy it, I... I just lost my head, honey. I'm going to marry you—and I'll be a good husband to you, Mercy, or I'll die trying."

And he meant it, he realized. He'd always intended to marry someday, anyway. And though he'd always assumed his bride would be some girl back home in Brazos

County, his someday had just come a little sooner than he'd planned, and in a different place. He wanted this girl. He'd been raised to do the right thing all his life, and he sure as hell wasn't going to fail to do right by Mercy Louisa Fairweather.

She stood staring at him, as if trying to decide whether she could trust him.

"And what about you, Mercy? You must have liked me, just a little, to agree to have supper with me, in spite of bein' taught all Texans were demons." His raised brows repeated the question, and he smiled at her encouragingly.

Her eyes avoided his. "Yes, I... I guess I did," she admitted.

He took a step closer to her. "And before... things got... out of hand, it felt *good,* what we did, didn't it, Mercy? Tell the truth, now—you *liked* it when I kissed you, didn't you?" He took another step, approaching her as carefully as one would approach a spooked mare.

"I—I'd never been kissed before. Not really."

He'd take that as a yes, he thought. Now that he'd decided she was going to be his wife, he was glad to have been the first man to "really" kiss her. And he'd be the only man to ever kiss her and touch her, and share her bed, he mused, as long as they lived.

He took the final step, which brought him close enough to reach out and stroke her cheek. "I'm—I'm sorry about the misunderstandin', Mercy, but I'm not sorry that we're here like this now, and I want you to be my wife. Marry me, Mercy, please? I'm going to make it so good for you, sweetheart."

For a moment she stood stiffly, resisting the caress, but then, trembling, gave in to it and leaned her cheek into his hand, closing her eyes. He could feel the wetness of her tears on his palm.

"All right, Sam Devlin, I'll marry you," she said.

He lowered his head and kissed her, tenderly, with none of the passionate aggressiveness he had shown before. It was a kiss of promise, a sweet sealing of a bargain. He tasted the salt of her tears as his lips left hers to touch her cheeks, and he pulled her close, her face nestling into his chest, his chin resting on top of her head, his fingers tangling in her hair. God willing, he'd never put any tears in her eyes again, though how he was ever going to be worthy of this girl he couldn't imagine.

Lord, he was going to have to take this innocent girl back over hundreds of miles of rough territory, to a farm that was still more a ruin than a going concern. He knew his family would welcome his bride—but how was Mercy going to feel about living among strangers, far from her own kin, especially while he was away on another trail drive for months on end? It would take at least one more drive to fully recoup the Devlin fortunes—especially now that he wasn't going to regain his poker losings from last night by bedding Abilene's prize whore for nothing, he reminded himself, smiling wryly at the thought. Well, he'd have to let Wyatt Earp have the last laugh, but Sam didn't feel as if he'd lost, after all.

"Papa won't marry us, Sam," Mercy said, breaking into his thoughts.

"He won't, hmm?" Sam couldn't say it surprised him. From what Mercy had said, it sounded as if her papa classed Texans lower than rattlesnakes, scorpions and other vermin. He sure wouldn't let one close enough to marry his precious daughter. Hellfire, he wouldn't put it past the reverend to put his Christian principles on the shelf just long enough to put a few holes in Sam for his audacity.

"Then we'll just have to get hitched before I go and meet your papa," he told her.

"B-but—there isn't another preacher in town," Mercy said, drawing away from his chest to look up at him.

"We'll...have to go to another town, won't we? Salina, maybe.... Only—Papa and Charity will be so worried, not knowing what's happened to me for so long. He may have missed me already, in fact. Heavens, how late it must be already," she said, looking at the moon, which had sunk low on the horizon. "Oh, Sam, what if he's already out looking for me?" she asked, anxiety written all over her face.

Sam thought for a moment. The sooner they were safely wed, the better. Mercy's father might stop at nothing to prevent his daughter from marrying some "good-for-nothing Texan," but Sam didn't think the preacher would have much to say once he and Mercy were joined in the sight of God, all right and legal.

"We won't have to go to Salina," Sam told her. "I know of another preacher in Abilene."

"You...you do?"

He told her about Deacon Paxton, the barkeep at the Alamo Saloon.

"He's really an ordained minister, Sam? You're sure?"

"He says he is, and I believe him. Look, let's just get married, so your father won't have any way to separate us, and we can get married again, anywhere you want. Maybe your father would even agree to perform the ceremony then. What do you say?"

"All right, Sam," she said simply.

Dawn was breaking by the time they had gathered up their things and hitched the horse—who'd been very content to munch on hedge apples while he'd been hobbled—back up to the shay.

"There'll be rain later on," Sam commented, casting an eye on the streaks of red and gold surrounding the fiery ball of the rising sun.

Mercy nodded. "What's that old saying, 'Red sky at morning, sailor take warning'?"

Sam snorted. "What would you know about sailors, living on the Kansas prairie?" he teased.

"I read it in a book," she told him archly. "Mama taught us to value books and learning."

"Honey, I'm just teasin' you," he assured her. "I purely love to see the sparks fly in those green eyes." He kissed the tip of her nose.

As the bay trotted along over the rolling prairie, the sunrise illuminated features that the darkness of night had only been able to hint at—the waving sea of grass, punctuated at intervals by sodbusters' cornfields, and clumps of cheerful, dew-spangled sunflowers that grew taller than Mercy. Cardinals and blue jays, hunting their breakfast, added splashes of darting color to the scene, while meadowlarks perched on hedgewood branches and sang about the glory of the day. One of the bedded-down herds they had passed last night was just beginning to move, but luckily they got on the road ahead of it so they didn't have to eat the herd's dust.

The ride back to Abilene seemed like a moment out of time. The sway of the carriage made Mercy drowsy, and she snuggled close to Sam as he told her more about her new home in Brazos County, Texas, and her future in-laws.

"Mama's goin' t' be so thrilled to have another daughter," he told her, his arm around her shoulders, keeping her warm against the early-morning chill. "And Annie will just love you to death, Mercy. Garrick, well, since the war, he's been a tad, ah, moody, and he takes some gettin' used to, but he'll come around, you'll see. . . ."

She listened, wondering how she would ever get used to all these new relatives. And what about Charity? How would her younger sister manage to stay out of trouble without Mercy to chivvy her away from the primrose path? If she wasn't there, would Charity fall for the next good-looking cowboy or smooth-talking drummer that blew into town? Perhaps her father would agree to let Charity join her down in Texas, as soon as Mercy was settled, or perhaps, if her father could be made to accept her inevitable marriage, he would learn to like and respect his unexpected son-in-law, and decide to move to Texas, as well! That *would* be a miracle, she mused, but on this bright morning, miracles not only seemed possible, but likely.

The town was hardly stirring when Sam tied the horse up to the hitching post in front of the Alamo Saloon and reached up a hand to help her down. Across the street the clink of broken glass accompanied the swish of a broom as a youth swept out the debris of last night's carousing, stopping for a moment to eye them curiously. From the Alamo, someone's snores whistled over the swinging doors, but the usual tinkling piano music was silent.

"Will he even be awake, this Deacon Paxton, do you think?" Mercy asked with a giggle.

"If he isn't, I imagine he'd consider this a good cause to wake up for," said Sam, grinning down at her. She couldn't help but smile back. He looked so handsome, even after a night without sleep, even with a night's growth of beard shadowing his lean, bronzed face, this man who was soon going to be her husband!

He led her inside. There was no one there but a pair of cowboys, one slumped over a table, his outstretched hand still clutching a whiskey bottle, another, a few feet away, slouched back in his chair, his head lolling back over the chair's headrest. He was the one Mercy had heard snoring from outside. At the sound of Sam's boot heels, a nervous-looking, plain-faced woman had scuttled out of a back room, fumbling as she tied her apron on.

"Sorry, mister," the woman said as she darted an inquisitive glance at Mercy, standing next to Sam with her shawl wrapped around her shoulders. "Didn't know nobody was here. You be wantin' some breakfast?"

"Maybe later," Sam said. "But right now, I'd sure like to see Deacon Paxton. Is he around?"

The woman looked surprised. "He's asleep."

Sam reached into his pocket and came up with a silver dollar. "Please, ma'am, would you get him for me? I don't think he'd mind, if you were t' tell him Sam Devlin from Texas wants him to perform a weddin'," he said with an encouraging grin.

The woman gasped, *"A weddin'? At this hour?"* then stared at Mercy, who felt herself blushing at the scrutiny.

She tried to return the woman's speculative stare, but failed. Could the woman tell she'd been out all night with Sam? Did she guess that the rumpled appearance of the red silk dress meant that she'd been lying on an old quilt with the man who now stood beside her? Was there some sign visible to any who looked closely that proclaimed Mercy Fairweather was no longer an innocent virgin? Oh, Lord, what had she done? Mercy had never had reason not to look a person in the eye!

As if he guessed Mercy's embarrassed thoughts, Sam put his arm around her waist and pulled her closer.

"That's right, a weddin'." He continued to stare back at the woman until she left to do his bidding.

Five minutes later a man sauntered down the stairs, still buttoning his shirtfront. He was tall, like Sam, but older, with silver mixed in with the dark hair, and wore a patch over one eye. The right side of his face, the side with the patch, bore several scars.

Mercy remembered seeing him around town. He'd always tipped his hat to her, and she'd wondered how he'd received those scars.

He looked surprised when he focused on her, and she realized with a sinking heart that he recognized her as the preacher's daughter. Would he now refuse to marry them, or insist on getting Papa's consent first? If he did, the plan was doomed. They'd have to elope, and they'd be lucky to get out of town without Papa trying to stop them.

Her hand, which by then had been resting on Sam's arm, must have tightened, for she felt him patting it reassuringly.

"Honey, this is Deacon Paxton, the minister I told you about," Sam announced. "Deacon, I'd like you to meet Miss Mercy Louisa Fairweather, my intended bride."

She and Deacon nodded to one another, the nod of townspeople who weren't exactly acquainted. Mercy had a feeling that Deacon missed little despite the lack of one of his eyes, and certainly had not failed to notice her rumpled dress and the shadows she knew must be under her eyes. And yet his gaze was not condemning, just curious.

He turned to Sam. "I hear tell you want me to perform a marriage service."

"That's right," Sam said.

"But Miss Mercy's father is a minister. Why are you coming to me?" Paxton asked Sam.

"Mercy doesn't think her papa will consent for us to marry," Sam answered, his voice level, but Mercy had felt him stiffen slightly.

"I see." Paxton turned to Mercy. "Miss Mercy, do you want to marry this man? Even if your father'd be against it?" His gaze penetrated to the deepest part of her soul, and she felt he could see the uncertainty she was feeling. He waited calmly, smiling slightly, and Mercy felt his smile warming that cold, doubting part of her.

"Yes, I want to marry him," she replied, her voice surprisingly strong.

"Then just let me get my Bible, and we'll begin," he said, and Mercy let out the breath she hadn't realized she'd been holding.

The barmaid must have told several people of the event taking place downstairs, for while they waited in the bar for

Deacon to return, a handful of people gathered on the stairs, whispering among themselves and pointing at the couple below. One of them, Mercy was displeased to see, was Tom Culhane, who smirked at her when she looked up. He had his arm draped around a sleepy-looking saloon girl. Mercy quickly glanced back at Sam, and saw him giving the bowlegged younger cowboy a look full of warning. Mercy forced her eyes away from Culhane and found herself gazing straight into the eyes of a red-haired woman leaning over the banister, her face full of amusement.

Though older by perhaps five years, the woman was pretty in a bold, worldly kind of way. Instinctively she knew this must be Mercedes LaFleche, the soiled dove that Sam had thought he was asking out to dinner last night. Again she darted a glance at Sam, and saw that he had seen her, too.

What is he thinking? Does he find her attractive? Does he wish he had taken her out to supper instead of me? If he had, he would not now be standing here, waiting to make a lifetime commitment to a girl he barely knew.

As if he were reading her thoughts, Sam pulled her closer, his action causing her to meet his eyes. They were so blue she felt he had brought the sky in with him, and the sun.

She couldn't help but look again at Mercedes. The woman grinned back, shaking her head in a rueful fashion, and when Deacon Paxton ascended to the landing and started to go past the woman, Mercy saw Mercedes reach out and touch his arm.

"Just a minute, Deacon," she heard the woman say. "The bride needs a veil. And did you think of a ring, Sam Devlin?"

Sam, his face stricken, had to admit he had not.

"Sam, it doesn't matter. You sure haven't had time—" Mercy began.

"Hmmph! Men never think of anything!" Mercedes said. She disappeared back up the stairs, only to return a moment later clutching something fluttery and white, and joined the trio standing in front of the great brass-trimmed mahogany bar. She opened up the cloth, and Mercy saw it was a delicate lace mantilla.

"Every bride should have a veil," she said, smiling at Mercy in the friendliest fashion as she draped the snowy lace over Mercy's hair.

Then she seized Sam's hand and placed a plain gold band in it. "I was engaged once, to a boy back in New Orleans. He...he died before he could put this on my finger."

"Hellfire, Miss Mercedes, we can't—" Sam started to say, but the woman placed a manicured finger over his lips.

"Oh, hush up, cowboy," she interrupted with a smile. "I've been saving it for the right occasion. And I believe this is it."

The unexpected kindness from a stranger, and a woman who did what Mercedes did at that, was so touching that it brought tears to Mercy's eyes as she tried to smile back at Mercedes LaFleche.

The woman chuckled and stared up at Sam for a few seconds before patting Mercy's shoulder. "Be good to this tall, handsome hunk of cowboy, honey. Sure, I wish I'd seen him first, but there are plenty of cowboys for me, and only one man for you, I'm thinkin'—and you're standin' next to him, honey." Then she stepped back and motioned to Deacon. "Well, let's start the weddin', Deacon."

Deacon opened his Bible and began, "Dearly beloved..."

Chapter Eleven

Her biscuits would never turn out as flaky and golden brown as Mercy's, Charity thought in despair as she labored to knead the heavy, sticky dough that would undoubtedly turn into gray lumps of lead when baked. *Where is Mercy? What on earth am I going to say to Papa?*

"Charity, where in heaven's name is your sister?" inquired the Reverend Jeremiah Fairweather after being greeted by the unusual sight of his younger daughter up to her elbows in flour. "And *what* is burning on the stove?"

Charity squeaked in alarm as she turned around, only to be confronted by clouds of smoke rising from the blackened strips that had been bacon fresh from the smokehouse only this morning.

"Uh, sick, Papa. Mercy's sick," Charity said quickly, grabbing for the skillet, but in her terror at being caught in the lie, she sloshed the grease and caused a small grease fire to blaze up. Her father muttered something that sounded suspiciously like a cussword while reaching for a pot lid to smother the flames.

"Sick, you say? Nonsense, Mercy's never sick," Papa said, lifting the lid once the danger was past and surveying with dismay the blackened strips that had been bacon. "Perhaps I'd better look in on her," he added, his face creased with concern.

"No!" cried Charity without thinking, then tried to moderate her tone. "That is, uh, it's just her, uh, woman's time...cramps, you know, Papa. She...wouldn't want you to."

Her father peered at her with the same soul-penetrating eyes that had brought sinners to repentance during many a sermon. "Charity, what's going on?" he asked in a dangerously quiet voice.

"Nothing, Papa," Charity whispered, miserably aware that she'd never been a good liar when her father asked a direct question. Now the secret of Mercy's failure to return last night was going to be discovered, all because she was not clever enough to dissemble until Mercy could reappear.

Her father gave her one last searching look before saying, "Even so, I believe I will go see her," and turned on his heel to leave the kitchen for the bedroom in the back of the house.

As fearful as she was of her father's anger, Charity was also relieved that the knowledge of Mercy's absence was about to be shared. She'd spent a restless night, listening for her sister and dozing fitfully, only to waken at every sigh of the wind, every random noise in and around the house. Gnawing worry had completely eroded the delicious feeling of keeping the secret of Mercy and her handsome suitor. What if, underneath his kind, charming exterior, Sam Devlin was really just as wicked as Tom Culhane had turned out to be, or worse? What if he'd harmed Mercy? Then it would be Charity's fault that she had kept the secret!

Her heart pounded as she listened to her father's footsteps echoing down the puncheon floor of the hallway to the back bedroom. She heard him calling Mercy's name, routinely at first, then his voice changed, sounding alarmed.

He was back in the kitchen in a moment. "Charity, could your sister possibly be, ah, indisposed out back?" he asked, referring obliquely to the outhouse.

Charity hung her head. The moment of truth had arrived. "N-no, Papa. She isn't."

"Then where is she, daughter? If you know something you're not telling me, the time to confess is right this minute," her father said in an icy, awful voice.

"I'm sorry, Papa—I thought she'd be back before you were last night or I'd never have gone along with it. I just wanted her to have a good time for a few hours, honest, Papa—"

"Where is she, Charity?"

Trembling and beginning to cry, Charity told her father that Mercy had gone to supper with a Texas cowboy, a trail boss named Sam Devlin, and had not returned all night.

The ensuing roar of rage could be heard, Charity was sure, clear to Texas Street.

"You may kiss the bride."

Cheers and whistles broke out as Sam Houston Devlin did just that. A few of Devlin's outfit, who had gotten wind of the boss's nuptials taking place in the Alamo, clapped and stomped their boot heels, creating a powerful racket that woke even the drunks slumbering at their table.

Tom Culhane watched from his position on the landing, his lip curling. *Well, isn't that sweet? Devil gets hitched, while I'm still stuck payin' for a few minutes between a woman's legs,* he thought sourly. *If he hadn't meddled in my business a couple of nights ago, I'd have gotten it for free from that stupid little blond bitch.*

"Now, where are you two lovebirds gonna spend your honeymoon?" he heard Mercedes LaFleche coo to the newly wedded pair, just as if she'd been the official maid of honor. "I hear the Grand Hotel has a room big enough to be a bridal suite."

Tom could see Devlin's bride blush as red as the hue of her dress, and even Sam looked a little taken aback at the thought.

"I don't know," Tom heard him say. "Guess we haven't taken any time to think about that yet. First we need to go tell Mercy's papa the news." He gave the girl an encouraging squeeze as her face turned anxious. "Don't worry, honey, it'll be all right."

"Well, why don't you stay and have some eggs and bacon first?" suggested the beaming bartender who had performed the ceremony. "There oughta be a weddin' breakfast, now that you're properly hitched."

When Sam hesitated for a second, looking inquiringly at his new wife, Mercedes spoke up. "Yes, a weddin' breakfast! Your little wife's gonna need her energy for the rest of the day, I'd bet," she added dryly, her remark punctuated by the renewed cheers of the cowboys.

"All right, let's have breakfast. Boys, Miss Mercedes," Sam said, his gaze including everyone in the Alamo Saloon, even Tom, "it's on me."

When pigs fly, Tom thought, clomping down the stairs and out into the dusty street.

He had no clear plan to do anything but avoid the sickeningly sweet sight of Devlin's happy face, and began to wander the streets, kicking sullenly at a stray cat, looking for something to occupy his time. Maybe he'd get his gear together and head out of town today. There was nothing to keep him here, and it was a damn sight better than going back to Texas with Devil and some of the outfit, as they'd originally planned. They'd promised each other that they'd race through the Nations, now that they were unencumbered by a herd of slow-moving longhorns, and once across the Red River, they'd whoop it up in Fort Worth. Since

Devlin had gotten hitched, though, things would change. No doubt he'd be wanting to travel in easy stages for the sake of that damned silly girl he'd married, and they'd be subjected to the sight of the trail boss billing and cooing with his wife every morning like a couple of doves. There'd be no getting drunk every night around the campfire, and he imagined they'd be glared at if they slipped and uttered so much as a "hell" in her presence.

Damnation, but he couldn't stand hypocrites. Two months ago in Fort Worth, Devil had been carousing and shooting up the town with the best of them.

Culhane was just passing the Bull's Head, another all-day, all-night saloon, when one of the half doors swung wildly open, crashing into his shoulder as a wild-eyed, middle-aged man rushed out, trailed by none other than the same little blonde he'd been kept from having his way with the other night.

"I—I beg your pardon, s-sir," stammered the frock-coated man. He was flushed to such an extent that Tom could see the red through his gingery, thinning hair. He uneasily eyed the pair of six-guns riding low on each of Tom's hips, murmuring, "No offense intended. I—I'm a little distraught right now, you see. I was j-just—just looking for one of my daughters. You haven't seen her, have you? A pretty girl, about as tall as her sister here, but with dark red hair? I'm the Reverend Jeremiah Fairweather, and her name is Mercy. I'm told she was, ah, foolishly associating with one of the cowboys in town right now."

Tom reckoned the old fool would have used stronger language about the man his precious daughter was with if he hadn't been speaking to a man who was also a cowboy. He darted a glance at the girl, and was amused to see her practically shrinking behind her father's frock coat, as if that would hide her from him. Her skin had turned a sickly pale.

Bet she hadn't told her doting daddy about the night she'd snuck out with him, Culhane thought gleefully. If he played his cards right he might get the chance to have her yet.

"Quite all right, sir. Think nothin' of it," he returned in a genial voice. "And, as a matter o' fact, I *have* seen your daughter, I b'lieve. If y'all was t' follow me, I reckon I could take you right to her and the cowboy you mentioned."

He heard the little blonde—Charity was her name, he finally remembered—gasp, while her father's face turned white as the belly of a newly caught perch. He gaped at Tom, his lips flopping open, much like the same perch.

"You can? In the name of God, do so immediately!"

"Papa," pleaded the girl, "please go easy on her! I'm sure she never planned to worry you!"

"Silence, you silly girl!" her father shouted, getting all red in the face and surprising Tom with the intensity of his anger. "Do not confound your sister's sin by your own foolish babbling! The time for you to speak was last night, when you chose to lie to me instead! You are to return to the house, Charity—no, I won't hear a word of argument from you—you are to go home right this minute and stay there, do you hear?"

The blond girl, white-faced, stared at her father for a moment, and then, sobbing, turned and ran down a side street.

Tom smiled in satisfaction. Charity had not had the gumption to tattle on him, since it would incriminate herself, too, and without her along to blacken his character, Tom could tell the outraged father anything he wanted to about Devlin. Revenge was going to be sweet indeed.

"I don't believe I caught your name, young man," the preacher said after a last look at Charity disappearing around the corner.

I don't believe I threw it, old codger. Aloud, Tom said, "It's Culhane, Reverend. Tom Culhane."

"Pleased to make your acquaintance, though I regret the circumstances. And now, Culhane, will you be so kind as to escort me to my erring daughter?"

Woo-ee, thought Tom, inwardly gleeful at the fire blazing in the older man's eyes. *Looks like there's gonna be hell to pay in a few minutes.* And if he was clever, maybe he could stoke the fire so it would burn the hotter.

"Yes, *sir.* Jes' follow me," he said, grinning as he reversed his direction and started back toward the Alamo Saloon. *Looks like there's gonna be an unexpected guest at the wedding breakfast.*

"Reverend Fairweather, there's some things I think you oughta know about the situation afore we get t' where yore daughter is," Tom said as they marched through the dusty streets.

"I'm listening, Mr. Culhane," the preacher said, his voice calm now, but Tom had seen the muscle jumping in Fairweather's rigidly held jaw.

"Well, sir, I'm ashamed t' tell ya, but the fact is, the man yore precious daughter is with is my boss—my former boss, that is, when I was trailin' cattle up here t' Abilene. But after I heard tell of the dare he took concernin' your daughter, sir, I was plumb ashamed to be associated with him, and that's the truth."

"*Dare?* What in God's name do you mean, Culhane?"

Tom took care to keep his outward expression shocked, though inside he was grinning for all he was worth. "Why, Reverend, when we hit town my boss happened to spy yore beautiful, innocent daughter. I'm afeared to tell ya he conceived an unholy lust fer her, and I'm mortified t' inform ya, Reverend, that he took a dare from one o' the cardsharps that he could... that he could bed her."

"He *what?*" Outrage made the man's face turn purple and the veins bulge in his neck.

He had just converted a man who was merely enraged to one who was homicidal, Tom thought, hanging his head in pretended sorrow at having to be the bearer of such awful tidings. "Yessir, though I blush t' repeat such sordid things, my boss made a bet he could seduce your innocent lamb of a daughter." *Tom, it's a good thing you're wearing boots, as thick as you're laying it down,* he told himself smugly.

Fairweather stopped dead in the street and faced Tom. again. *"What is the name of this instrument of Satan?"*

"Waal, you ain't gonna believe this, but he couldn't be better named—we call him Devil. That's Sam Devlin, Reverend, outta Brazos County, Texas, but Devil's his handle."

The Reverend Mr. Fairweather said nothing more for a few seconds, but a muscle jumped in his temple and he gritted his teeth as if fighting for control.

"Take me to him. At once."

If there was ever murder in a man's eyes, Tom thought, it was in this preacher's eyes. Perhaps he would be able to achieve revenge without even getting his own hands dirty, especially if the preacher was angry enough to shoot first and ask questions later. It might not be as personally satisfying for Tom to see someone else kill Devlin, but it would mean he wouldn't have to race out of town to avoid a hanging.

"Sir, you ain't armed, are ya?"

The preacher looked startled at the thought. "Certainly not. I'm a man of the cloth."

What had he been planning to kill Devlin with, his bare hands? "Here—you kin borrow my pistol," he said, offering the older man the gun butt first.

The Reverend Jeremiah Fairweather hesitated. "That my daughter's foolishness should bring me to this..."

"It ain't her fault. I reckon he seduced her with purty words an' liquor an' all—prob'ly raped her when he got her alone."

It was all the push the man needed. He reached for the gun.

"Besides, he'll probably be wearin' his Colts. You be careful, Reverend," Tom advised, motioning him to follow.

The man nodded soberly and marched after him, and a minute later they had reached the Alamo Saloon.

"Right across the street there, in that there saloon, I do believe you'll find yore Mercy an' that devil who's ruint her."

He watched as the preacher plowed purposefully across the street, his boots raising clouds of dust in his righteous wake.

Chapter Twelve

The wedding breakfast had gotten louder and merrier as some of the guests progressed from bacon, eggs and flapjacks to whiskey and beer. The Alamo was as raucously noisy as if it were nine o'clock at night, rather than in the morning; nevertheless, some sixth sense alerted Sam immediately that the man silhouetted against the swinging doors was trouble.

He straightened in his chair, putting a protective arm around Mercy, who didn't notice because she was responding to a question from Deacon. The bright sunlight at the newcomer's back prevented Sam from seeing anything except that the man wore some sort of dark frock coat much like the one he himself was wearing now. His face was shrouded in shadow, but he seemed to be staring in Sam's general direction. He wished the man would move forward, or say something—not being able to see his expression made Sam fidgety.

Silence had fallen over the saloon. "Can I help you?" Sam asked the figure at last.

Mercy looked up from a forkful of scrambled egg, and allowed her fork to clatter to her plate. *"Papa!"*

But Mercy's father seemed oblivious to his daughter's outburst, raising a hand that held a pistol.

"Now wait just a minute, Reverend," began Deacon Paxton. "We want no trouble here."

The man ignored the barkeep, too. "Are you Sam Devlin?" he demanded as he aimed the barrel of the six-shooter at Sam's head.

"I am," Sam replied, watching the man carefully, as one would watch a coiled rattler. "But there's something you ought to know before you shoot that thing, Reverend Fairweather."

"Papa, wait!" Mercy shrieked, starting to rise, only to sink back down at a jerky motion of her father's other hand.

"Be quiet, Mercy. I'll deal with you later. Right now I am going to kill the man who has so callously stolen your honor." He raised the pistol again and cocked it.

"Papa! Stop! If you fire you'll be shooting at my *husband!*" Mercy screamed.

The gun wavered, but he did not lower it.

Fairweather's jaw dropped, and he became a little paler, if that was possible. "*Husband?* You *married* this man?"

Mercy nodded, white-faced, her eyes round with terror as she eyed the gun, which was still aimed at Sam's head.

"*Who performed the ceremony? I'm* the only ordained minister in Abilene. And don't lie to me, girl," her father warned her.

"I did, sir," admitted Deacon Paxton, taking a step or two forward.

"You? You're no minister," scoffed the Reverend Mr. Fairweather. "Daughter, you've been foolishly duped by evil men."

"I dislike arguing with a man holding a pistol, Reverend, but I *am* an ordained minister," insisted Paxton.

"Oh?" Fairweather made the one awful syllable full of doubt and condescension. "And might I be allowed to see your certificate, sir?"

Paxton's eyes fell. "I, uh, don't have it with me, Reverend."

Fairweather spread his arms wide in a mocking gesture. "Well, of *course* you don't have it here at the *saloon!* Let's go to your lodgings, Deacon. I'd like to see the document."

Deacon lifted his head and looked the preacher squarely in the eye again. "I'm afraid I don't have the certificate in Abilene at all, Reverend."

"I see. Well, perhaps you could impart to me at least *where* you attended seminary?" Fairweather asked, his pale eyes glittering behind his spectacles.

There was a long moment of silence. Sam waited, his heart sinking, as Deacon seemed to struggle with the words. "No, sir...I...can't."

"Oh, and why is that?"

Deacon darted a glance at Sam, his eyes full of anguish, before turning back to Mercy's father. "It's hard to explain, Reverend. Things happened to me a few years back and I...I just don't remember. But I *know* I'm a minister, Reverend. I just know I am."

Fairweather looked scornfully from Paxton to Mercy. "Congratulations, daughter. You've been 'married' by a minister who not only cannot prove he is one, but cannot even tell us where he attended seminary. And did you surrender your precious virginity *before* or *after* your supposed nuptials?"

Sam watched as the doubt brought on by Deacon's admission was joined by shame in Mercy's eyes. It was past time he spoke up, he decided, anger rising inside him.

"I believe Deacon's tellin' the truth, Reverend. If he says he's a minister, then he is." He saw Deacon's grateful face. "But there's an easy remedy here, if you choose to disbelieve him. I married your daughter in good faith, sir, because I wanted to be her husband. I'd be perfectly willin' to have you marry us again—immediately." He reached for Mercy's hand as he spoke, and squeezed it reassuringly. It was cold and trembling.

"Please, Papa," Mercy said. "I want to be Sam's wife."

Ever so slowly Fairweather lowered the gun. "I—I'll have to think about this... take time to pray," he said, his voice quavering with uncertainty. "W-would you please, um, excuse me for a moment?"

As Sam and Mercy watched, he turned and lurched unsteadily out of the saloon.

Staring at her father's departing figure, Mercy rose and looked as if she was going to go after him, but Sam reached out and grasped her wrist. "Give him a few minutes, Mercy. He's spooked, and it's better if you don't crowd a man when he's spooked. He'll be back."

Mercy gave him a tremulous smile, and sat back down.

Fairweather blinked as he went back out into the blinding sunshine. It took him a moment for his eyes to adjust sufficiently to look for Culhane. He was nowhere in sight.

Now what was he to do, Fairweather wondered. Perhaps he would have to do as he had said, and pray for guidance.

"Hsst! Preacher!" came a voice. Fairweather whirled around to see Culhane's head sticking out from the side of the building. Culhane beckoned, then put his finger up against his lips to indicate he was to be quiet.

Casually Fairweather strolled around the corner of the building as if deep in thought.

Culhane was rolling a cigarette as he lounged indolently against a rain barrel.

"Yore daughter still in there with that cowboy?" Culhane inquired in a lazy drawl after blowing a perfect smoke ring.

"Yes. Culhane, she says she's *married* Devlin! That—that *barkeep* claims he's a minister, and he married them! Of course, it can't be true.... Why, the man can't even produce any proof!" Fairweather told the younger man, feeling righteous indignation swelling his rage once again.

"Heck, I shore wouldn't b'lieve that. What's he doin' tendin' bar in a saloon, then?"

Fairweather guiltily remembered Paxton having approached him about helping him in his ministry, and how he had rebuffed the man. "My point exactly," he said quickly.

"Well, it don't sound as if they're likely to be hitched legal. What are you going to do about it, Preacher?" Culhane challenged him. "Ya went in there with my pistol, an' I didn't hear no shots."

Fairweather looked down at the six-gun he was still clutching, amazed that he had forgotten he was holding such a heavy thing. "I...I don't know...."

"Ya tell me Devlin's hornswoggled yore daughter inta thinkin' they're hitched, but you don't believe it. Y' could marry 'em again yoreself, but ya don't believe he's a fit husband for your child, do ya?" He waited until Fairweather shook his head. "Preacher, I cain't tell ya how ashamed I am t' know this man, especially now that I've met a fine, upstanding man such as yoreself. If there's anythin' I kin do t' help ya punish that sorry cowboy, I'm yore man—even if ya had somethin' *permanent* in mind."

"Permanent?" Fairweather echoed. He searched Tom's face for confirmation that Tom was saying what he thought he was. "Oh! Oh, no! Surely killing Devlin would be wrong, even as evil as he is! Oh, my Lord, I just can't think right now...." He felt so confused. Hadn't he just gone into the saloon, intending to put several holes in his daughter's debaucher? And yet, now the idea of having someone *else* do so sounded so cold and repellent.

But if Culhane thought he was an indecisive fool, he didn't say so. "Yes, sirree, I kin shore understand that. You're certainly a saint not to want this bastard dead. *I* would, iffen it was my girl. But I could just, uh, make him disappear *without* killin' him, ya know."

Fairweather paused, considering the idea. It *did* sound less wrong.

Culhane pressed his advantage. "Looky here, Preacher. All ya'd need to do is get them separated for a while. If ya can get yore daughter to go with ya—tell her ya jes' want t' talk to her—I kin find a way t' make Devlin vanish. Okay?"

"What will you do...exactly...to accomplish such an end?"

"Preacher, if ya don't know nothin', ya cain't be held accountable fer nothin', kin you? I'll jes', uh, capture him, and knock him out...and by the time he comes to he'll be so far away he won't bother comin' back. Maybe I'll put him on a train to Californy, or somethin' like that—without no money, even if he was of a mind to, he ain't gonna work his way back here very quick, is he? Meanwhile ya kin larn that girl o' yers not to trust cowboys, right?"

It sounded as if it would work, but doubts remained. "I...I don't have much money, Culhane—what would you charge for such a favor?"

Culhane gave him a big smile, and Fairweather suddenly wondered if he'd just made a bargain with the devil. "Nothin', Preacher. I'd consider it a Christian service."

"You...you wouldn't allow it to become open knowledge what happened to him, would you? Or that I was...associated with it—in any way?"

Was that contempt he saw flashing across Culhane's face? It was gone so quickly he could not be sure, and when Culhane replied, his face was as bland and reassuring as his voice. "No, sir. He'll just...vanish, as if he's thought better o' matrimony and vamoosed outta town, scairt o' yore fatherly wrath."

Fairweather took a deep breath, hoping he'd decided on the right course. "All right, then. I...I hope she'll consent to go with me," he added, as new doubts assailed him.

"She will. Wimmen love t' talk things over. Now, iffen you're not gonna use that iron on that sumbitch Devlin, give it back t' me."

Fairweather returned to the saloon and found Mercy and Devlin waiting for him near the door. There was a wary look on the Texan's face as he returned the minister's gaze.

"I...I have decided to consider the matter," Fairweather announced. "To do that, I need to speak to my daughter, Devlin. Privately. I'm sure you'll understand that I must be sure that marriage to you is what my daughter really wants, that she hasn't been merely seduced by foolish promises."

Sam didn't like the man, and he didn't like the idea of Mercy going off with him even for a little while. Mercy's smile was trusting as she met his gaze now, but her eyes were still troubled and doubtful. This was Mercy's father, and she'd been raised to obey him, to trust what he was saying. Apparently before last night she'd never disobeyed him—ever. He was afraid of the ways this man had of making Mercy doubt him, ways that were reinforced by years of his fatherly authority.

"Don't go with him, Mercy," he said, not as an order but as a plea. "You don't have to go with him. You can stay with me."

Mercy looked distressed as she stared at Sam, then back at her father. "I—" she began.

"I merely want to talk to my daughter, Devlin," Fairweather repeated in ultrareasonable tones, speaking to Sam but impaling Mercy with those penetrating, pale eyes. "She will rejoin you in an hour or so. In fact, if you will come to the house in two hours, I will marry you two if that is still my daughter's wish after we talk."

"Oh, Papa!" exclaimed Mercy, and closed the distance between herself and her father in a bound. "I *knew* you'd understand!" She flung her arms around her father.

Fairweather shot him a look of pure triumph over his daughter's head.

Sam tried one last time. "Mercy, I want to go with you. I don't like the idea of him talkin' to you, tellin' you things, an' me not bein' there t' know what he's sayin' about me."

Mercy was back at his side in a heartbeat, her eyes full of entreaty. "Sam, please," she said, taking his hands in hers. "It'll be all right, I'm sure of it now. I won't let Papa turn me against you, I promise. And if you're not right there, glowering at him like you're both doing to each other right this minute," she added teasingly, "I'm sure I'll better be able to persuade Papa that you're going to be the best husband in the world for me!"

Sam hesitated, still sure he couldn't trust the ginger-haired preacher with the light of fanatic, outraged fatherhood still glittering in his pale eyes. But surely Mercy knew her father, and perhaps she *could* talk Fairweather around if he didn't insist on coming along. Besides, it would give him time to check out of the Drover's Cottage, and get his money from the safe, and arrange the trip home—after a honeymoon night in the Grand Hotel, of course. He liked the idea of making love to his bride in a clean, soft bed, under a roof, before introducing her to the rigors of camping out.

"All right," he said finally. "I'll be there at eleven-thirty. That's two hours," he added, staring at Fairweather.

Now it was his turn to receive an ecstatic hug from Mercy. "Good! And when you come, you'll find me all packed and ready to go," she promised, her green eyes sparkling with joy.

Sam was dazzled by the smile. Surely he had married the most beautiful girl in the world.

Chapter Thirteen

Sam watched as Mercy and her father went through the swinging doors, then turned back to those of his outfit that had taken part in the impromptu wedding breakfast.

"Well, I'd better go gather up my things and pay my bill at the Drover's Cottage," he said. "You boys who still want to ride back home with me, let's plan to meet about noon tomorrow at that little creek where we bedded down the herd that last night before we drove 'em into town—wasn't it about five miles south of here?"

"Aw, boss, you won't be wanting any of us rough brushpoppers for company," teased Jase Lowry. "This is your honeymoon trip!"

The rest of the cowboys guffawed and clapped their agreement.

Sam grinned. "Well, ordinarily I'd have to agree with you, and any hand that feels it necessary to go hurrahing under our window at the Abilene Grand Hotel tonight may find it difficult to sign on with me come next spring, but I sure don't relish the idea of just my bride and me travelin' through Indian territory alone. I'd be much obliged by your company, and that's a fact. And I promise to limit smoochin' Mercy to times when none of you are lookin'."

There were hoots of disbelief.

"You got yerself a purty one, boss, that's fer sure," announced Cookie Yates. "Cain't rightly see what she sees in you, though, especially this mornin'. You look like you bin rode hard and put away wet."

Sam smiled ruefully as he rubbed his whisker-roughened face. "Perhaps I'd better take time for a bath and a shave before I go pick up my wife."

"Hell, she looks at ya like ya hung the moon and the stars anyway, but it might help sweeten that old sourpuss of a father of hers," Clancy McDonnell opined. "Maybe if ya showed up lookin' respectable ya wouldn't have to sit through a fire-an-brimstone sermon afore he lets her go off with ya. Lord, I don't know as I'd want him for an in-law."

Sam had noticed that Tom Culhane had crept back among the Devil's Boys in the past few minutes. He'd noticed the young cowboy hadn't joined them for breakfast, though he had been coming downstairs when he and Mercy had arrived. Sam supposed Culhane had assumed he wasn't welcome, since they had not parted friends after their last meeting. Now, though, he might be thinking about mending his fences with Sam so that he'd have a job lined up for the trail-driving season next spring.

Hellfire, he was in a mood to let bygones be bygones. He nodded to Culhane in a friendly fashion, and Culhane nodded back, though Sam noticed he wouldn't meet his eyes. Still a mite ashamed of himself, maybe. Well, he was still welcome to join them on the trip back to Texas, as long as he could behave. He was adequate as a cowboy, and on trail drives Sam needed as many as he could get.

"Deacon, I'd like to thank you for performing the wedding ceremony," Sam said, holding out his hand to the bartender. "Just for the record, *I* believe you're a minister. Fact is, you kinda put me in mind of my brother, who was also a man of the cloth, before the war."

Deacon eyed him oddly.

Sam thought he'd embarrassed the man, and went quickly on. "I hope that you don't mind me sayin' that it was all right for Mercy's father to marry us again himself, if he was of a mind to. I just figured he might be more at ease if he said the words over us, too."

"No need to apologize for that. I understood," Deacon said, returning his handshake warmly. "Say, I hope you'll stop in to say goodbye tomorrow mornin', before you leave Abilene with your lovely bride. There's something I'd like to talk to you about."

Sam studied the man for a moment, then sat back down. "No time like the present," he said with a wave of his hand. "Tell me now."

Paxton looked at the curious faces of the cowboys still lounging around the bar, then gestured at the dirty dishes piled up behind it. "No, you've got things to do before you can pick up your bride, and it's nothing that can't wait until tomorrow. You're a lucky man, Devlin. Besides, I've got work to do here. I'll see you tomorrow."

Sam nodded, a little puzzled by the man's mysterious attitude, but just then Wyatt Earp came in.

Wyatt looked around the saloon, then his eyes came back to Sam. "Dang it, am I too late to kiss the bride? I just heard, Devlin! Congratulations, cowboy!" he said, slapping Sam on the back.

"Yep, you're too late. Mercy's gone off to unruffle her papa's feathers," Sam told him.

Wyatt rolled his eyes sympathetically. "Pray for a miracle, boy. That won't be easy," he told him with a grin. "I gather there was a little case of mistaken identity. A pretty *expensive* case of mistaken identity."

Sam laughed. "You might say that. But I'm not sorry with the way it worked out, not sorry at all."

Earp slapped him on the back again. "That's the spirit. Me and your Miss Mercy, we aren't exactly introduced, if you know what I mean, but she looks like a real fine, sweet lady. Can I buy the groom a drink to celebrate?"

"Thanks, Wyatt, but no, I've got to do some things before I pick up my bride."

"Papa, I'm *really* sorry that I worried you like this," Mercy began, running to keep up with her father, who was looking neither to the right nor the left—and certainly not at his daughter. It seemed as if he wanted to put distance between himself and the Alamo Saloon as quickly as possible, as if he feared being turned into a pillar of salt if he lingered a second too long. "But I need to explain to you—"

"We will not speak of it until we reach the house," her father snapped. Apparently he was not inclined to speak of anything else, either, for he just kept putting one foot in front of the other, maintaining an icy, tight-lipped silence.

As they walked along without speaking, they passed a few townspeople coming in and out of stores, driving past in buckboards, going about their morning errands. Normally, her father would have called out greetings and returned their good-mornings, but today he seemed not to see them. He just kept walking, his shoulders rigidly erect, head held high.

Mercy tried to wave and smile as if nothing were wrong. She was painfully aware, though, of the odd looks on their faces as they noticed the preacher's daughter, following in her father's wake and wearing a fancy, though rumpled, gown, far different from the modest, everyday apparel they were used to seeing her in. Once, after greeting two ladies of their congregation, she looked back and saw them speaking earnestly to each other behind cupped hands as they watched her go. She kept her head down after that.

It was a small town, and the gossip would spread fast. Before nightfall all of Abilene would have heard about the preacher's daughter being led through the streets in a grass-stained dress, the very picture of guilt.

Let them talk—what do I care, she thought rebelliously, resenting all those years she had been the very epitome of moral rectitude, the shining example, not only for Charity but for every other child around. She hadn't realized what a heavy burden it had been until she had dropped it. *I'm a married woman now, and Sam is going to take me away from Abilene, Kansas, forever. I'll be Mrs. Samuel Devlin, not "the preacher's daughter" anymore. Why, I don't even have to tell anyone in Texas my father is a preacher, if I don't want to!*

She maintained her stubborn hardness of heart until they reached their front porch. Then her father paused, as if reluctant to go inside, and turned back, looking at her.

"I...I was just recollecting the last time your dear, departed mother wore that dress," he said, looking at her, then quickly looking away as his voice seemed to catch in his throat.

Immediately her heart softened. Papa only wanted what was best for her, didn't he? Her mysterious disappearance must have been frightening for him until he had found her this morning, and coupled with her sudden, drastic change in behavior, it was no wonder the poor man appeared to be in shock. The morning sun shone on his face, emphasizing the tired lines around his eyes and his tightly held mouth, and the thinning hair upon his head. Why, he was old!

She had been a wicked, wicked girl to deceive her father the way she had, she decided as she studied him, and felt overcome with remorse. She wasn't sorry she loved Sam, and had married him, but surely, with patient, loving persistence, Papa could have been gradually convinced that Sam was a good man, worthy of his daughter.

"Papa," she began again.

All at once the door opened, and her sister hurtled through it. *"Mercy!"* Charity cried. "Are you all right? Oh, tell me what's happened!"

"I'm all right, Charity," Mercy said quickly, speaking before her father could. "And I'm married. I'm Sam's wife. See?" She held out her left hand, on which the plain gold band that Mercedes had given them rested loosely on her ring finger.

"You're *what?* Oh, Mercy, tell me *everything!*" her sister shrieked, hugging Mercy and laughing and crying at the same time.

"Daughters, the veracity of that statement is *still to be determined,*" her father interrupted heavily, putting a restraining hand on Charity, who was jumping up and down. "Charity, I need to speak alone to your sister about what has transpired. Please find some chores to do in the barn until I call you."

"But..." It looked as if she were about to argue, something she had never dared to do with Papa before, but after a warning look from Mercy, she nodded. "All right, I'll gather the eggs," Charity said, and went back inside. A moment later, after hearing the back door being shut, Mercy followed her father into the house.

They sat at the table, where the ruins of Charity's attempt at cooking breakfast were still in evidence. Mercy shoved a plateful of congealed scrambled eggs away with a rueful sigh. "I see Charity's still no cook. I've tried to teach her, Papa, honest I have. She just doesn't keep her mind on things."

Her father said nothing, just kept looking down at his Bible lying there.

"I know, we didn't sit down to discuss the dreadful state of Charity's culinary ability," she said, attempting to keep her voice lighthearted and failing. "Papa, I've gone about this business all wrong, and it's my fault you've gotten a bad first impression of Sam—but he's a really good man, Papa."

She wanted to tell him about the way Sam had rescued Charity from the aggressive cowboy, Culhane, but to do so would have revealed her sister's sneaking out, which had caused Mercy to meet Sam. One sister in trouble was enough. "If you'll just give him a chance, I'm sure you'll get to like him! In time, I'm sure you'll see he's the right man for me...."

Her father raised his eyes then, pale eyes that were full of sorrow. "Mercy, I don't believe for a moment that that marriage was a valid one, or that he ever meant to contract a valid marriage with you."

Mercy stiffened. Did they have to argue about this again? "If Sam thinks Deacon's an ordained minister, then I believe it, too," she asserted. "But just as Sam said, Papa—if you choose not to believe it, then *marry us yourself*, if you want to be sure."

Her father pounded his fist on the table. "I am not willing to join my daughter, my own flesh and blood, to that limb of Satan—why, he's even nicknamed 'Devil'!"

Mercy leapt to her feet. "Papa, that's just cowboy foolery, and you know it! Sam's told me about some of the rowdy hijinks they got up to along the trail and when they hit town. But he's a good man, Papa, and I love him, and I believe he'll settle down and make me a good husband, and a good father to our children."

"Mercy, *I am not willing to let you take that chance.*" He said the words as if that decided the matter.

Well, she'd tried the gentle, easy way, and he wasn't listening. "Oh? And if you insist on not believing Deacon Paxton was qualified to marry us, are you willing to take the chance that your daughter will bear a baby out of wedlock?"

His head came up at that and he stared at her as the blood drained from his face.

She was sickened that she had had to be so brutal in her honesty, but he had to see that she would not back down.

"Yes, Papa. Sam and I...well, we should have waited until after the wedding, but we didn't. It is very possible, after last night, that I'm already carrying Sam's baby."

She saw her father blink several times and clutch his Bible convulsively.

She rose and went to put her arms around him. "Oh, Papa, I'm so sorry. I never did this to hurt you," she said again, sick at heart. Was he about to cry? She had never seen him cry, except when her mother had died!

But apparently he mastered himself, for no tears fell. "I...I knew that must have happened, of course," he said with difficulty, speaking to his trembling hands. "I...just didn't expect to hear you say it...in so many words, I suppose. I didn't want to have to tell you this, but I can see imparting a painful truth to you is the only way I'm going to get you to listen to me."

She froze. "And what painful truth is that, Papa?" she asked, trying to sound unconcerned. "Are you going to try and tell me Sam Devlin already has three wives back in Texas?" *Oh, God, that isn't it, is it?* Sam wouldn't have asked her to marry him if he was already a married man—*would he?*

"You sound mightily cheerful about the possibility of Devlin being a bigamist," her father said, fire flashing from his pale eyes, "but no, that's not the case—at least, as far as I know."

He took a deep breath. "Daughter, this man that you believe is so good and honorable—aside from the fact that he callously seduced you outside the bonds of matrimony, of course—saw you, lusted after you and then made you the subject of a lewd, lascivious *wager*. If he could seduce *you,* the preacher's daughter, Samuel Devlin was to win a considerable sum of money. And from what you've just admitted, we can safely say he is now richer than he was before."

Mercy felt as if she had been punched in the stomach. "I—I don't believe you," she said quickly. She thought about the night before and felt a quick jolt of relief. She knew it couldn't be true. "Sam didn't know I was a preacher's daughter. He thought I was M—"

No! She couldn't tell her father Sam had taken her to supper thinking she was Mercedes LaFleche, a prostitute! "He, uh, didn't know who I was when he asked me to supper," she said.

Her father blinked, and she thought for a moment he was going to ask her what she had been about to say, but he didn't.

"Mercy, why would I have heard such a thing if it were not true?" her father asked, his face full of regret.

"And who told you such a thing—Abigail Barnes? Heavens above, Papa, we all know what a gossip *she* is! It *was* her, wasn't it? She was in the mercantile that day Charity and I first saw Sam standing across from the store," she said. *That day I watched him watching the soiled doves parade down the street.*

"No, it wasn't Abigail Barnes."

"Well, I for one don't believe it, whoever told you that," she said staunchly, even as her mind was filled with images of that very lie making the rounds of the good folk of Abilene.

"I'm sure you don't," her father retorted. "You imagine yourself to be in love, and in your blissful dream you think that this Texas rowdy is also in love with you. But others who are not so impressionable will find it easy to believe, and your good name will be ruined."

"It's already ruined," she replied, trying to keep the bitterness out of her voice. "I saw the way the people looked at me as we walked home from the saloon. I might as well have had a scarlet *A* sewn onto my bodice. But I know the truth, Papa, and in any case the gossip will die down after I leave town with Sam," she added coolly. "Your congregation won't be stained by my presence."

"You...you mean to go to Texas with this man? You'd leave Abilene, and your father? And your sister?" He looked stricken.

"Papa, Sam's home is in Texas," she observed gently. "But I was hoping to persuade you and Charity to join us down there, just as soon as we get settled. Just think of it, Papa! It'd be warmer down there—you wouldn't have these cold Kansas winters to contend with—and we could all be together. You could start another church there. Please, Papa?"

Her father cleared his throat. "There'll be time to think of all that later," he said, consulting his pocket watch. "Right now, if I were you, I'd be worried about whether or not you're ever going to see this cowboy again. We'll just see if he ever shows up to claim you, Mercy—or if he just rides out of Abilene as if the wrath of God were on his tail."

The calm certainty with which her father made this pronouncement sent a chill down her spine. "You think Sam will just run off and leave me here?" she cried, incredulous. "Well, you're wrong! He's not that kind of man! Sam will be here in two hours, just as he said. And I hope you'll be ready to say goodbye then!" she challenged him.

Her father got to his feet. "Very well, Mercy. In the meantime I must write a funeral sermon. Old Mr. Turnbull passed away last night—not that you had time to give *him* another thought, let alone a prayer, last night after you used my presence at his deathbed as a means of escaping from my guidance," he added.

His words sent guilt arrowing through Mercy as she stared back at her father. It was obvious he had been up most, if not all, of the night. So had she, but her father was no longer young.

"I'll be in my room when your supposed husband arrives," her father said, leaving the parlor without a backward glance.

Sadly, Mercy watched him go. She wished there was a way that she could do it all over again, from her first meeting with Sam to their wedding, so that her choice of a mate would not be the cause of her father's grief. Well, that wasn't possible, but she could hope that by the time Sam arrived her father would have accepted the situation. Time and prayer would have to bring about healing after that.

The grandfather clock in the parlor chimed the hour, startling her. Thirty minutes was gone already! She had very little time left to pack. Perhaps Charity could help her while she told her sister what had happened.

"Charity!" she called, running out the back steps to the barn.

Chapter Fourteen

"Congratulations on yer nuptials, young feller, and have a good trip home," Colonel Gore, the manager of the Drover's Cottage, said as he handed back to Sam the money he had kept in the hotel's safe. "Just sign here," he added, handing him a stub of a pencil and pointing at a line in the register.

Sam reckoned there was as much chance that Gore was a real colonel as he himself was a general, but this morning the innkeeper could have called himself the president of the United States and Sam wouldn't have cared. His mind was too full of amazement and joy.

Gore's wife spoke up from her husband's side. "You don't want to go to claim your bride with *guns* strapped on," she said, eyeing his Colts disapprovingly.

Sam glanced down at the six-guns that were holstered on his hips. It was so natural to have them there, he hadn't given them an extra thought when he was redonning his clothes after his bath.

"Why don't you leave them here?" Mrs. Gore suggested.

Sam started to protest that he never went anywhere without his Colts, but before he could tactfully refuse, the innkeeper's wife spoke again.

"We can keep them in our safe overnight. You don't want to go to that young girl's father looking like a gunslinger, do you?"

He supposed not. Leaving them off might make him look more favorable to the preacher, and anyway, he wasn't going to need them between now and morning. Except for when they went down for supper, he fully intended that he and Mercy were not going to leave their hotel room—or their bed. And anyway, he'd still have his "boot gun," the little derringer he kept tucked inside his right boot, and the throwing knife he kept in the other boot.

"All right," he said with a sigh. "I suppose you're right, ma'am, and thank you. I'll be back for 'em before we leave tomorrow mornin'."

Mrs. Gore accepted them with a satisfied cluck. "You're getting a good girl, you know. I know young Mercy. She's a sight smarter than that flighty flibbertigibbet of a sister of hers," she said with a sniff. "And if you ask me, Mercy has the kind of beauty that will last longer, too."

"Thanks," he said with a grin, deciding not to comment about Charity. He knew Mercy wanted to be able to have her sister move down to Texas, sooner or later, and he thought it was a good idea. It would keep Mercy from being so lonely, and might even save Charity from the primrose path. "You know, I never thought I'd leave Abilene with a wife, that morning we brought the herd in."

Colonel Gore chuckled, scratching his head. "Life is full of unexpected happenings. You sure you want t' take all that cash with you, since you're not leavin' till morning?"

"Yeah, I'll be transferrin' it to the Grand Hotel's safe, but I want to give my wife a fancy supper tonight, with champagne an' everything."

My wife. He couldn't help the grin that spread across his face whenever he said the words, or even thought them, in spite of the fact that the biggest hurdle still remained before him—going to the Fairweather house and facing the reverend, who in all likelihood hated his guts for what he had done to his daughter.

He certainly wasn't afraid of Jeremiah Fairweather, not by a long shot. He just hated the fact that the reverend's anger and Mercy's ambivalence about parting from her father under such circumstances had marred their wedding day. He hoped that Mercy had been able to talk her father around, to make him see that while their relationship had not begun with the highest motives on his part, he aimed to be the best husband Kansas and Texas had ever seen. Maybe in time the old coot would even learn to like him, but whether he did or he didn't, Mercy was his wife and the Reverend Jeremiah Fairweather was going to have to learn to live with that fact. *What God hath joined, let no man put asunder.*

When he had returned to the Drover's Cottage after stopping off at Sloan's Bathhouse for a bath and a shave, the sky had been darkly overcast, and now, as he left the hotel carrying his saddlebags and bedroll, the air was heavy and close and the sky rumbled with thunder. Maybe the threatening weather, after all those days of endless sunshine, had a lot to do with his feeling of unease.

He glanced at the lowering sky. *I'll be lucky if I get to the Fairweather house before the downpour starts,* he thought. *Shoot, a little rain won't hurt me.* He'd ridden through lots of gullywashers on the Chisholm, usually riding hell-for-leather to keep up with panicked, stampeding cattle. Just walking through rain, or sitting at a window watching it fall, might be downright peaceful.

He wanted to stop in at the livery stable to check on Buck before going on to join Mercy. It was on the way to the Fairweather house anyway, and the clock on Gore's wall had indicated he still had a few minutes to spare. He looked in on the gelding daily, even though he knew he was getting fat and eating his fool head off in the stall Sam's money had rented—it was the least he could do after the sturdy cow pony had carried him surefootedly through stampedes, across rivers and over hostile territory all the way from Texas. And the livery owner had shown an obvious attachment for his jug of whiskey—Sam wanted to make sure he wasn't so drunk that he had forgotten to muck out Buck's stall.

A few minutes of walking took him past the stockyards and over the train tracks to the Twin Barns livery. Just as he reached it, a jagged stroke of lightning rent the sky, followed by a large clap of thunder, and he dashed into the dim shelter of the stable.

"Just in time," he called out, indicating the rain, which had begun to fall in sheets just as he reached the shelter, to the figure slouched in the chair, a hat covering his face. The chair was tipped back against the outer wall of a stall.

The figure snored just then, the sound muffled by his hat. "Drunk," Sam muttered disgustedly, "and it's not even afternoon."

He could smell the familiar odors of horseflesh, hay and manure. All around him, above the drumming of the rain upon the corrugated tin roof, he could hear the sounds of horses chewing, stamping, and then the nicker that meant Buck had caught his scent and was calling out a greeting. Sam ambled in the direction of Buck's stall, which was midway down the aisle, pausing for a moment to admire the tall black Thoroughbred he had seen before, the one who was the spitting image of Goliad, Cal's horse. Then he went on to the next stall, and when Buck lowered his head, Sam scratched behind the buckskin's black-tipped ears, a motion that could be counted on to send the horse into equine bliss.

"How have you been, boy? Gettin' fat and sassy, are you? Have you had a chance to look over the other horses here—can you maybe recommend a filly for my wife to ride to Texas?" he asked the horse, feeling not the least foolish at speaking out loud. There was many a night this horse had been the only creature he had to talk to, and Sam didn't doubt for a minute that Buck understood him better than most humans.

He went into the stall and slapped the gelding's shoulders affectionately. "Yep, that's right, a wife. Your master went and got himself married. And just wait till you see her, Buck. She's the prettiest little thing, with big green eyes, pretty dark red hair and a waist no bigger than this...." He caught himself indicating Mercy's waist size to the horse—who just wuffled on his hands when he saw that they were empty—and laughed at himself. "You don't care about her waist size, do you, old boy? You just want your sugar, and if she brings it to you, you'll like her even better than me, won't you? Well, don't worry, I didn't forget your treat."

Reaching inside his pocket, he brought out the lumps of sugar he'd brought from the Alamo Saloon this morning for just such a purpose. "We'll have to make sure we stock up on some of this, or I suppose you'll dig in your hooves and refuse to carry me out of Kansas, won't you?"

After letting the buckskin lip the sugar cubes from his outstretched palm, Sam ran a gentle hand exploringly down Buck's sturdy legs, checking for cuts and swellings. Buck was not overly tall, with chunky, powerful shoulders. It wasn't his fault that he was just a cow pony, Sam thought, thinking wistfully of the splendid horses that had been raised on the Devlin farm before the War Between the States had changed everything. Conformation-wise, Buck wasn't a patch on that first stud his father had brought over from Ireland, though he reckoned Buck had more sense than any horse in Kansas or Texas. Maybe one day he'd be able to rebuild the stud, and he'd make sure that smart cow ponies were crossed with the line occasionally so that the

Devlin horses were known for their intelligence as well as beauty and speed.

"I think he's favorin' that off hind leg a little," came a voice suddenly, causing Sam to start and whirl around, and Buck to snort at his master's sudden motion.

As he was turning around, Sam was thinking that the livery owner must have awakened and heard him in Buck's stall, but just then the lightning flashed, and in the short-lived illumination Sam saw that it was Tom Culhane, rather than the liveryman.

"Oh, it's you," Sam said. "Thought it might be that drunken sot of a liveryman, wakin' up to see if one of the horses was bein' stolen."

Culhane took off his hat, and rainwater flew as he shook it a few times. Then he smiled, a smile that did not warm his narrow features or reach his bloodshot, close-set eyes, Sam noted before going around Buck and pushing the horse's hindquarters over a little so he could bend to pick up the gelding's hoof.

"Naw, he's still snorin' out there," Culhane replied. "My guess is you could steal every nag in the stable and he wouldn't wake up." He looked pleased about the fact.

Sam peered at the underside of the hoof, wishing he had a lantern so he could see better in the dimness, but what he could see looked normal, and Buck didn't object to Sam picking up the hoof, a pretty good indication that his leg didn't hurt.

"I think it's all right," he announced as he straightened and brushed off his hands. "Probably just the way he was standing." Blast it, now he'd be going to Mercy smelling of horse. Well, she knew she was getting a cowboy.

Culhane just continued to stand there, staring. Outside, the thunder rolled overhead, and the lightning flashed again.

Sam felt a prickling at the back of his neck, and wished the liveryman had been awake. "Somethin' you wanta talk about, Culhane? I don't have long—in fact, I probably should have been at the Fairweather house a coupla minutes ago."

"Right, to pick up yore bride," Culhane said with a snicker. "You, a married man. Who'd have thought it?"

Sam suppressed a twinge of annoyance. It was one thing to accept his crew's good-natured ribbing at breakfast this morning, quite another to watch this young pup sneer at him—the very same young pup who'd only recently threatened to make sure he wasn't around to hire any of the crew come next spring, just before he tried to draw on him. He suspected Culhane was drunk, and he hoped the liquor hadn't given him the itch to pick a fight—again. Sam didn't want to have to show up at the Fairweather house dirty and sweaty from wiping Culhane all over the barn floor, his appearance proof that he was much too rough a character for the reverend's daughter, but he'd do it if he had to.

"Yeah, well, miracles happen," he said shortly, stepping out of the stall and closing the half door behind him. "Now, if you'll excuse me. . . ." He caught a whiff of stale whiskey on Culhane's breath. Yeah, he'd been drinking.

But Culhane hesitated, eyeing Sam strangely. All at once Sam wished he hadn't let the innkeeper's wife talk him into leaving off his guns. He'd have felt a lot safer with their familiar weight riding at his hips.

"That preacher don't like you at all. He tole me so," Culhane said all at once.

Sam studied the younger man, seeing the glitter in the red-rimmed eyes. "I don't know what he was doin' talkin' to you about it, Culhane, but I don't believe that's any of your affair." Earlier in the encounter he'd been about to repeat his offer to have Culhane join the hands who were riding back with them, but the invitation would go unsaid now. He wouldn't trust the younger man if he was the last cowboy from Texas.

Culhane snorted. "Mebbe not. Mebbe so. I jes' thought you'd like t' know," he replied.

"Much obliged," Sam said shortly. He had better things to do than trade gibes with a drunk this afternoon. "I've got to be goin' now, though it looks like I'm in for a soakin', too," he said, referring to the rain, which was still drumming on the roof.

"All right, be seein' ya," Tom said as Sam started to walk past him, heading for the door.

Why was Culhane lingering? Probably too lazy to go out and get wet again, Sam thought—or was he waiting to do something to Buck, after he left? He decided to walk down the street for a minute, then double back and make sure Tom wasn't up to mischief. He could always claim he'd forgotten something.

The thunder crashed again, just as the butt of Culhane's pistol connected with Sam's skull and the inside of his head filled with flashing stars and red lights. The stable floor rushed up to meet him. Sam felt an explosion of pain in his head simultaneously with the impact of the hay-strewn, hard-packed dirt.

A black curtain was threatening to descend, a curtain that might never rise again. Through a crimson haze of pain, Sam heard the click of a gun. Damn, with all the lightning and thunder out there Culhane wouldn't even have to worry about the noise of a gunshot, Sam thought, trying to will his numb body to move.

"Told ya the preacher didn't like ya. An' neither do I, you sumbitch," Culhane mumbled, and fired. Sam felt a hot, searing pain as a bullet slammed into his thigh. Using his last, desperate reserve of energy, Sam twisted, grabbing for his boot gun as Culhane shot again.

He never reached it. The impact of the bullet in his chest slammed him back against the floor and he lay there, stunned, feeling the hot, sticky blood oozing from both wounds, and waiting to feel the barrel of the pistol against his head, waiting for Culhane to fire the shot that would finish him off.

The grandfather clock had never tick-tocked so loudly, thought Mercy, eyeing it balefully. Just then it chimed once, twice.

Two o'clock. Sam was now two hours and thirty minutes late.

She heard Charity, who was standing vigil at the front window, open her mouth to speak. She sensed her sister was going to ask again, "Are you sure you got the time right? Are you sure he knows where the house is?" followed by a worried look, and "Well, are you sure he's coming?"

Mercy was sure she'd go crazy if she heard the questions again, especially if she had to see their father, who was pretending to write a funeral sermon at the table, tighten his lips in grim satisfaction once more.

"*Yes,* he knows where the house is, I told him. And *yes,* he's still coming, and no, I don't know why he's late," she burst out before Charity could frame the questions again. Mercy straightened against the stiff, unyielding back of the horsehair sofa. She'd begun doing some darning, determined to keep her hands busy, at least, so that her fidgeting wouldn't betray her inner panic. She laid the stocking down and smoothed the striped blue lawn skirt of her Sunday-best summer dress, which she had thought would be perfect as a going-away dress. "I'm sure he's just been... held up... somewhere."

Her father took off his spectacles and smiled that maddening, pitying smile. "Daughter, when are you going to face it? He's had more than twice the time you two agreed upon. Devlin's thought better of it—he's not coming. You're going to have to accept that, sooner or later."

Mercy gritted her teeth with the effort it took not to call her father names, or burst into tears. *"He's coming. You'll see,"* she snapped. "And when he gets here, he'll be able to tell us why he was delayed. I'm sure we'll all look silly for sitting around fretting like this," she added, trying to laugh and failing miserably.

Her father just gave her that look again and went back to his sermon.

Two hours later she could stand it no longer. "I'm going to go and find him," she announced. "Charity, why don't you come with me?" she called to the kitchen, where her sister had been desultorily snapping peas.

"You're going nowhere!" roared her father, jumping up from the table. "I will *not* allow you to leave this house, *do you understand?"*

"Papa!" she protested, tears stinging her eyes. He'd never taken this fierce tone with her, never.

"Have some *pride,* Mercy!" he snapped. "Can't you see you've been jilted? Practically left at the altar—or should I say *at the bar?"* he inquired with heavy irony. "I won't have you running desperately all over Abilene, looking for your paramour, who has seemingly seduced and abandoned you!"

"I don't believe you," she insisted, but the tears were streaming down her cheeks now, and she couldn't stop them.

"Oh, Mercy," Charity murmured, having come in from the kitchen. Sitting by her sister on the horsehair couch, she put an arm around her. The kindness was too much for Mercy just then, and she collapsed against her sister, sobbing.

"I've already told you about the wager," their father went on. "You didn't believe that when I told you, either.

Doesn't his failure to keep his word confirm the truth of it? Face it, daughter, he's already gotten what he wanted from you—your honor—and now he's taken the money he won and he's either drunk as a fiddler in one of the saloons or he's halfway out of Kansas by now. You should be on your knees in gratitude for your lucky escape, daughter!"

"But we're *married!*" she protested.

"Hmmph. As I told you, I doubt that completely. But I'll make inquiries, and if by some mischance Paxton *is* a true ordained minister, we'll just have to see about getting it annulled. Provided you don't prove to be with child, of course," he added heavily. "In that case we'll cling to the falsehood just as if it were true—and after a time, we'll let it be known that we've received word that Devlin has died in some kind of accident, so that you can have the honorable status of a widow."

An image of the future stretched out before Mercy, bleak and cheerless. She could see herself walking through the town with a child clinging to her skirts, a child that had no father. Could it be true? Had Sam Devlin been nothing but a clever, smooth-talking trickster, who'd talked her right out of her virginity with his honeyed drawl? Was he even now laughing and joking with his outfit about the gullible little preacher's daughter he'd seduced? No, it couldn't be, she insisted to herself. The look in Sam's eyes, the sincerity that rang in his voice, those things were real. He hadn't lied to her. But the thoughts rang hollow even as she said, "He's coming. I *know* he'll be here."

Chapter Fifteen

"And now I gotta make yore carcass disappear, like I promised that stupid yokel of a preacher," Tom said, addressing Sam's crumpled body. "Well, not *ezzactly* as I promised him, 'cause he was dumb enough to b'leeve I could just *kidnap* ya or somethin'—how the hell did he reckon I wuz gonna do that without gettin' hurt when I let ya loose? Huh! He jes' didn't want nothin' to feel guilty about, that's all," he muttered.

After assuring himself that the liveryman still slept on, Tom went to work. First he backed the livery's buckboard into the barn so that its wagon bed couldn't be seen from outside. Then he took hold of Devlin's pant legs and, careless of the way the corpse's head scraped and bumped along on the rough dirt floor, dragged the body to the wagon. Grunting and sweating, he finally managed to heave the taller man's body into the wagon bed, where he left it in the bent, side-lying position in which it had landed. He covered it up with a tarp that had been lying in the wagon bed, saying, "There! Now no one will even suspect what I'm haulin'."

Tom had been boarding his own mount there, a rangy sorrel, but he hadn't wanted to pay the higher board for a stall, so the horse had been turned out in the corral with several others. He went back out to the corral now and lassoed the sorrel. Hoping his horse wouldn't mind pulling a buckboard, he backed the sorrel between the traces, then retrieved his saddle, horse blanket and bridle from the tack room and threw it into the wagon bed, careless of whether or not it struck Devlin's body. What did it matter? The bastard was beyond feeling.

After he'd dumped the body somewhere it wasn't likely to be found any time soon, he planned to leave the buckboard somewhere else, then ride his sorrel back into town as if nothing had happened. Tom was drunk, but not so drunk that he didn't know better than to just take off, much as he wanted to. It was well-known by all of the outfit that he and Devlin had been at odds. If he and Devlin disappeared at the same time, the Devil's Boys would set up a yelp that would send any posse straight on his direction. In fact, they'd probably come after him themselves. So it behooved him to put himself in some public place, where he could be easily observed, yet where the observers were likely to be vague as to exactly when he had come and gone. It might even be kind of fun to watch the hue and cry develop. The Devil's Boys might still accuse him, but if he acted surprised enough, and could get a few witnesses to say he'd been just idling about town, he'd be able to ride off in a few days, scot-free. And he'd be sitting pretty, too, he thought, now that he had several thousand dollars in his pocket after robbing Devlin's body. Devlin had been a fool to take it all out of the safe before leaving town, he thought with disdain.

But what if they accused him anyway, and his accusers found the money on his person? They'd know it couldn't possibly be his, and the noose would be as good as around his neck. Culhane thought quickly, and a few minutes later he had hidden it where no one but him would ever find it.

After checking once again to make sure that the liveryman was still fast asleep, Tom exited the barn carefully, peering through the downpour to see if anyone was abroad to observe him. No one was.

"Giddap!" he called to the sorrel, and headed the wagon out of Abilene.

Supper, badly cooked by Charity, was a late, silent affair, during which Mercy tried to ignore her sister's concerned glances and the fact that her father wouldn't look at her at all.

Only twenty-four hours ago, she thought dully. How much could change in the course of twenty-four hours. *Twenty-four hours ago I was dining with Sam. We were laughing and talking and I thought he was the handsomest, kindest man I'd ever seen. And I'd never known a man, especially not in what Papa would call "the biblical sense"—and more importantly, I'd never learned how a man could lie. I guess that's the real meaning of a "loss of innocence" to me.*

Oh, he'd never actually said that he *loved* her, not really, Mercy realized, thinking back. He'd said, when he had laid her back on the blanket, that he wanted to *make* love to her, and when he was about to take her, that he was going to love her like she'd never been loved before. But now she understood, with a certain bitter wisdom, that men didn't mean anything by it—at least, they didn't mean the same thing a woman did. When Sam said love, he had meant love in a purely physical, sexual sense. The *act* of love. He hadn't been lying then, exactly, but all he meant was *mating*. Like the animals did—and just like an animal, when it was over, so were his feelings. But he was sure enough lying when he'd said he wanted to marry her, evidently, or he would have come for her as he promised.

She was sure now that he hadn't believed that Deacon Paxton was a minister, any more than her father had. Either that or Sam *was* already married, and knew he could not contract a legal union with anyone else. Why else would he have felt so free to abandon her, once she was out of his sight? If they were well and truly married, one would think he'd at least have wanted to enjoy his marriage rights a few times, before being married became even a minor inconvenience!

Liar. He was a liar, that was all. Were all men like that, liars, just out to get what was between a woman's legs? She stared across the table at her father, who was solemnly chewing a mouthful of the peas that Charity had cooked to the point of mushiness.

"Papa, did you love Mama?" she asked him.

He looked startled by the fact that she had spoken at all, and even more by the question. "Well, of course I did! The Bible commands it—'Husbands, love your wives.' Yes, I loved her. She was a good woman—much too good for this earth, it seemed," he concluded, meeting her gaze. His eyes seemed to say, *And she would have been heartily ashamed of you.*

Then where had she—Mercy—come by this wild streak that had resulted in the disastrous events of the past twenty-four hours? Mercy remembered her mother as a calm, serene, sweet woman, one who never raised her voice, never seemed to get more than mildly and transiently annoyed at the difficulties of life. Had she ever been overcome by passion? Mercy wondered. Had she ever felt that fire heating her veins, overcoming her common sense, causing her to surrender her entire soul to a man? Was it possible that she had ever felt that way about *Papa?*

Looking at her father now, with his thinning reddish hair, his watery, pale eyes and his bony chin, Mercy found that hard to imagine. Had her mother come virgin to her marriage bed, or had there been some other, wilder lover who had taken her, then abandoned her and left her with child?

"Papa," she asked carefully, "when were you and Mama married?"

"In July of 1848," her father snapped, "as you will see if you look in the family registry in the Bible. Mercy, why are you asking all these questions about your mother, tonight of all nights? *Haven't you put me through enough today?*"

She dropped her gaze. "I'm sorry, Papa. I didn't mean to make things worse," she said meekly. Well, so much for that theory. She had been born in October of 1849, more than a year after her parents were wed. Unless he was lying.... But no, Papa wouldn't lie in a *Bible.*

But what did it matter, really, whether she was her father's child or not? No matter whether she had gotten this sudden wild, unruly streak from some phantom sire or through simple, sinful willfulness, the result was the same—she had fallen victim to a smooth-talking charmer and had lost the right to hold her head up high ever again.

Her father rose from the table, signaling that supper was at an end. She had hardly eaten anything, but it didn't matter. Maybe she'd never be hungry again. Maybe she should just forget about eating and starve to death—it would be easier than living with the shameful knowledge of how easily she'd been fooled.

"I think this evening we should drive out to the Abels farm and check to see how the family's doing," their father announced as Mercy and Charity began to gather up the dishes.

Mercy looked up from the dish she was scraping. "No, Papa, I don't want to. I...look horrible, and my head is aching." *And if I go with you I'll miss Sam if he comes,* a tiny voice whispered inside her.

She hadn't known she still had any hope, and the realization dismayed her. *Fool,* she called herself. If he hadn't come by now, he wasn't coming at all.

"I want you to go, Mercy," her father said in that I-don't-expect-to-be-argued-with way he had sometimes. "The sooner you begin to start walking the right path again, the better. The Abelses have suffered a grievous loss, and it's your Christian duty to go out and comfort them, not lie mooning around the house, wrapped up in your selfishness."

The thought of having to go anywhere and be seen by anyone was too much to bear. "I don't think I could be of any comfort to anyone, Papa," she said brokenly, her vision blurred by tears as she raised her eyes to plead with him. "Don't you see? They'd...they'd be able to tell in an instant that I wasn't this sad over Mr. Turnbull. Please...please don't make me go, Papa!"

"I'll go with you, Papa," Charity offered.

He ignored Charity and just stood there, arms akimbo, studying Mercy. "You still think he might come, don't you? And you want to be here, just in case?"

How had he guessed? How had Papa known about that wee little voice she was trying so hard to crush within her? "No, Papa, not really, and I wouldn't go with him now if he were the last man on earth," she lied, picking up another plate.

He sighed. "Well, I suppose you've got to get it out of your system. Go ahead and stay home this evening. But Charity, I want you to remain with your sister, not come with me. *And I'm going to hold you responsible for whatever happens, Charity, is that clear?*" their father demanded.

Charity said, "Of course, Papa" in a startled voice, and then shot Mercy a commiserating look.

His eyes went back to Mercy, who knew she'd been checkmated. If there had been even the smallest chance that she would have weakened and gone looking for Sam, she couldn't now. It wasn't that Charity could stop her, even if she would. But Papa knew she wouldn't get Charity in trouble now, after everything else that had happened.

"Tomorrow, however, we will begin to put this foolishness behind us once and for all. I will expect both of you to attend the funeral tomorrow afternoon at one," Papa added before leaving the kitchen.

The rain had stopped. He couldn't believe his luck when he found the obviously deserted soddy. "Ain't no one likely to find ya in there, 'least not until the varmints have eaten most of ya," Tom said after hauling the body out of the wagon with his arms underneath Devlin's shoulders.

As he was dragging Devlin under the low entrance of the rude dwelling, a pair of bats, disturbed by the unexpected human company, flapped out right over Tom's head. In his fear that the bats would fly into his hair, he dropped Devlin and waved his arms above his head.

As Devlin's head hit the dirt floor, he suddenly moaned, and the shock of it nearly stopped Tom's heart.

It gave wings to his feet, though. Tom ran a good hundred yards out on the prairie, as if he feared Devlin's vengeful ghost was about to rise and punish him. Then, realizing how foolish that was, he slowly returned, watching the crumpled body still lying half outside for any further movement.

It didn't move as he came near. "Ain't dead yet, huh?" he said, his voice sounding preternaturally loud in the stillness. Gingerly he reached trembling fingers to Devlin's neck.

A pulse still fluttered there, but it was faint, very faint and rapid. The trail boss's shirt was drenched with darkened, still-moist blood, while his face was waxy pale. Tom gave him a poke with the toe of his boot, but Devlin moaned no more.

"Well, if you ain't dead yet, you will be b'fore long," he muttered, dragging Devlin the rest of the way into the deserted, cobwebbed interior of the soddy. He heard the squeaks of mice rustling overhead in the sod roof of the rude dwelling, and the sound further gnawed on his nerves.

He knew he should put another bullet into the trail boss, just to make things sure, but he was still too spooked by the bats flying right over his head and Devlin's unlooked-for signs of life. He just wanted to get out of there. Devlin was going to bleed to death anyway, and if his heart was still beating when he left him, Tom could say with perfect honesty that he hadn't killed him.

Then, as he exited the soddy into the dusk, he noticed his shirt was bloody from contact with Devlin's blood-soaked shirt when he had been carrying the body with his arms under the shoulders.

"Shee-it," he muttered in disgust. He'd just bought that danged shirt two days ago when they'd struck Abilene, but he couldn't very well ride into town with Devlin's blood covering his chest like a brand.

He glanced back at the soddy, wishing it hadn't rained. The prairie had been tinder-dry before the rain today, and if he could have set a match to the soddy, tossed the shirt inside it to burn up along with Devlin and then backed the buckboard against the flaming dwelling so that it would burn, too, then all of the evidence would be ashes and charred bones.

But there was no telling whether he could get the soddy alight now that it was damp, and, once burning, whether it would keep burning long enough to do any good. Besides, the sight of the fire or the resulting pillar of smoke might attract unwelcome attention.

No, he was better off leaving Devlin here to slowly bleed to death, and he'd find a gully or something to leave the buckboard in. It'd be dark by the time he got back into

Abilene. He climbed back onto the wagon seat and, after loosing the brake, clucked to the sorrel again.

When Sam awoke, it seemed as if the thunder had chosen to rumble inside his brain. And when he struggled to open his eyes, the lightning joined the thunder to put on a blinding display. At first all he could see was a blur. The atmosphere was musty and earthy. Dear Lord, were those roots dangling overhead? Was he dead and buried, or worse yet, *buried alive?*

Panicked, he threw out his arms, expecting to meet the solid dirt of a grave around him. His right arm struck an earthen wall, but his left encountered nothing. *Pretty roomy for a grave.* So maybe it wasn't one, though he had no idea of where he *was.*

But the burning pain in his side distracted him from pondering his whereabouts. *Hellfire, if I'm not dead, I sure ought to be, after I let Culhane get the drop on me like that.* Gingerly he used his right hand to explore the left side of his chest, locating the site of the oozing stickiness at last, and following the open, stinging groove just below his nipple around the curve of his rib to where it ended about a handspread down from his armpit. *Well, there's an honest-to-God miracle,* he thought. A graze wound. The bullet that should have gone right to his heart and ended all his problems—his earthly ones, that is—had skittered along the rib and apparently never embedded itself in the skin. If Culhane hadn't been drunk, it never would have happened that way, Sam thought. There was no reason the younger cowboy should have missed a close-up shot like that at a helpless man.

But what of the other bullet, the first one, which had entered his right thigh? Grimly he felt the blood-stiffened cloth over his pant leg, and winced. He must have lost a lot of blood, judging by how big an area was caked with dried blood. Just brushing the cloth over the wound burned like fire. That one sure as hell wasn't a graze, and if he didn't get some help it might be the end of him.

But was it safe? He had no idea if minutes, hours or only seconds had passed since Culhane had shot him. Was Culhane still lounging around, just a few feet away, just waiting to see if he'd finished him off? Slowly, cautiously, he raised his head and tried in vain to focus. He still saw double, but there was nothing human standing around, singly or in pairs. Wherever he was, there seemed to be some kind of square hole a few feet above his shoulder, which apparently communicated with the outside, for a faint silver light came through. Moonlight.

The world began to spin around him as he attempted to push himself up with his hands and, groaning, he gave up for a moment, sinking back down, feeling the cold sweat pop up on his forehead and the nausea churn in his stomach.

Now what was that liveryman's name? "H-Help!" he called, his voice a mere croak. His voice seemed to bounce off close walls. "E-Engle?" he called, remembering the name at last. Still no answer. Probably the old drunk had lurched off to get his supper, or merely gone to seek his bed to sleep it off, Sam thought in disgust. He'd get no help there.

But he had to get out of here, wherever *here* was. Culhane might very well come back to see if he was dead, under the pretense of looking for him, now that some time had elapsed. He had to get some help, had to get word to Mercy about what had happened....

Mercy. It all came back to him now. Culhane had said, "That preacher don't like you at all," and repeated it just before he had shot him. God Almighty, had the righteous Reverend Jeremiah Fairweather hated him so much for what he'd done to his daughter that he'd paid Culhane to *kill* him?

He didn't doubt the possibility for long. There had been real fire and brimstone in the preacher's eyes when he'd looked at Sam, and he'd been so very eager to get his daughter away from him—*so Culhane could ambush him,* Sam realized, sick at heart. Had he been so caught up in a romantic haze that he hadn't noticed Culhane was following him from the moment he'd left the Alamo and gone to get his bath and shave, just waiting for the proper moment when he could catch him alone? Cowards like Culhane wouldn't usually take a chance with challenging him to a draw, where the odds would be overwhelmingly in Sam's favor. He was a better shot than Culhane could ever hope to be.

But how had the preacher had enough money to persuade a greedy bastard like Culhane to do his dirty work? From what he'd seen of the ordinary folk of Abilene—the ones not directly connected to the trades that catered to the cowboys—no one had any money to spare, least of all the preacher. He'd been wearing a frock coat shiny and threadbare with age.

Oh, God, the money, he thought with a sickening lurch of his heart. He reached for the wallet he'd put in his left breast pocket when he'd left the Drover's Cottage. It was gone. *Damnation.*

But the loss of several thousand dollars, as vast a sum as it was, was actually the least of his problems. Culhane had assumed he was dead and left him...somewhere...and he was wounded, how badly he wasn't sure. It was probable that unless he got some medical attention—and he wasn't sure there was even a horse doctor in Abilene, let alone a sawbones—he could die of blood poisoning, assuming Culhane didn't come back to finish him off. He had to get to safety and at least name his attacker before Culhane returned.

But where was safety in a town like Abilene? There was no lawman here and no jail; such justice as there was was of the vigilante variety. He'd have to find the scattered remnants of his crew. The Devil's Boys would see that justice was done.

"Buck?" he called, but the only answer was the nearby hoot of an owl. Well, he sure couldn't walk anywhere, not tonight. The very effort of raising himself up on his elbows made him gasp in agony. He'd worry about revenge tomorrow.

At the moment, Sam thought drowsily, all I want to do is live long enough to tell someone Culhane shot me so that he hangs for it.

But what about Mercy? his conscience accused him. What about the girl you married only this morning, or at least think you married, who's been waiting for you all afternoon? None of this was her fault. He didn't for a minute think that she knew anything about her father's part in the plot to do him in. Was she even now looking for him?

No, another part of him argued, in a town this small, by now she would have found me. Probably she'd never left her house—probably she was still pacing the floor of her home, damning his eyes and every other part of him for humiliating her like this.

Well, explanations to his bride would have to wait until he had gotten help, at least, and told his story. Then, if he was still alive, he could send for Mercy.

Chapter Sixteen

The next day's funeral, followed by dinner for the mourners served on plank tables outside the Fairweather house, seemed endless to Mercy, who had slept little the night before. She longed for peace and solitude, needing time to come to terms with what had happened, but everywhere she looked there were members of the numerous Abels and Turnbull clans, as well as other citizens of Abilene, not all of whom belonged to the First Baptist Church.

"If you ask me, I think some of these people just like to eat," was Charity's tart comment as she and Mercy went back to the kitchen to bring out more platters of fried chicken and corn on the cob. Many of the guests had brought cooked dishes, cakes and pies, and several of the women had been helping to serve the dinner, but at the moment the sisters were alone in the kitchen.

Mercy smiled in rueful agreement, taking a swipe at her damp brow with the edge of her apron. She'd been aware of curious looks, but as yet no one had had the insensitivity to ask her about her hasty, questionable "wedding" yesterday, and the fact that she was still at home, with the groom nowhere in evidence.

"Heavens, do you think they'll ever leave? My head aches so!"

Charity's expression was full of sympathy. "When they're all full to the eyelashes twice over! But when they do, Mercy, you go on up and lie down, and don't you worry about the dishes. I know you didn't sleep much last night."

Mercy gave her sister a second look. Charity had made a real effort, ever since her disastrous outing with Tom Culhane, to be a thoughtful, levelheaded person. Was she finally beginning to shed some of her flightiness?

"Thanks, honey," Mercy said, putting an arm around Charity and giving her a quick, appreciative squeeze. "But I couldn't leave you with all that. There's going to be enough to keep you busy until nightfall if you're doing it alone."

"Oh, I'm not doing it alone," said Charity with a wink. "I hope you don't mind, since he used to be *your* beau, but Ned Webster asked me what he could do to help, and I said he could wipe while I washed."

"And he said he *would?* My, my, Charity, he must be sweet on you to do that!" commented Mercy. "No, of course I don't mind. There was never anything really between us—Ned always seemed too shy around me to do anything more than just stare."

"You're just so forthright and capable, Mercy," Charity explained. "It scares boys like Ned off."

"I've sure demonstrated how forthright and capable I was lately, haven't I?" was Mercy's bitter rejoinder, and she took the platter of chicken out to the funeral guests before Charity could say anything more.

It was late afternoon. George Abels and his wife were the last to leave, after thanking the minister profusely for his eloquent eulogy. Then, when Papa went out to the barn to tend his horse, and Charity and Ned were already hard at work on the dishes, Mercy was at last free to seek a nap.

But sleep wouldn't come. Anger, self-pity and a stubbornly persistent hope had been battling all day in her brain, and so far, anger was winning. How dare Sam Devlin expose her to public humiliation by pretending to marry her then never showing up to claim her? Was he still in town, boasting of his easy conquest and his trickery, or had he left Abilene, only to repeat his sins in other towns on the way home to Texas?

No, the stubborn voice inside her—the one that believed in the trustworthiness of the man who had stood up with her in front of God and her outraged father and said he wanted to be her husband—insisted. Something had happened to Sam, or he would have been there. And yet, ever since yesterday afternoon she hadn't done anything but sulk, as if she didn't care even enough to go and check.

Idiot! Do you think it's even possible for you not to hear if there'd been a gunfight or something? There's a handful of gossipy women in Abilene who'd enjoy nothing more than to come report on Sam's misdeeds to you. No, nothing ill had happened to Sam—nothing ill ever befell men like that.

He might already have ridden out of town, making it too late, but if he was still there, she'd be dadblamed if she'd let him go without telling him off. It might be the sole satisfaction in her life, before the lonely years began.

She got up off the bed, smoothed her hair and went out to the kitchen, where she was amazed to find Ned Webster laughing and talking, perfectly at ease with Charity, who looked flushed and happy. If that didn't beat all! A girl could never tell about boys like Ned.

"I couldn't sleep," she told Charity when her sister noticed her standing there. "If Papa comes in just tell him I went for a walk. I think I need a breath of air."

Charity nodded, and looked as if she would have said more except for the presence of Ned by her side.

She knows, thought Mercy. *She knows I'm going to look for him.*

Thank God for the rain yesterday, Mercy thought as she marched grimly away from her house. At least the dust had had a good wetting down, and she wouldn't return home all dusty—or muddy, either, for the fierce summer sun had already dried the puddles that had been in the road yesterday.

She hadn't gotten ten yards from the house when she encountered a trio of cowboys on horseback. She recognized them as some of the Devil's Boys from yesterday morning when she had been introduced to them at the "wedding" breakfast. While she was still wondering whether she should acknowledge them, and shame herself by asking about Sam, the foremost of them jumped off his horse and touched his hat to her. His face looked worried.

"Miz Devlin, we were just comin' to see if you was at yore father's house," said the man, who she remembered was called Jase. "Do you know where Sam is? We went out to meet y'all five miles out like we planned, only no one ever showed up. Did y'all change yore plans, ma'am?"

The question made her forget all about pride. "He hasn't been with you?" she asked. "I haven't seen him since the wedding yesterday. He never came to the house afterward, as we had agreed." Her pent-up fury was rapidly transforming itself into alarm.

"Sam didn't never show up fer yore weddin' night?" Jase asked. The three cowboys exchanged looks while Mercy waited in an agony of impatience.

Could she trust these men? This couldn't be part of an elaborate ruse, could it? "No, he most certainly did not! And you're telling me you haven't seen him, either? I was just going to look through the saloons for him. Please, tell me the truth! I'll understand if he had second thoughts, and told you he didn't want to be married after all—*just tell me the truth!*"

There were more exchanges of looks, which made her want to scream, but she kept a ladylike silence until at last the one Sam had called "Cookie" said, "Waal, ma'am, I don't rightly know what to say, 'cepting to repeat that we ain't seen hide nor hair of him, either. Last we saw, Sam was walkin' toward the bathhouse."

"No, I saw heem just after eleven—he was heading toward the livery," put in the Mexican wrangler, whose name she couldn't remember.

"Well, he ain't in the saloons, Miz Devlin, neither the big ones nor the little ones in shacks and tents, neither," said Cookie, "so I guess we can spare ya the trouble of lookin' there."

She believed him, though she couldn't have said why. "Perhaps you should check the, uh... the..." She felt the crimson tide running up her neck to her cheeks.

"He ain't in no stores, ma'am," supplied Jase helpfully.

"No, I meant the houses of ill repute, as I believe they are called?" Mercy said. There was no point in being delicate. She'd only waste precious time.

Jase, though, seemed twice as embarrassed as she was at her frankness. "Umm, ma'am, I don't believe Sam would do such a thing, but we'll check them for you."

"Thank you," she said, "I'd be much obliged. Well, gentlemen, I believe I'll just take a walk through town just the same. I, uh, need something at the mercantile, in any case," Mercy said. "You'll send word if you hear anything?"

They nodded and touched the brims of their hats. Mercy resumed walking, thinking hard.

One of the cowboys had seen Sam at eleven, heading toward the livery. Why would he go there? Then she remembered him telling her he was boarding his horse there, as did many of the cowboys. But why would Sam go to the livery *at that particular time*—unless he was indeed planning on leaving Abilene yesterday?

But would he have left without telling his outfit? Though they had been polite to her, none of them were likely to condemn a man for not wanting to be tied down to a wife!

But the cowboy had not said he saw him go *into* the livery, just *toward* it, she remembered as she reached the Twin Barns. Had Sam actually gone *into* the livery? Well, there was only one way to find out.

Mercy had walked from one end of the first barn to the other before Engle finally put in an appearance, backing out of one of the last stalls with a pitchfork full of manure.

"Kin I help ya?" the red-faced liveryman inquired, standing poised with his load of manure, as if he wasn't quite sure what to do with it now that a lady had shown up.

"Yes. I'm wondering whether Sam Devlin, a cowboy from Texas, has been boarding his horse here, and whether he's taken it and gone?"

She had no idea if the liveryman knew who she was, for he just blinked. "Yep, he was, ma'am, and yep, he still is. It's that buckskin down at t'other end, on the left."

She thanked him.

There was a buckskin in the stall Engle had indicated, all right. The beast raised his head and stepped forward, nickering a greeting, when Mercy looked in at him.

"How are you, boy?" she murmured, patting the dark, velvety nose that had been extended inquiringly at her. "No, I didn't bring you any treats. Has Sam got you spoiled?"

The horse snorted but didn't withdraw.

"Did you see Sam yesterday, big boy?" How silly, to be expecting answers from a horse! She looked back down the aisle to ask the liveryman, but he'd vanished again.

And then she noticed the flies feeding on a dark brownish red pool of something to the left of her lace-up boots. It was too reddish to be animal waste or tobacco juice. It looked like. . . *blood.*

And over there—there was some more! A frisson of unease tingled between her shoulder blades. *What had happened here?*

Mercy bent and looked further at the livery's hard-packed dirt floor. If she peered very closely, she could see an irregular path through the hay-strewn dirt, leading toward the back entrance. . . almost as if a big heavy sack or something like it had been recently dragged along there.

Following the path, she came to its end at the same time she refound Engle, just inside the door.

"Mr. Engle, was Sam Devlin in here yesterday, about eleven in the morning?"

Engle stopped and leaned on the pitchfork handle, apparently oblivious to the fact that he had just dropped his load of manure. "Well. . . as to that I cain't rightly say, ma'am. I—I wasn't feelin' too well yesterday. . . ." His voice trailed off and he refused to meet her gaze.

She tried a different tack. "Did you see the stains on the ground, down by the buckskin's stall? They look like blood."

The liveryman blinked again, reminding her of a big red-faced owl. He shook his head, but obligingly went and looked. "Shore 'nuff *could* be blood," he said as he straightened from an awkward crouch.

Mercy waited, but he offered nothing more. No ideas about what she, or anyone, should do if the stains were, in fact, blood. She kept her exasperation in check with difficulty. *Dear God—what if that blood on the ground is Sam's?* There was no sheriff to go to. She had to look for Sam herself. But if the Devil's Boys had already looked through the town, there wasn't much point in her looking there, too.

"I see. Well, would you mind very much if I borrowed Mr. Devlin's horse? I'm Mercy Fairweather, uh, *Devlin*—we just got m-married yesterday, you s-see," she stammered, aware of the stableman's curious regard.

"Yes, ma'am, Miss Mercy. I heard tell before I, uh, fell ill.... No, I don't 'spose there'd be a problem if you was to take Mr. Devlin's gelding out. He's paid fer a week. I'll even saddle 'im for ya, you bein' the preacher's daughter an' all," he said with an abashed smile.

So he did know who she was. "Thank you, Mr. Engle," she murmured.

She had time to worry about her impulsiveness while the liveryman saddled and bridled the buckskin. The livery didn't have a sidesaddle, so she would have to ride astride, and she hadn't come dressed for riding. She was going to be revealing a lot more than her ankles when she rode out of town.

Mercy hadn't been on a horse since coming to Abilene, for the town was small enough to walk through in five minutes, and if they paid calls to farm families out on the prairie, Papa mostly hitched up the buckboard. What if Sam's horse resented leaving the comfort of his stall at the whim of a strange rider—or took offense at the feeling of her skirts brushing his flanks—and threw her somewhere out on the prairie, far from help?

The gelding seemed to have no such intentions, however, after Engle obligingly gave her a leg up into the saddle, for he waited placidly while the liveryman shortened her stirrups.

"He calls him Buck," the liveryman offered as he headed back into the stable.

"Buck," Mercy repeated aloud. "How original." *Don't men ever use any imagination?*

The horse flicked his ears as if listening, then, when Mercy tentatively nudged him with her heels, moved forward at a jarring trot.

Mercy had no definite plan in mind, and in any case she was too preoccupied with keeping her seat to guide Buck in any particular direction. But once she had adjusted to the bone-rattling gait, she saw that the gelding was heading out of town over the west road—the same way Sam had taken her when they went for their moonlit picnic.

It was already getting on toward suppertime. She didn't want to be caught out on the prairie alone in the dark. She'd just ride out for a while, and see if she could find any trace of Sam, and if not, she'd start her search again in the morning, she decided. Maybe she could involve some of Sam's outfit, if they were still around. She gave the horse his head, and he settled into a canter that was as easy to tolerate as sitting in a rocking chair.

Just two nights ago, she thought. Two nights ago she'd been riding out over this same prairie with the very man she was now looking for. Would she ever find him, or had he vanished without a trace?

I ought to go back, she told herself as she topped a rise. Twilight on the prairie could be deceptive. The sunset could be blazing in all its glory and then, seemingly in the blink of an eye, the light would seem to drain away, leaving the sea of grass in darkness.

Then on the next knoll she saw the deserted soddy, the very one she and Sam had had their picnic by. Drawn by sadness and regret, she urged the horse forward.

There it was, she thought sadly as she reached the spot, the very place in the waving grass where Sam had spread the quilt for the picnic, the place he had made love to her. The place where she had become a woman. Oh, God, would she ever know what had happened to Sam?

And then Mercy heard a sound, like a little cry.

Mercy froze on Buck's back, thinking at first it was the cry of an animal. She had no firearm with her...were there cougars out on the prairie?

But the gelding pricked his ears forward and nickered, as if in response to the sound.

And then she heard the cry again. It was human, and it was coming from the deserted soddy.

Chapter Seventeen

The hair prickled at the back of her neck, and she felt an icy knot of fear forming in her stomach. Was the soddy haunted? Papa had always maintained that there were no ghosts, but—

There it was again! She laid the rein against Buck's neck, trying to turn him, but the gelding moved forward instead, whinnying as if in reply to the eerie cry.

"No, Buck!" she muttered, drumming her heels against his flanks, but the gelding had suddenly turned stubborn. He walked right up to the door of the soddy before stopping.

"I'm *not* going in there!" she insisted to the obdurate horse. Even if it wasn't a ghost, it could be something as dangerous—an outlaw who had seen her coming, and now was trying to lure her inside, for example. But Buck wouldn't budge. If she was going to flee, she would have to do so on foot.

The sound—more like a moan this time—came again. It sounded like a man in pain.

Then she remembered the blood she had seen on the livery stable floor. *Can it be—?* If there was even a chance that it could be Sam, she had to look. Her heart thumped against her rib cage as she dismounted. Trembling, her legs like jelly, Mercy stepped forward and ducked her head to peer inside the soddy.

She could see nothing at first, and her first tentative step forward brought her squarely in contact with a low-hanging cobweb. With a shriek of horror she wiped the sticky substance away from her face and swiped at her hair, fervently hoping its maker was not now creeping somewhere on her. A side step resulted in a sudden squeak at her foot, and she heard some tiny creature scurrying away.

"Hello?" she called in a quavering voice. "Where are you?" And then, as her eyes adjusted, she saw a crumpled form lying in front of her.

"Sam?" she called, kneeling to peer at the face. *"Sam!"*

He lay so still. She thought at first he was dead, and that the moan she had heard seconds ago had been his final utterance, but then he stirred and struggled to open his eyes.

"M-Mercy?"

He said it like a man who has been presented with a handful of hope after he had lost every last ounce of his own.

"Yes, Sam, it's me!" she told him, stretching out a hand to touch his cheek. Its cool clamminess frightened her. "Sam, what's happened to you? What are you doing here?"

"S-shot..." he mumbled. "Here..."

She smothered a whimper with her hand as she saw the dark stain on the left side of his shirt. "Oh, Sam, not in the chest!" she cried, her heart sinking. Even if the bullet had missed the heart, men who were shot in the chest didn't usually live long.

"J-just a gr-graze," he answered, even as her trembling fingers were unbuttoning his shirt and exposing the angry furrow in his ribs. "But also...in the leg.... Th-think it's stopped...bleedin'...."

She felt the blood-encrusted cloth over the thigh wound. Clearly, it had bled a lot, though she felt no warm moistness that would indicate it was still bleeding, but the amount he had already lost was dangerous.

"Sam, we've got to get you some help," she informed him. "I've got Buck out there. I'm going to take him and get help. Pa'll come back with the buckboard, and we'll get the doctor for you." She prayed at the same time that the man who passed as the town's sawbones wasn't passed out from the laudanum he took for his frequent "toothaches."

Sam's hand shot out and gripped her wrist, surprisingly strongly for a man in his condition. *"No. D-don't get... your f-father,"* he rasped. "He—he's in on it. P-paid Culhane—"

"Don't get my father?" she repeated, staring at the white, drawn face. "Paid Culhane? Sam, what in heaven's name are you talking about?"

Sam blinked and shifted slightly, then winced as if some fresh spasm of pain were shooting through him. "Culhane...shot me. Tol' me...your papa...wanted him to," he said through gritted teeth. "He wouldn't do that... for free."

"*My* father paid Culhane to shoot you?" she repeated in astonishment. "Sam, that's impossible! He wouldn't do such a thing! Culhane must be lying!" But even as she denied it, she remembered her father's calm certainty that Sam had abandoned her, that she'd never see him again. But why would he have been so sure, *unless the incredible things Sam was saying were the truth?*

Something in her face must have hinted at her thoughts, because his face looked sad and he said, "S-sorry, honey. Know it's... hard t' believe... but your father hates me. Thinks I'm no good for you.... Reckon it... made him do somethin'...he wouldn't ordinarily do. But you see why you can't tell him...where I am...."

"Yes." She could see that. "But I have to get you help some way," she said, trying to imagine how she could get garrulous old Doc Tatum here to help Sam without him telling the whole state about it, let alone her father.

"Anyone...in Ab'line would tell him. I'll be all right...jes' need t' sleep," Sam insisted.

"You will not be," she argued. "Both of those wounds need to be cleaned, and if the bullet isn't removed from that one in your, umm, *thigh,*" she said, feeling herself blush at saying a word that sounded almost...*intimate,* "you could get blood poisoning."

"I'll be all right," he repeated, a stubborn edge to his voice. "Now g-go home. I'll...come for you," he said.

But she could see the beads of cold sweat on his forehead. "I'm not leaving you here alone," she told him. "If you're going to be so mulish, then so am I. I'm staying right here with you tonight."

He just blinked at her. For a moment she couldn't tell if he'd understood. Then he muttered, "Thirsty."

"Well, I imagine you are, losing all that blood," she murmured, wondering how she was going to get him some water. The same creek whose bullfrogs had furnished music for their midnight picnic was just below the knoll on which the soddy stood, but how was she to get it to his lips?

Mercy got up and peered around the dirty corners of the soddy, being careful to watch out for cobwebs. Perhaps the settlers who had abandoned this dwelling had left something behind.

Sure enough, she found a dusty, cobweb-covered old wooden bucket. She turned it over, thumping on the top, and shuddered as she saw a big black spider scuttle into the shadows. But she said a prayer of thanks for the things that had been left in the bucket—an old dried, hollowed-out gourd that would serve as a cup, a fat candle stub and a cake of lye soap.

The creek had been replenished by the day's rain, and was gurgling merrily when she dipped her bucket into it. She took a moment to wash her face with some water in her cupped hands, then returned to Sam.

He drank a whole gourdful of water, then mumbled, "More."

"I don't think I should give you very much at a time," she said, uncertain if she was right. "Now help me get you out of your shirt and pants—I've got to wash these wounds."

She helped him sit up to remove his shirt and pull down the top half of his union suit, a maneuver that had him wincing against the pain of movement. Beads of sweat broke out on his forehead. Then, after pulling off his boots and kerseymere trousers, Mercy cut away the blood-stiffened patch in the union suit beneath.

"Do you have a knife?" she asked.

Sam's eyes widened. "You're not plannin' on cuttin' the bullet out, are you? Just let me die in peace, woman."

The look of terror that flashed over his face would have been comical if it hadn't been for the circumstances.

"No, silly, I'm afraid that's a little beyond my talents," she said, trying to smile. "I just wanted to cut some strips off my petticoat to wash your wounds, and then to bandage them."

"Oh." He nodded toward the boots she'd removed. "In the right one."

The blade was short but wicked looking.

"Wish I'd had time to use that on Tom Culhane, that sneaking bastard," he growled, then fell silent and watched as she raised her skirt and casually cut off the lower half of her embroidered muslin petticoat.

She supposed a proper lady would reprove him for such language, but at the moment she could only agree. But how was she supposed to feel about her father, now that Sam had told her he had paid the cowboy to do this to Sam?

She deliberately shoved that question to the back of her mind until she could deal with it. "Why did he bring you clear out here?" she asked, hoping her question would distract him a little from the painful business of scrubbing the dried blood away from his wounds. "He shot you in the livery, didn't he? I found blood not far from your horse's stall. Why didn't he just leave you there?"

Sam shrugged. "I 'spect he figured he'd be the first person they'd blame," he said, his voice stronger since she'd given him water. "My whole outfit knew there'd been bad blood between us ever since the other night when I stopped him from taking liberties with your sister. He tried to draw on me a couple of mornings ago in the Longhorn. Ow, woman, do you have to take my hide off like that?"

"Sorry," she said, sitting back a moment to give him a respite. She decided she rather liked him calling her *woman,* even though his voice had been exasperated both times he had said it.

He'd set his teeth against the pain as she began to scrub again, so his words were ground out. "I guess he figured on just makin' me disappear. I don't know how he got me here, but I was comin' to as he was draggin' me through the door. Where *is* here, anyway?" Sam asked, taking a deep breath and looking around him as she stopped to rinse out her rag.

"That very same soddy I said I wouldn't go into just two nights ago," she said with a wry look overhead at the roots of sod that protruded from the low ceiling like thin, dried icicles. "It's every bit as horrible in here as I'd thought it would be," she added, brushing away some dirt that had sifted down onto his face. She tore off part of the strip from her petticoat and folded it against the wound in his thigh, which had begun to bleed again after her scrubbing. Then she moved to the wound at the side of his chest.

"I reckon Culhane figured I'd just die in here and no one'd find me till I was just bones," Sam said. "But at least it's shelter. How did you come to find me here, anyway?"

Mercy told him, shuddering inwardly at how easily she might not have come this way. He could have died alone, just as he had said. If she hadn't wanted to tell him off for abandoning her, if she hadn't seen the blood and gotten suspicious, if she hadn't taken his horse and gone wandering out over the prairie...

"Good ol' Buck." He sighed. "If I ever get back to Texas I'm going to see that he never does a lick o' work ever again. He can just graze all day in a pasture we have that runs down to the Brazos, and when it gets too hot he can stand under the cottonwoods...."

Mercy watched Sam's eyes get a faraway, wistful look as he spoke of home. "Oh, you'll get there, all right," she said lightly, "but don't you think Buck would get bored with nothing more than that to do?"

"I don't know," he admitted. "I expect I would."

Mercy applied the last patch of torn petticoat to his chest wound, then cut off some long, thin strips to hold the bandages in place.

"I'll buy you a new petticoat, I promise," he said with a grin that didn't entirely hide the pain and weariness Mercy knew he must be feeling. Then he glanced out the glassless "window" of the soddy. "Honey, it's almost dark," he added, turning back to her. "You'd better get on back to Abilene."

"I'm not leaving you here, wounded and helpless!" she exclaimed incredulously, then knew she had said the wrong thing.

"I'm not helpless," he growled. "And you can't possibly stay in this dirty soddy all night. Go on back—I'll be fine." There was a stubborn glint in his dark eyes.

"How can I go home, knowing my father wanted you *killed?*" she protested. "I'm never going home, ever! I hate my father for doing this to you!" Angry tears spilled over her cheeks.

Sam laid a gentle hand on her cheek as she knelt there beside him. "Don't say that, honey. I don't want you hating your papa because of me. He loves you, you know that. He's just a mite... misguided right now, that's all."

She bit her lip. Two could play at being stubborn. "Maybe you're right, but I'm not going back there, and I'm not leaving you alone here. You're hurt, and I'm your wife, and I'm staying here to take care of you." She went on before he could argue. "I found a candle in that bucket—I'd better use one of those matches from the little box I found in your trousers pocket and light it while I can still see."

She lit the match against the stone step, then lit the candle, screwing it into the looser earth in the corner of the room.

"Better unsaddle Buck," Sam murmured, his eyes drifting shut as the flickering circle of light illuminated the shadowy corners of the soddy. "Take the bridle off, too.... He won't...go far...."

Mercy picked up the bucket, intending to empty the bloodied water. She'd forgotten about Buck, but he was grazing close to the door of the soddy. Giving him an appreciative pat, she loosed the cinches and dragged the heavy stock saddle from his back, then pulled the bridle off, too.

The gelding gave a pleased snort, then got down and rolled blissfully in the grass. He was still thrashing around when Mercy went down to the creek for fresh water, but came ambling down for a drink of his own as Mercy was coming back.

By the time she reentered the soddy, carrying Buck's saddle blanket, it was fully dark. Sam was already asleep, lying on his back where she'd left him.

Lord, I hope I'm doing the right thing, she prayed as she lay down beside him and pulled the saddle blanket over him. *But surely You don't expect me to just go back to Papa as if he weren't responsible for Sam being here like this.* Not only would he never let her return to Sam—he might even send Culhane back to finish the job!

But would Sam recover out here in this dirty soddy, with just her to watch over him? she wondered as she lay next to her husband under the blanket that smelled of horse and leather, and listened to Sam's even breathing. She was so frightened, and so tired.... But surely God would watch over them during the night, and in the morning she'd have a clearer idea of what she must do to protect Sam until he was well again.

She lay on her side facing Sam, afraid to lie against him for fear of causing him pain. At last, worn out by her exertions and fear, she slept.

Chapter Eighteen

"Hey, Deacon, there's a bunch o' folks walkin' this way carryin' torches," announced the piano player as he came back through the swinging doors, first throwing his still-lit stub of a cheroot into the dirt behind him. "You don't suppose they're figurin' to burn down the place again, do you?"

Deacon laid his damp towel down beside Tom Culhane, to whom he'd just served a beer, and came out from behind the counter. Then he stood in front of the bar, uncertain what he should do. He surely hoped no one was in a saloon-burning mood. Last year when Abilene had first been open to the cattle trade, some indignant townspeople had torched a couple of saloons in a vain attempt to try to prevent "sin" from coming to their town. That was before many of the same settlers had learned what vast profits could be made in selling their produce and services to the Texans, though, and since then there had been little but grumbling about the rowdy Texans who kept Abilene roaring all summer long.

Mercedes LaFleche and Wyatt Earp, who'd been having a cozy late supper together at a corner table, rose and went to look outside.

"Deacon, it's that preacher fella, the one who was all riled up about you marrying his daughter to that Texas trail boss yesterday morning," Mercedes said over her red-satin-clad shoulder. "Looks like he's brought the whole congregation."

"Deacon Paxton, come forth!" shouted a voice from outside.

Deacon shot a what-now look at Wyatt, who rolled his eyes. "Don't worry, I'll cover you," the cardsharp promised. "But they all look to be sodbusters. I don't reckon any of them are armed."

He started for the door, wondering what the preacher wanted. Out of the corner of his eye, Deacon saw three of the cowboys from Sam Devlin's outfit who had remained in Abilene get up and head for the door also. He noticed that Tom Culhane, however, remained at the bar, drinking his beer, watching the door with wary eyes.

The five of them—the three Devil's Boys, Wyatt and Mercedes—formed a solid, reassuring phalanx behind Deacon as he stepped onto the wood planking outside the Alamo.

"Good evening, what can I do for you, Reverend?" Deacon inquired as his eyes took in the flickering torches held by three of the men among the score of townspeople surrounding the preacher. Most of the crowd were sodbusters, as Wyatt had said, bearded, tired-looking men, accompanied by plain-faced farm wives in drab, serviceable clothing. He saw Charity Fairweather, the preacher's other daughter, hovering close to her father. She looked as if she'd been crying.

But it was the preacher himself who took most of Deacon's attention. His pale eyes burned with an angry intensity in his flushed face as he stepped forward.

"You can tell me where he's taken my daughter, that's what you can do," he commanded. "We've searched all the rest of the town, and I have reason to believe she is here with that scoundrel, or that you may have seen her."

"Where he's taken your daughter? You mean Sam Devlin and Miss Mercy? I haven't seen either of them. What makes you think I have?" he asked. He'd heard that Sam was missing, of course. The three cowboys, who'd been sitting at the corner table of the saloon since early evening, had spoken of little else.

"Don't treat me like a fool, Paxton. You're the one who *married* them," Fairweather said with a sneer. "Why wouldn't you provide him a place to carry out his dishonorable intentions toward my daughter?"

Paxton controlled his anger with difficulty. He sure didn't like Abilene's only "official" minister, but if he wasn't careful, this fanatic might well direct his congregation to set their torches to the Alamo, and in spite of the rain earlier today, the wood was dry enough so that he might just succeed in burning the place down.

"Yeah, that's right, I married them," he replied. "But you can ask anyone here, and they'll tell you, *Sam Devlin hasn't been seen around here.* No one's seen him since the wedding, though his boys, here, mentioned seeing your daughter just a few hours ago, walking into town. They told me she was surprised that they hadn't seen him, either."

There was an angry buzz in the crowd after he spoke, and Deacon saw one of the farmers whisper something into the preacher's ear.

"Of course all of you would say that, Paxton," Fairweather said scornfully, his eyes raking the cowboys, the cardsharp and the soiled dove standing behind Paxton.

"Well, you're welcome to look upstairs for them, Reverend, if you don't think the sight of cowboys using their hard-earned money to *fornicate* with the saloon girls'll contaminate you too much," he challenged Fairweather. "Better leave the women and your daughter outside, though," he couldn't resist taunting.

Fairweather went almost purple. "I think I'll just do that," he said. "Charity, you are to remain right here on this very spot," he commanded the blond girl beside him, who looked as if she might die of embarrassment and shame. "Come, men," he said pompously.

"Wyatt..." Paxton murmured as the Devil's Boys behind them stepped aside to let the minister and the sodbusters pass.

"Don't worry, Deacon," Wyatt murmured with a grin. "I'll go with 'em and make sure none of the cowboys shoot the fools."

Deacon followed as far as the foot of the stairs, listening as the farmers stomped upward in the wake of the preacher and started opening doors. With all the racket that they made approaching, it was unlikely that any of the couples occupying the rooms above the bar would get caught in the act, though, and Deacon could hear the catcalls and jeers that greeted the farmers as they pushed open each door.

Then Deacon saw Tom Culhane leave the saloon and go outside. Curious, he went to the open window and saw the young cowboy motion Charity over to him. Deacon ducked back so that he could hear without being seen.

"You have your nerve, even trying to speak to me," Deacon heard Charity say, her voice an indignant hiss. "What do you want, you—you snake in the grass?"

"Why, Miss Charity, I was just goin' t' offer my sympathies on the disappearance of yore sister," came the wounded reply. "I reckon you're plumb worried about her, or you wouldn't be so mean to a fella who just got a little carried away by yore beauty," he added.

Deacon was pleased with her terse reply. "Horsefeathers. You lie like a tombstone."

"I'm sorry to have offended you, Miss Charity," Culhane said after a moment. "Sure you don't know anything about where your sister vamoosed to? You wouldn't keep a secret that upset your father, now, would you?''

''Tom Culhane, you just tend your own knitting from now on, all right? And don't you come near me, ever again, or I'll sic Ned Webster on you.''

Oh, ho, so the preacher's younger daughter had a beau now, and had gotten sensible since the evening he had seen her in here with the shifty-eyed young cowboy who'd been in Devlin's employ. Good for her, he thought as he heard the sound of Charity's footsteps taking her away from Culhane.

Fairweather descended the steps a couple of minutes later, his shoulders sagging. ''Very well, she's not here,'' he said as he stopped to point a bony finger at Deacon. ''But if I ever hear that you knew anything about her whereabouts and failed to inform me, hell will have no fury equal to mine. Have I made myself clear, Paxton?''

''Abundantly, Reverend,'' Deacon answered him, mentally forgiving him for his pomposity. He supposed if his daughter was missing he'd be hard to get along with, also. ''Sir, I think it may be significant that his cowboys thought your daughter was with Devlin, and yet when she spoke to them, she'd thought he was with them, and now she's missing, too—''

But Fairweather wasn't listening. Deacon saw him looking at the bar, where Culhane was once again sitting. A look passed between the preacher and the young cowboy. Then the preacher strode out to where his congregation was waiting with their torches. Deacon followed, just to see what they were up to.

''Reverend, it ain't no good tryin' to search out on the prairie in the dark,'' one of the grim-faced farmers was telling the frantic father. ''One of the horses is liable to put his leg in a gopher hole. We'll start again in the mornin', and meantime, we'll be prayin'.''

Deacon saw the preacher shrink like a balloon with a slow leak as his congregation dispersed. And then, to Deacon's surprise, the preacher walked back into the saloon and crooked his finger at Culhane, who got up, leaving his beer half-drunk, and followed Fairweather out of the saloon.

Well, well. What can those two possibly have to talk about? Again Deacon went to the window, to see where they were going, but they had already been swallowed up in the darkness. Lord, he had a bad feeling about Sam Devlin's disappearance, and the subsequent vanishing of his new bride. Was he ever going to get a chance to tell Sam what he'd remembered?

"Well, did you do as I asked you? Did you capture Devlin? Where is he? Don't you lie to me, young man," demanded Fairweather when they'd walked down the dark alley a little way.

Tom smothered the urge to knock the silly old fool down. "Yep, I got him, all right. All you need to know is he ain't ever gonna be seen in Abilene agin," he said, hooking his thumbs through his gun belt as he faced the preacher.

"Then where is he? And where's my daughter? Why did she disappear, too?" Fairweather demanded.

"Rev, I cain't tell you where I've got Devlin penned up, now, kin I? As long as you don't know, you cain't be made t' tell nobody where he is so's he kin be rescued, kin you?"

He watched as the preacher considered this. "No, I suppose not. But what about my daughter?"

"I haven't seen her," he said truthfully. His head ached from all the whiskey and beer he'd been drinking and the inquisition he'd been subjected to by the Devil's Boys. He'd told them he knew nothing about Devlin's disappearance, but he had a feeling they didn't believe him. The strain of sitting at the bar as if he'd done nothing wrong was giving him a gut ache, too, and he didn't feel like being bothered by this picayune preacher. "I'd say yore slut of a daughter was probably out lookin' for her lover."

"You foul-mouthed little swine. Don't you—"

He saw the preacher clench his fists and swing, but he was able to duck it easily and come back with a right cross that knocked the preacher back into the mud.

"Ole man, jes' leave me alone from here on. I did yore dirty work, an' I don' know nothin' about yore daughter," he said, and stalked off. *Huh! What an idiot, to hit a man packing iron!* The old fool was lucky he didn't fill him full of lead.

"Cold..."

The murmured word woke Mercy instantly in the pitch-black darkness. The candle had long ago guttered out.

"So col'..." Sam murmured again, his voice slurred. She reached a hand out to his forehead. It wasn't cold, it was as hot as a boiling teakettle! He began to shake, just a little quiver or two at first, then it became a constant rippling as the chill took hold of him.

"Oh, Lord, Sam, you're burning up with fever," she murmured as he pulled the horse blanket up to his chin, his shudders getting more and more pronounced. But the horse blanket wasn't that long, even unfolded, and now his legs were left uncovered.

To bring the fever down, should she bathe him with the cool water she'd collected in the bucket? But that seemed downright cruel when he was already so cold.

Sam huddled against her, clutching her to him as his teeth began to chatter. She could feel the cool dampness of sweat breaking out on his skin. He seemed barely conscious.

"Cold..."

Was this the beginning of pneumonia? Lord, she had to do something besides pray for more blankets to magically appear! In the complete darkness she couldn't even find the matches, but it didn't matter—there weren't any other candles, anyway.

A shocking idea came to her. What if she removed her own clothing and spread it over him, then lay against him so that he could absorb the warmth of her body? The idea of lying naked while holding Sam, who was wearing what was left of his underwear, made her blush, even in the darkness. But he was ill, and more than half out of his head. He'd never know. If there was even a chance it could help him she had to try.

He's your husband, anyway, she told herself. *There's nothing wrong with lying naked with your husband.*

Sam moaned a protest as she extricated herself from his shivering embrace. She stood and unbuttoned the bodice of her dress, then, after pulling it off over her head, spread it over his legs. Her three petticoats followed, and then her corset cover.

Mercy took a deep, appreciative breath as she unfastened the corset itself and tossed the obnoxious thing into the corner. She didn't wear one with everyday dresses, but she had donned it—how many hours ago?—for the funeral and the dinner that had followed. Then, after a glance back in Sam's direction to reassure herself that it really was too dark to see anything, she removed her chemise, leaving on only her thin muslin pantalets.

Burrowing under the clothing she'd spread over Sam, she lifted his arm so she could snuggle up against the right side of his chest. He resisted at first, and then, as if his brain was finally registering the idea of warmth, he gave in with a sigh and held her close.

Just as the first gray light of dawn made it possible to see the outline of the window cut in the sod wall of the house, Mercy woke to feel Sam pushing her away. He had thrown off everything—the petticoats, her dress, even the horse blanket. She felt his forehead, and he groaned in his sleep.

"Sam, you're as hot as hell's doorknob," she whispered in despair. After pulling on her chemise, she brought the bucket over beside her, tore another strip off her outer petticoat and started sponging.

Chapter Nineteen

During the next hour, while she wiped him down with the cool water, removing his union suit so that she could reach his arms and legs, she realized that she was going to have to leave the dangerously ill man and go to find help. She would have to try to do it stealthily, somehow, so that her father or Culhane did not see her and follow her back out here.

She had decided something else, too, while Sam was muttering in his delirium. If God allowed Sam to recover, she would have to steel herself to let him go back to Texas without her. She would do it because she loved him. He didn't love her, and she could no sooner possess him than one could possess the wind. There was no way she could expect him to honor his promise to be her husband now. Her father's plotting had destroyed any possibility that such a mistaken union could ever succeed.

As for herself, she wasn't sure what she would do, but she could never live with her father again. Perhaps she would have to leave Abilene and take a job, a respectable job, somewhere. Surely there was a place for her in this world that did not involve joining Mercedes LaFleche's sisterhood.

Sam's forehead seemed cooler now, and he slept. Glancing out the window, she noted that it was fully light, and so she began to dress. Perhaps if she rode very quietly down the back streets of Abilene she could get to Doc Tatum's before most folks were up and about—and before he'd sipped any laudanum. Maybe she could also find a way to get a message to Charity secretly, for her sister was bound to be worried.

Just as she was about to go catch Buck, though, she heard the gelding nickering, and the sound of hoofbeats. *Oh, Lord, we've been found already!* She dived for the floor, grabbing Sam's bootgun out of his left boot. The derringer would be a feeble defense, but she wouldn't give him up without a fight. Her heart pounded in her ears as she crawled to the window and inched up until she could see out.

It was Jase Lowry and Cookie Yates! They had apparently spotted Buck, and realized the horse's presence nearby might mean Sam was inside.

"Sam, you in there?" she heard them call.

Trembling with relief, she went to the door. "Thank God it's you," she told the startled cowboys. "Yes, Sam's here—I found him yesterday after I left you. He's been wounded. It's bad."

She stood aside as the two men rushed past her, then followed them into the soddy.

"Please don't wake him," she cautioned them. "He's had a bad night, out of his head with fever. The one in his chest is just a graze wound, but he lost a lot of blood from the one in his thigh. I'm so frightened...."

"Don't you worry, ma'am, we'll get him to the sawbones in town," Jase Lowry told her. "Who shot him?"

"I..." There'd be time enough later to worry about Tom Culhane's punishment, and she feared what these men might do if they knew her father's part in the shooting. "Never mind that for now," she said firmly. "But you can't take him to town. There are folks that don't wish him well.

It'd be better if you could bring the doctor here, without them knowing where we are."

"Well, I kin pretty well figure who mighta shot him, anyway," Jase informed her. "And you might like t' know that yore papa was out looking for you last night, him and his whole church," Jase said. "They aimed to be out bright an' early this morning, searchin' fer ya."

She'd been afraid of that. Eventually they'd find them here, too, and then what would happen?

Cookie had been gently examining the wounds without waking the sleeping man. Now he straightened and the two men exchanged looks.

"Jase, you go find the sawbones, and get him out here—at gunpoint, if you have to. I'll stay here and help guard Sam. Mebbe I kin find some plants nearby to brew up some medicine while we're waitin'." He glanced around the soddy. "And bring some supplies with you—blankets, some grub, a lantern, that sort of thing, so the boss an' his missus can hole up here long enough for him to get better."

Cookie's brisk organization and his apparent assumption that Sam *would* get well reassured Mercy. "If there was only a way to get them to look in the wrong direction—make them think we've gone on back to Texas, or something," she mused aloud.

"Put 'em on a false trail, ya mean," Jase said, rubbing his bristly jaw. "Yeah, that might work. What about yore sister? Would she help us, or would she jes' tell yore papa?"

Mercy thought for a moment, twisting a fold of her skirt. "She'd want to help, but it would be wrong to get her tangled up in this any more than she has been already," she said at last. If her father even thought there was a possibility Charity was lying to help her sister, he would make Charity's life hell—and Charity was too young to be on her own. "But if you see her alone, try to let her know that I'm all right. Can you really do all those things?"

"I aim t' try, Miz Devlin," he said, looking at his booted feet. "I'd do anything for Sam, an' that's a fact. I guess the sooner I git started, the better." He turned on his heel and left the soddy.

She watched him go, hope beginning to take root in her heart. It had warmed her, the way he had called her "Miz Devlin," and Cookie had referred to her as Sam's "missus." She could revel in that identity, at least for a little while yet.

Sam awoke a couple of hours later when the door of the soddy was pulled open, sending a welcome breeze across his hot face. He heard the clink of spurs.

"You didn't bring the doctor?" he heard Mercy ask, her voice sounding disappointed—and worried.

"Naw, he'd have been worse'n useless. I found him, all right. His housekeeper said he'd gone out to a farm to deliver a baby, so I went out that way and found him, only he was passed out in his buggy. The horse was just grazin' by the side of the road. He had some flask in his hand. Guess he'd been drinkin'," Jase concluded with disgust. "I couldn't even rouse him, Miz Devlin. But I did the next best thing—I stole his bag. Figgered Cookie might be able to do somethin' with what's in it, seein' as how he was our doctor on the trail, leastways."

"Mr. Lowry," he heard Mercy protest, "you shouldn't have stolen—"

"Jase," Lowry corrected her. "I'll take it back soon's Sam's on his feet, ma'am. But I did get the other things. Jest let me go unload my horse."

Sam felt the breeze on his face again as Jase left. He wanted to open his eyes and let them know he was awake, but it was just too hard.... He felt too weak to even move his little finger.

A moment later Jase was back. "I saw Manuel in town, told him what we was doin'. He's gonna stay there, keep an eye on things, like, so we know what the reverend's up to, beggin' yore pardon, Miz Devlin. But I didn't get no chance to talk t' yore sister, ma'am. Sorry."

"Did you see any sign of a search party?" Sam heard Cookie ask.

"Yeah, they was organizin' in town jest as I rode in," Jase said. "They was fixin' to split up and go in parties of two or three in all directions. Don't know if I convinced 'em, but I told 'em I met Sam and his missus on the road t' Wichita. Figured they wouldn't believe he'd be headin' any other way but toward Texas, but at least that way they won't be lookin' for him to stop anywhere close to Abilene."

Sam succeeded in opening his eyes at last, and saw Mercy rummaging through one of two flour-sacking pokes. "You did well, Mr.—Jase," she said. "Flour, and bacon, and eggs, and bread, and beans, and cornmeal, lard—even a little jelly and sugar! And candles and soap," she added with an appreciative sigh. She explored the other one. "Oh, and a pot and a skillet and more matches. Thank you."

Jase held out something else, a bundle wrapped in brown paper and twine. "Figgered Sam'd be needin' a change of clothes, too, once he's on the mend."

"My, you've thought of everything," Mercy praised. She stopped and looked up at Jase. "No one...got suspicious, seeing you buy all those things, did they?"

"No, ma'am, it's stuff we might be buyin' fer the trip home, anyway. Anything useful in that doctor bag, Cookie?"

Sam focused with difficulty on the wiry old chuck-wagon cook, who was busy pulling out a variety of stoppered vials and strange-looking instruments. "*Salix alba,*" the cook read aloud, squinting at the inscription. "Sure looks like willow bark t' me, but he's gotta be awake enough to chew it. But I spied some boneset growing down by the creek, and gathered some cow chips fer a fire, an' I reckon that'll work jest as well if I make a tea. Picked some purple coneflower out on the prairie, too. The flowers are about gone but that don't matter—it's the roots that do the most good. I'll make a poultice for the wounds outta that." He paused and pulled out an instrument that had apparently been at the bottom of the bag. "Sure hope we don't have to resort to usin' this," he said, his brow furrowing.

Even Sam could see well enough to realize it was a saw. "You even try...t' come near me...with that thing, Cookie," he said, the words forming with difficulty on his thickened tongue, "and you'll never...w-work for me again."

Mercy emitted a glad shriek. "Sam! You're awake!" She dashed over to kneel beside him, her hand stroking his cheek. No woman had ever looked more beautiful to him—or more frightened and tired. As he stared up at her, her eyes became suspiciously moist.

Jase and Cookie had come to stand behind her, too, and were peering down at him. "Don't you worry, boss, we'll get ya well, and we'll watch over the both of ya till ya are. Ain't no one gonna threaten you or the missus till you're on yore feet agin," Cookie told him stoutly.

"Who done this, boss?" Jase Lowry asked.

Mercy was holding out a dipper full of water, and he took a drink first. "Culhane," he said after swallowing the blessed, soothing wet stuff.

The two men bristled, clenching their fists.

"That little sawed-off, bowlegged weasel," Cookie growled.

"I'm gonna go fill him so full of daylight they'll think he's the sun, boss," Jase promised, giving a meaningful tap to each holster.

"He's...*mine,*" Sam said with all the firmness he could muster. "Don't...do anything...to him."

"All right, Sam, if you say so," Jase said at last. "I shoulda guessed it was him last night—I thought he was actin' funny at the Alamo. Wouldn't look nobody in the eye. He was nervous as a frog in a frying pan."

"Just...keep an eye on him...." Hellfire, even that little bit of talking had worn him out. He felt his eyelids drifting shut, and he was powerless to stop them.

As the sun rose high overhead, Sam's fever soared again. He lay with his head in Mercy's lap while she alternately coaxed and begged him to take sips of some bitter-tasting liquid. Now why would she want him to drink such nauseating stuff? He wanted water, gallons and gallons of it, cool and sweet from the Brazos!

His thigh burned as if the Comanches had stuck a burning arrow in it. In fact, his whole body was so hot that he thought he might have entered hell prematurely. Minutes later he felt as cold as if he were sitting at the bottom of a well during a norther.

Then he felt some cool substance being spread over his chest and thigh. Once the pain from having the wounds touched subsided, he lost all sense of what was going on inside the soddy and drifted into some filmy world of his own. In it he was a boy again, playing on the Brazos with his two brothers. Garrick was whole in his dream, missing none of his limbs, and both Cal, whom the war had taken from them, and his long-dead father were alive.

But his father kept his back to him, and Cal looked different than he remembered, more like... There was a startling revelation just beyond the foggy edges of his dream.

He reached for it, but the disclosure hovered tantalizingly just out of his reach....

To be replaced by images of Mercy on that moonlit night—was it only two nights ago? Mercy lying back on the old quilt, and him following her down, feeling the soft, welcoming warmth of her body, the lush softness of her lips, hearing her cries of delight as he stroked her and urged her to open to him... breathing in the scent of her womanly essence....

On the edge of the mist that surrounded him he heard the sound of a woman crying. *Don't cry, Mercy. Why are you crying, when I love you?*

"That wound's infected. The poisonin' is spreadin' up his bloodstream," Cookie told her after Jase had talked her into eating some beans and corn bread and a little bacon.

"No! It can't be! He's been sleeping so peacefully," Mercy gasped, going over to see.

Cookie's grim look told her more than his words. His face told her that Sam might slip directly from this "peaceful" sleep into a permanent one.

The wound in Sam's thigh told the same story. From the puckered, reddened edges of the bullet wound ran a thin reddish streak, going up toward the crease between his leg and his trunk.

"Blood poisonin'," Cookie repeated. "Ya sure ya don't want Jase to go fetch yore father, an' see if that doctor is sober yet? I know ya had yore differences with yore papa over Sam, but surely he'd do some prayin', him bein' a preacher an' all. Ya oughtn't t' be alone durin' this. An' that sawbones, mebbe he knows somethin' I don't...."

She didn't even waver. *"No,"* she said fiercely, forgetting that she wasn't going to say anything about her father's responsibility for Sam's shooting. "It's more than differences we had—it's my father's fault that Sam's lying here like this, maybe d—" She couldn't say it. "God wouldn't listen to prayers from a man like that. And I don't think Doc Tatum knows even as *much* as you do, Mr. Yates. He'd just want to use that saw—and Sam would end up dying, anyway." Or end up a miserable cripple, unable even to ride a horse, she thought. Sam wouldn't want to live like that.

"If he dies I'm goin' straight into Abilene and killin' Culhane with my bare hands, as slowly and painfully as possible," Jase vowed behind them.

"Shuddup, Jase. We ain't gonna let Sam die," hissed Cookie, but his eyes betrayed his uncertainty.

"I'm going out to stand guard," Jase said later, after taking one last look at Sam. "Let me know if..." His voice trailed off as he avoided Mercy's gaze. He didn't need to finish the sentence for her to know what he meant.

She settled herself with Sam's head in her lap. His fever was up again, his head so hot she could feel the heat radiating right through her skirt and petticoats. His breathing was rapid and shallow.

"His lungs is clear, at least," Cookie announced after leaning over with his ear to Sam's chest.

"What does that mean?"

"If he gets rattly, we're gonna lose him, Miz Devlin. So far it ain't. But if it does... I just thought you should know."

She hardly dared to ask her next question, but she had to know. "What about that red streak?"

"It's spread mebbe an inch."

The light was fading. Jase had already lit the lantern before he left.

"Shouldn't we give him some more of the tea?"

"He ain't awake enough to drink it," Cookie told her. "He'd just choke on it, and that would give him the chest rattles all the faster. I just reapplied his poultice, Miz

Mercy. There ain't nothin' more I can do fer a while. I'm gonna get some shut-eye," Cookie told her. "Wake me in a coupla hours—sooner if ya need me."

She nodded, though she wanted to cry out at being left alone to watch over Sam, as ill as he was. He could die between one breath and the next! But the old man was obviously fatigued, and as he said, there was nothing more he could do for a while.

It was up to her, then. All she could do was pray. Her father wasn't here to do the praying for her.

She began a litany—*God, please let him live, please save Sam, God.* But her prayers seemed to rise no higher than the root-pierced earthen ceiling of the soddy. The shallow, soft sound of Sam's breathing punctuated her silent entreaties.

If God was there, He was mute. No comforting assurance bathed her soul. Had Sam's breathing grown shallower, more irregular?

Please, God, save him. Don't let him die. I'll do anything...

Anything? whispered a still, small voice within her.

Yes, anything! Haven't I already said I'd give him up?

Forgive....

Forgive? Forgive Tom Culhane? You must be joking! The man wanted Sam dead! she protested.

The voice within was silent.

Then she saw her father, holding his arms open to her as he had when she was a girl. She saw the little girl that she had been, running into his embrace and hugging him with all the fervor of a child.

Forgive.

Forgive Papa, Lord? But it was by his order that Sam was shot! Surely You don't mean—

Forgive, the voice commanded.

All right, she thought, the tears streaking down her cheeks as she smoothed the sweat-dampened dark hair away from Sam's forehead and stroked his beard-darkened drawn cheeks with her wetted handkerchief. *If that's what it takes. But I don't understand.*

Just forgive.

Chapter Twenty

"Cookie, wake up! You've got to wake up," she insisted, shaking the slumbering chuck wagon cook just after dawn.

Mercy had just relieved Cookie of watching over the desperately ill man an hour ago, after getting a few hours of sleep herself. The old cowboy had fallen instantly asleep, his snores filling the shadowy soddy.

"Wha—? What is it?" he mumbled, then suddenly sat up. "Is he worser? Is he—?" The unfinished question lingered in the still morning air.

"You've got to look at this," she said, tugging on the grizzled old chuck wagon cook's sleeve until he came over to where Sam lay. She pulled the blanket off the sleeping man. "Am I just seeing what I want to see, or is that red streak a little less red?" she asked, pointing. "And it hasn't gone any farther up, has it?" Mercy held her breath as she waited for his answer.

Cookie peered at the wound in Sam's thigh for so long that Mercy thought she would die of fear.

"Yes'm, I do believe it is a tad lighter," he said at last, "and no, I don't believe it's gone no higher."

That acknowledgment emboldened her to seek another encouraging confirmation. "And doesn't he seem cooler to you? At least a little?"

He yawned hugely before reaching a gnarled, weathered hand down to feel Sam's forehead. "I believe he is, jest a little."

"Then he's going to live?" she asked, holding her breath again.

"Waal, it's a mite soon t' say," he hedged. "Seems like the coneflower poultice is workin', so I don't reckon the blood poisonin's gonna kill him. But now the fever's down, we got t' keep it down, so the pneumony don't ambush us. We got t' keep encouragin' him to drink that tea, ever' time he's awake. And lots of water, too."

She smiled tremulously, trying not to give way to tears of relief. "I'll do that," she promised, then felt guilty as she looked at the old man's tired face. "I—I'm sorry I woke you up, Cookie. It's still early—why don't you go back to sleep?"

He stood and stretched, a grin splitting his weathered features. "Aw, I always figger ya kin sleep when ya cain't do nothin' else, Miz Mercy. I reckon I'll go build a fire and get th' coffee goin', an' check on Jase."

The voices had blended into his nightmare. Cookie's voice had become Tom Culhane's voice, repeating the words, "Told ya the preacher didn't like ya. An' neither do I, you sumbitch." He twisted wildly, trying to get away before the cowboy fired, wondering why his thigh already burned as if he'd been shot.

"Sam! Sam! What are you trying to do? Lie still, Sam! You'll start bleeding again if you keep thrashing like that!" a feminine voice insisted, and he felt the pressure of hands on his shoulders, holding him down.

Panicked, he fought the hands. Why was she holding him still just as Culhane was about to shoot? Did she want him to get hit? The hands holding him were small hands, the pressure light—why couldn't he struggle free? Why was he so weak?

He opened his eyes and looked wildly around. For a moment he had no idea what he was doing in the soddy, and then he was able to focus his eyes on Mercy's anxiety-filled face, bent low over his as she pressed him down against the bedroll beneath him.

It all came back to him. He'd been shot. Culhane had dragged him in here to die, and by some miracle, Mercy had found him. He stopped trying to struggle upright, and lay back on the bedroll as waves of dizziness washed over him.

"You were dreaming, Sam," Mercy told him. "It's all right, you're safe now."

He wondered vaguely if he'd caused her any trouble, if he'd looked ridiculous when he'd been struggling against her. All his life Sam had had a dislike of looking foolish, of earning the contempt of those around him. But he saw no contempt on Mercy's face, just concern and love. Surely women, with their cool, soft hands and their caring eyes, were the most superior species on earth.

Just then a sleepy Jase Lowry stumbled in with a steaming tin cup of coffee halfway to his lips.

"Gimme that," Sam demanded, his voice sounding small and slurred to him. He cleared his throat.

Jake surrendered it with a grin. "Pullin' rank, huh, boss? You're gettin' better, all right."

"Sam, here, drink this instead," Mercy urged, holding out a cup of the boneset tea. "You need this more than coffee. It's to keep the fever down."

He made a face, and held up a hand to push the tea away. "I'll die for sure if I have to drink any more of that awful stuff," he told her, but softened his words with a smile. "Besides, if Cookie's coffee can't fix it, Mercy, it ain't worth fixin'. Cookie's coffee's so strong it walks right into the cup, isn't that right, Cookie?"

"I'd tell you what yore opinion is worth, Dev, but there's a lady present," the old man retorted, but it was obvious he was pleased.

Cookie ambled out then and made breakfast, returning minutes later with two tin plates of bacon and eggs for Sam and Mercy. Cookie's cooking had never smelled so good to Sam, and he gruffly declined Mercy's offer to feed him, but he found that he was so weak he couldn't sit up. He could only eat in a reclining position, and even then, he was only able to eat a few bites before he sank back on his back, exhausted.

"You looked like a picture I saw once of a Roman senator reclining at the banquet, Sam," she teased as she took his plate away. "Don't worry, your appetite will come back. It's always a little puny after a high fever."

Mercy smiled over her shoulder as she exited the soddy, but there was a haunted look in her eyes that made him suspect just how close he'd come to dying in the past twenty-four hours. By God, he'd make Culhane pay for frightening Mercy half to death. He wondered how long he was going to have to wait before he was strong enough to do so, or if Culhane would still be there when he was ready.

Mercy was back in a few minutes with a kettle full of steaming water and a folded shirt and pants. "You need a bath and a change of clothes, Sam," she said matter-of-factly, taking a rag and beginning to work up a lather.

"Hey, I can do that," he protested, reaching for the rag. He wasn't going to let her bathe him as if he were a squalling, toothless baby!

There was a flash of impatience in her green eyes as she faced him. "You couldn't even sit up to eat, Sam, remember? Can't you just be patient for a day or so until you regain your strength? It doesn't make you any less of a man. After all, I am your wife," she reminded him, two spots of hectic color appearing high on her cheekbones. Then, as if he'd already agreed to submit, she pushed the blanket aside and calmly began to soap his chest.

"But—" How could he explain to this innocent girl, without embarrassing both of them, that his slumbering manhood had awakened like a sleeping dragon at her first touch and was already beginning to stir?

"Don't worry," she told him, her voice teasing again, "Jase is going to town to check with Clancy, and Cookie's going to stand guard outside. Your men aren't going to see you getting bathed."

Sure enough, the sound of a horse whinnying, followed by the fading thud of hoofbeats, confirmed her words. And then there was only the sound of songbirds and the hum of cicadas coming in the little window.

"Jase was good enough to buy you some new clothes when he bought the supplies," Mercy was saying as she finished his chest and went on to wash his arms. "We didn't know what happened to your clothing, whether you had left it at the Drover's Cottage, but in any case, it was probably better not to show any interest in your things—it'd be just like saying Jase knew you were still alive, and where you could be found, wouldn't it?" she chattered brightly as she dried his arms and moved on to his legs, starting at his left foot and soaping upward.

"Yeah, Jase's a real smart feller," Sam said through gritted teeth. He wasn't in pain—leastways, the stinging pain of his wound hadn't increased, but his manhood was definitely responding to the attention being paid to his lower leg and the promise of those soft, feminine hands coming ever nearer. And there was nothing he could do by the force of his will to get it to sink back into polite quiescence before she noticed....

"I'll give you a shave next," she informed him, "and after I get you washed up, I'm going to go outside and do up the breakfast dishes, then I'm going to take the old broom Cookie found out back to the inside of this place."

"Such ambition," he mocked, feeling her hand get nearer, nearer.... Why she had not *seen* his erection already he couldn't imagine.

"But it's just awful how the dirt sifts down onto everything," she went on, demonstrating by brushing it off her arms. She returned to his leg, soaping up past his knee now. "If there was a woman living here before, I don't know how she put up with the constant dirt on everything.... Oh, my..." She jerked her hands away from his thigh.

His eyes flew to her face. He saw Mercy staring at his manhood, which was standing proudly erect, as if in mockery of his weakened state.

"I—I'm sorry, honey," he said, trying not to grin at her discomfiture. "I guess parts of me still don't realize that I'm really weak as a day-old kitten."

"Yes, well..." Mercy didn't looked reassured. She turned away from him, but not before he could see that her face was flaming. "I suppose you could finish your bath, after all," she said, and fled outside, leaving him to deal with the torment of his throbbing manhood, which remained stubbornly hard as he thought of how good her hands had felt upon him.

When she returned, bringing the washed dishes, Mercy made no reference to the embarrassing incident, but went about making good on her threat to clean up the interior of the soddy. First she braided her long, auburn hair, tying the ends with a strip of leather she took from her pocket, and pushed the fat plait over her shoulder.

There was nothing much she could do with the hard-packed dirt floor, but he watched as she wielded the broom, evicting spiders and nests of mice from all the shadowy corners and overhead. Then she swept off the plank shelf that remained along one wall, and began to set on it the supplies that Jase had brought, humming under her breath as she did so. Finally she went out for a few minutes, and when she returned he saw that she had picked a bouquet of purple, white and yellow wildflowers. She put them in one of the tin cups and set it in the middle of the shelf, then stood back to admire the effect.

It was just like a female, Sam thought as he watched her, to try to make even the humblest shelter a home. She'd seemingly forgotten all about his presence, which allowed him to savor the fluid grace and economy of her movements, the gentle swell of her bosom when she leaned over, the glimpse of stocking as her skirts swirled around her legs with her exertions. Her face had grown flushed as she worked, but her eyes sparkled.

Sam was growing drowsy as she took the dirty bathwater outside. He heard her exchanging words with Cookie, though he couldn't tell what they were talking about. And then he slept.

He awoke to the flickering light of a coal-oil lantern. Had he slept all day? No, scraps of bright sunlight were stealing through the sides of the window, which was now mostly covered by a blanket-curtain that had been fastened to the wall with some nails driven into the sod.

Without raising his head or moving, he turned his eyes to search the soddy until he found Mercy, and when he saw her, what she was doing nearly made him gasp aloud.

Now that she had cleaned the soddy as much as such a dwelling could be cleaned, she had taken advantage of his dozing to heat water for her own bath. She had removed her dress and petticoats, and these lay folded nearby. She had peeled her chemise down to her waist and was kneeling on one of the spare blankets next to the kettle full of water.

As he watched through his lashes, dry mouthed, she soaped first one breast, then the other, and rinsed each with water until both nipples stood out proudly from her supple young body. Then she pulled the chemise over her head and threw it to her pile of clothes. Now she was clad only in the lace-trimmed pantalets. He sensed that she was going to look to see if he still slept, and so he closed his eyes, shutting out the enticing sight.

He opened them to see that she had removed the pantalets and was laving her belly and legs. *Oh, God*... He was hard again, wanting her more than he'd ever wanted a woman in his entire life, even though the shadowy room spun around as he raised his head to see her better. He wished she'd come over and lie down next to him... and if she did, that he was strong enough to bury himself in that freshly washed, sweetly scented feminine flesh. He wasn't, he knew, but he'd sure like to give it his best attempt, he thought wryly, closing his eyes to make the spinning stop.

When he opened them again her washrag-covered hand had dipped between her legs.

He must have groaned aloud, for Mercy whirled around, turning her back on him and grabbing for the blanket.

"You might have let me know you were awake," she snapped, clutching the blanket to her as she turned to face him again.

"You're beautiful, Mercy, did you know that?" he said, disarming her in the best way a man can disarm an indignant woman, but he meant it. "I think the sight of you naked has got to be better medicine than that vile stuff you made me swallow."

"Oh, is that right, Mr. Devlin?" she retorted, then tried her best to pull on her unmentionables while holding the blanket in front of her with her teeth. It was impossible. She just stood there, frustrated, her eyes flashing fire at him.

"Yes, that's so, *Mrs*. Devlin," he told her, grinning. "Don't hide yourself from me, sweetheart. You're my wife, as you reminded me just a little while ago, so I guess that gives me the right to look."

Mercy gave up with a sigh of exasperation, settling for turning her back on him, so he was gifted with a lightning glimpse of rounded pink buttocks and slender, lovely shoulders before she covered herself again in chemise and pantalets.

"You Texans think we ladies believe every flattering word that drawls out of your mouth," she told him tartly, but a hint of a smile lingered at the lush corners of her mouth.

He watched as she donned three petticoats and then her dress, appreciating the fact that she had apparently forgotten all about the corset that lay folded by her boots. A woman as slender and lithe as Mercy didn't need a corset, anyway, and he liked the hints the bodice of her dress gave of her soft bosom beneath, without the severe molding of the corset.

"I thought you were going to give me a shave," he reminded her. Actually, he didn't give two hoots if he shaved now or next month, but it would force her to come closer. Right now she was standing at the other end of the soddy, eyeing him like a frightened deer.

"Yes..." she said, biting her soft underlip as if undecided. "You will behave if I do, won't you? It...it wouldn't be good for you to...exert yourself, after being so sick."

He raised a hand. "I promise. Honey, all I can do at this point is look, I swear to you."

He lay back as she came near him, bringing the soap and water and the razor Jase had bought.

If all he could do was look, then he wouldn't miss a second of looking, he thought as she lathered his face, then began to scrape the stubble off his cheeks. He watched her earnest face as she shaved him as expertly as if she'd been doing it all her life. Perhaps she'd had to shave her papa at some time, Sam guessed, savoring the sight of her unconsciously licking her lips as she studied him to see that she'd missed no stray whiskers. Damn, but she had to have the most kissable-looking lips of any woman in Kansas, he thought, wishing he had the strength to just pull her down with him and see what he could do with her, in spite of his dizziness.

"Mercy—" he began.

She stared at him, again wary, and sat back on her heels.

"Thank you," he said, and saw some of the tension leave her face, to be replaced by a pleased little smile.

"You're welcome, Sam," she said. "You look a lot better, and that's bound to make you feel better. Now, why don't you just rest," she suggested, and leaned over, planting a soft kiss on his newly shaven cheek.

It was just natural to turn toward her, so that after a heartbeat or two her mouth kissed not his cheek but his lips, and to follow with his hand at the back of her head, holding her there, while his lips and tongue began a slow, sensual perusal of her mouth.

Mercy struggled for only a moment, then sighed again, a softer sound this time, and gave herself over to the kiss, sinking lower on her knees as he gradually, gently increased the pressure on her neck until she had to either stiffen and resist or allow her upper body to rest against his. All the while, he kept kissing her. With his eyes closed, it was easier to ignore his light-headedness.

She did not resist, but sagged a little, so that he felt the deliciously wonderful sensation of her breasts crushing against his chest. Whether by accident or wisdom, she had chosen to kneel by his right side, so she wasn't brushing against the still-painful graze wound.

"Mmm," he breathed, still kissing her, as his body clamored for more. "Honey, lie down next to me," he breathed, moving his lips only enough to speak.

"No... I shouldn't... you're still weak," she protested, her voice a breathy whisper that warmed his neck and made him want her even more.

"Mercy, I can't do anything," he insisted. "I'm harmless—it's just that my head spins plumb around when I try to raise it. I just want to hold you." Well, that wasn't strictly all the truth. He wouldn't be able to fully make love to her, but he was hoping to be able to unbutton her bodice, and cup those delectable breasts while he kissed her. No doubt it would set him to aching again, but it would be worth it. He wondered how she'd react if he went so far as to suckle on one of her nipples, right through the bodice of her dress....

"Anybody want any dinner in here?" a voice suddenly said, just outside the window.

Startled, Mercy gave an involuntary shriek of embarrassment as she wrenched herself out of his grasp, looking over her shoulder. The door was still closed, the makeshift curtain still in place, but she looked as discomposed as if Cookie had actually seen them in the heated embrace. "Wha-what did you say?" she called out. "I was just c-cleaning up."

Sam mentally cast every lurid curse he knew on Cookie's head.

"I *said,* do y'all want any dinner? I caught a prairie chicken, an' made some broth fer Dev, and you and I kin have some of the meat and some beans, I reckon," Cookie called through the closed door.

He seemed mighty proud of himself, Sam thought sourly. He'd like to tell Cookie just what he could do with his damned prairie chicken broth.

Chapter Twenty-One

On the second morning after her sister's disappearance, Charity was in the barn collecting the eggs. At least, her hands picked them up and dodged the pecking of the more aggressive hens, but her mind was far away.

What had happened to Mercy? Had she found Sam after she had left the house for "a breath of air?" Had her sister and the Texan made up their differences, and were they even now on a blissful honeymoon somewhere? She could be happy for them if she knew for certain this was so, but this not knowing... this anxiety that Mercy had been the victim of foul play—it was awful!

Charity understood now what mental agonies Mercy had suffered the night she, Charity, had stolen out to meet Tom Culhane. The difference, though, was that Mercy had a great deal of good judgment, and any trouble that found Mercy was not as likely to be her own fault.

She thought about Tom Culhane and their encounter in front of the Alamo Saloon. How could she ever have found that swaggering braggart of a cowboy the least bit attractive? He was nothing but an underhanded sneak, and a lecherous underhanded sneak, at that. It bothered her that Papa had seen fit to even speak to him—and both times he had not been willing to do so in front of her. Why?

She felt a deep inner certainty that Mercy's disappearance had something to do with Tom Culhane, though she could not have said why.

"Psst! Miss Charity!"

Charity was so startled she almost dropped the full basket of eggs. She spun around and saw a man in the entranceway of the barn, a man holding a horse, but he had the bright sunshine at his back and she could not make out his features. Clutching the basket of eggs like a shield, Charity started to back up.

"Pardon me, miss. I didn't mean t' startle you," he said, his deep-voiced drawl identifying him as a Texan. "I reckon you cain't see me too well." He stepped forward slowly, as if he guessed she was still nervous. "I'm Jase Lowry, one of the Devil's—uh, one of Sam Devlin's outfit."

"Oh!" For a moment, all she could feel was relief, for she had thought for one terrifying second that it was Tom Culhane, and she was all too aware of how isolated she was out here in the barn, especially with her father gone to look for Mercy in the settlements south of Abilene. As he slowly came forward, though, leading his horse, she saw he was taller than Culhane, and she recognized him as one of Sam's cowboys she had met that night in the saloon.

"I jest wanted to let you know... that is, yore sister just asked me to bring you word she was all right."

Charity rushed forward. "Mercy's all right? Oh, thank you, thank you!" she exclaimed. "I've been so worried—so has Papa! Is she with Sam? Have they made up? Have they started back to Texas? Some cowboy told my father and the search parties they were on the road to Wichita...."

He smiled a little. "Whoa up, there, missy! You ask questions faster than a prairie fire with a tail wind!"

She put a hand up to her mouth. "I'm sorry." She was struck by what a nice smile the cowboy had. He was even a little . . . handsome, though his lean, beard-shadowed features gave him a rather untamed look. . . .

Stop it, Charity, she told herself sternly. *Thinking that way—that a man is attractive before you know what he's like inside—is just what got you in trouble the last time.*

"Yes, miss, yore sister's with my boss," Jase said, "and no, they haven't started back to Texas. They probably won't be doin' that fer a while."

Something about his expression warned her all was not well. "What do you mean, 'they probably won't be doing that for a while'?" she asked. "Where are they? What's wrong?" She lifted her chin so that she could look up into his eyes, for Lowry was much taller than any man of her acquaintance, even Papa.

He looked down at her, clearly uncomfortable. "Now, I don't want t' scare you, Miss Charity, so let me tell you first that Sam's alive—"

"Scare me? Alive? What *are* you talking about, Mr. Lowry?" Charity interrupted, her hands clenched near her face.

"Sam was shot," he said bluntly. "See, I knew it was no good just blurtin' it out. You're purt' near white as a sheet, ma'am," he said, reaching out a hand to steady her.

Until then she hadn't realized she was swaying, but she seized upon his strong arm gratefully. "But he's alive? Who shot him, and why?"

"Yes, he's alive. It's goin' to be a while before he's up raisin' hell again—sorry, ma'am, I forgot myself," he apologized. "As to who shot him, I ain't at liberty t' say right now, but I'd say pure, rattlesnake meanness would be my guess as to the reason."

"But where is she? Will you take me to her? If he's wounded she'll need help," she pleaded, taking hold of his hand in an effort to get him to see how earnest she was.

He looked down at his boot and toed a line in the dirt. "I cain't tell you where, Miss Charity—not right now, at least. It's obvious some folks don't mean well by my boss, and as long as you don't know where Sam and Miz Mercy are, you cain't be made t' tell no one," he observed. "Are the search parties still out there lookin' for them?"

Charity hesitated. "They're looking south of here, since that's where the cowboy saw them," she said at last, holding back the fact that her father was out of town and had only taken a couple of men with him. She didn't want to make the mistake of trusting too easily again.

Jase seemed satisfied with that. "Don't you worry about help, neither. Cookie Yates is helpin' your sister tend Sam. There ain't a better doctor between here and Houston, even tho' he ain't got no formal trainin'. Cookie's took care o' ever'thin' from snakebite t' broken bones on the trail."

"But... will I see her? You can't mean I'll just never see her again," she insisted, letting him see the tears that were stinging her eyes at the thought, and hoping he would be moved by them.

He was. He put an awkward hand out and touched the tears that had strayed down her cheek. "Now, don't you be frettin', Miss Charity. Miz Mercy wouldn't want you to, I know. And I reckon you will see her, jest as soon as Sam gets better and he gets a few things settled," he said, smiling encouragingly. "Now I better get goin', afore yore papa comes out—"

"No, wait!" she cried, seeing that he was about to leave. "Mercy's bound to be needing a change of clothes. Can you stay just a few minutes while I run in and get them?"

The Texan looked uneasy. "Won't yore papa wonder why you're doin' that? I don't want him t' know I'm out here—*no one kin know,* Miss Charity. It ain't safe fer Sam. Do you understand that?"

Charity nodded. "Don't worry. Papa's, umm, writing a sermon. He... he won't even notice what I'm doing," she assured Lowry, then ran out of the barn.

Minutes later she was back with a bundle of clothing wrapped with twine. She'd put Mercy's unmentionables in the middle and folded the dress around them, so that Jase wouldn't see them.

Jase remounted and she handed the bundle up to him. "Nice seein' you again, Miss Charity," he said, fingering the brim of his hat that he had just put back on.

She remembered that the last time this cowboy had seen her she'd been in the company of Tom Culhane, and she wondered if Jase had thought her a whore that night just as Tom had. She hoped she had made a better impression this time.

"Goodbye, umm, Mr. Lowry."

"I'm just Jase, Miss."

"Jase," she agreed. "Thank you for letting me know my sister is all right. And tell Sam I hope he's feeling better. I'll be praying for his recovery," she added, conscious of a reluctance to let the tall cowhand go. It was for the best, though. Papa had asked several ladies of his congregation to check on her while he was gone. She sure didn't need that nosy Abigail Barnes to find her alone in the barn with a handsome cowboy!

Jase's next stop was the Alamo Saloon, where he found Manuel idling over a beer.

"I figured you would stop een today," the vaquero said as Jase sat beside him and held up a hand to motion the barmaid over. "The boss, he will live, no?"

Jase told him about Sam's being out of his head with fever, and about their worry that he was developing blood poisoning, but that he seemed a little better this morning.

"He's back in his right mind agin, but weak as a pat o' butter in the noonday sun," he concluded.

Manuel grinned. "That will not last long, weeth Cookie and his pretty *novia* to take care of heem. But he still don't want us to do nothin' about that *malvado* Culhane?"

Jase shook his head. "He wants t' take care of it hisself. Cain't say as I blame him. If I was the one that little stumpsucker let daylight into, I'd be wantin' to be the one riddin' the ground of his shadow."

Manuel took a long draft on his beer. "He looks—how do you say—*nervous* every time I see heem around. And what if he thinks to vamoose? After all, amigo, we would all be gone from this Abilene now if thees thing had not happened."

Jase nodded. "I expect we'll jest have t' cross that river when we come to it."

Jase got lucky and shot a buck on the way back to the soddy that afternoon. By supper that night Sam was able to sit up against the sod wall and eat a venison steak as big as a saddlebag, as well as half the apple pie the cowboy had bought at the mercantile. It was obvious his strength was coming back by leaps and bounds. He admitted the wound in his thigh still hurt like hell, but he was starting to chafe over the restrictions Mercy and Cookie tried to impose.

"Stop fussin' over me, you old coot," he grumbled when the chuck-wagon cook informed Sam it was time to change his dressing. "I'm trying to listen to Jase talkin' about his trip to town."

"Some people are startin' t' feel better an' are gittin' a leetle big fer their britches," Cookie growled back.

Sam had the grace to look abashed. "Sorry, Cookie. I don't mean to sound ungrateful. It's just that when I think of Culhane leavin' town before I get the chance to come to an understanding with him, I feel sick all over again."

Mercy, who had been enjoying her relief that Charity, at last, had been told that she was safe, suddenly realized what Sam had been saying, and she felt queasy. What did Sam mean to do, have a shoot-out with Culhane? What if Culhane was the faster draw? And if Sam emerged the victor, how did he mean to take his revenge on her father for his part in the plot?

"Sam, let it go," she urged. "Let *Culhane* go. It's not worth the risk." *Let's just ride on out of here for Texas,* she wanted to say, *and forget about Tom Culhane.* But of course she couldn't say that, for once Sam was well enough to leave, she had to let him go. Because she loved him, she reminded herself, but her heart ached stubbornly at the thought.

"The day I let a little bowlegged weasel like Culhane shoot me down and go off scot free is the day I stop callin' myself a man," Sam snapped, looking at her with eyes that were suddenly as chilly blue as the prairie sky after a sudden frost.

Mercy looked away, biting back a retort in kind. Men and their pride, she thought, exasperated. *One may as well try to stop a blizzard on the plains as get a man to stop doing things in the name of pride.* And once he had achieved his revenge against Culhane, what about her father? What kind of revenge would satisfy him there?

She must have looked as upset as she felt, for suddenly Sam was putting his arm around her shoulder. "I'm sorry, Mercy. I reckon I sound grouchy as a range bull with hydrophobia. I just don't take well t' sickness, I expect." His smile was so winning that she forgave him his cross tone, but the icy lump of fear remained in her heart.

Cookie and Jase both elected to sleep out under the stars that night, since the old cook thought Sam was "on the mend" enough that he didn't need anyone sitting up with him.

"B'sides," he admitted, "we've been sleepin' out so long we get right fidgety if we cain't see the moon an' the stars. But you jest holler out the door if you need me."

Mercy didn't think she would, but she thanked the old cowboy with a kiss on his leathery cheek.

"Shucks, Miz Devlin, you didn't have to do that, but mind you, I ain't complainin'" was Cookie's only comment as he walked out into the gathering darkness.

When she turned around she saw that Sam had already fallen asleep sitting up, his head sagging forward, his hands still holding his plate and fork. Gently she nudged him into a more comfortable sleeping position on his back.

Well, that solves one problem. Since she had become aware of his continued desire for her this afternoon while she was bathing him, she had thought there might be an awkward moment or two as they settled into sleep. It was foolish to risk aggravating his wound, as much as she wanted him to make love to her, too.

Mercy gazed at his sleeping face for a moment, then blew out the lamp, removing her dress, petticoats and pantalets in the darkness. Smiling in the now familiar, earthy-smelling soddy, she lay down in her chemise beside her husband and pulled the blanket over them both.

Some time close to dawn Mercy awoke from a dream of the one and only time Sam had made love to her, to discover there was a very good reason that she had been imagining him touching her intimately. He was doing so at that moment, though his deep, regular breathing told her he still slept. In his sleep Sam had rolled against her, and now his hand was cupping her breast, its warmth heating her right through the thin muslin. At some point while she slept, her knee-length chemise had gotten hiked up around her waist. His leg—the uninjured one—was thrown casually over hers, which brought her bare buttocks into close proximity with his turgid manhood, straining against the confines of his union suit.

She tried to inch away, but even in his sleep the Texan was having none of that. Mumbling something incoherent, he pulled her back, his hand moving down to her waist to press her back against him again.

Well, at least she could angle her buttocks away from him so that she didn't feel his unconscious arousal, while keeping her upper body against him, couldn't she? She rather liked the safe, protected feeling she got while lying in his arms, though surely it was wrong to continue to encourage his...well, his *aroused state* to continue, she thought, blushing in the darkness.

As soon as she tried to move even just her buttocks away, though, he followed, his underwear no impediment to her feeling his manhood swelling and firming against her as the moments went by. Worse yet, his head had shifted so that his lips were now against the back of her neck, and she could feel the tickle of his mustache against her skin, and his warm breath. The scent of him was in her nostrils, a scent compounded of the soap she'd washed him with, his own musky, male smell and the whiskey he'd drunk at dinner. She found both the scent and the warmth of his breathing very arousing.

Mercy felt him thrust against her, just once, gently, tentatively. She went hot all over, just remembering what his erect manhood had looked like when she had accidentally stimulated it during his bath this afternoon. She had to lie still, she thought. He seemed to still be asleep, and if she lay quietly and did not respond, Sam would surely slip back into a deeper slumber.

But she didn't *want* to lie still, she realized as the heat his touch was engendering refused to subside, and built instead. She wanted to thrust back against his maleness and feel him react to her response, even if he was not consciously aware of what he was doing.

She did just that, pushing back against him at the same time as she burrowed more deeply against his chest.

At first he went motionless, as if he couldn't quite believe he had felt her action correctly, and so she wiggled against him again.

The response was immediate.

Chapter Twenty-Two

His arm tightened around her, and he thrust against her once, and then again, his manhood probing against the folds of her flesh, almost as if his underwear wasn't there, or he was unaware of it, until it found just the right spot. She gasped involuntarily. He groaned as his hand slid lower, caressing that sensitive bud from in front at the same time he thrust from behind.

She had become certain that he was fully awake even before she felt him fumbling behind her at the buttons of his union suit and freeing himself to thrust against her without any cloth impediment between them. And if he was awake, it meant he was aware of the sudden dampness between her legs, which made his manhood slide with increasing ease and quickness as he kept moving against her. He had to have heard the changed, ragged quality of her breathing, too. Did he think she was a shameful wanton for her desire? From what little she'd been able to glean about the subject of physical love, she'd guessed that only women of the caliber of Mercedes LaFleche were supposed to enjoy what went on between men and women.

She didn't have the courage to ask what he thought of her, to interpose words—even words asking for reassurance—into the near-silent haze of passion that surrounded them.

And then he groaned again, and she became aware from his head, which lay against hers, of the rigidly clenched teeth that ground tightly every time he thrust against her.

"You're in pain!" she whispered. "Oh, Sam, we have to stop—I had forgotten how this must be hurting you—I'm sorry!"

Incredibly, she heard him chuckle against her neck, a deep, rich, sensual chuckle. The motion caused his mustache to tickle the sensitive skin, and she shivered.

"Darlin', I promise you, I'm going to hurt a lot worse if we stop now. Please," he coaxed, and he stroked her some more, until she barely had the will to keep protesting.

"But...I'm sure we should stop. This can't be good for you, an injured man," she whispered, then wondered why they were whispering. Even if Cookie and Jase were camped right outside the door, it was doubtful they could have heard them.

"It can't be anything *but* good for me," he argued. "And you want me, too—you can't deny it, 'cause I can feel it's true," he added as he touched her again. She knew that he was feeling the dampness that indicated her arousal.

"And remember, this time it's not going to be painful for *you*, darlin'. But if you're really serious about sparing me pain, I'll show you a way," he offered as he angled his mouth so he could kiss her on the neck, right behind her ear.

The touch of his lips there made her dizzy with desire. "There's a way...so you won't hurt?" she asked, aching to feel him inside her, especially since he'd promised her there would be no repeat of the humiliating pain of losing her virginity.

"There sure is, honey. Just let me show you," he breathed against her. She felt an immediate loss as he pulled away from their close, spoonlike embrace to lie on his back.

She turned to protest, but he pulled her against him so that she was lying half on, half off him. Then he took her chin between his thumb and fingers, bringing her head down and kissing her, deeply and more thoroughly than she had ever been kissed in her life, his tongue mimicking the motions of coupling so hypnotizingly that she scarcely noticed his hands pushing her chemise down off her shoulders and farther, until her breasts lay bare against him. She was so on fire she would have done anything he asked as he kissed her and caressed her breasts until the nipples were firm and throbbing.

"Come on, Mercy, cover me," he urged hoarsely, one hand gently pushing her hip against his, until it seemed the most natural thing in the world to raise her leg over his body and lie full-length upon him so that they touched belly-to-belly, thigh-to-thigh, her soft breasts against the hard planes of his chest. Between them, his long, swollen manhood throbbed, and she moved against it—gently at first, feeling it pulse as her womanly folds enclosed it, just a little, and then feeling it withdraw, again and again, as she took a little more of it into her each time.

He raised his head and, using one hand to guide her breast to his mouth, closed his lips around one of her tingling nipples and suckled upon it until this time it was Mercy who was groaning with pure pleasure.

His suckling made her want to give him ecstasy, too, and so she raised up over him, acting with an instinct as old as time. Taking his shaft, she guided it inside her, and then sank down upon it as far as she could.

The sudden rush of heat from taking him so deeply inside her made her cry out, and she pulled up, feeling the exquisite slide of his member against her as she nearly slipped off him, only to feel it again as she sank back again.

"Oh, Mercy, *Mercy,*" he growled as his hips began to pump in time to her rising and falling against him. The world, which had narrowed to exclude anything beyond the earthen walls of the soddy, contracted still further so that nothing existed for Mercy beyond this man and the things he was doing to her, which finally caused that world to splinter around them in white-hot streaks of rapture.

Mercy collapsed upon him then, panting, and he held her to him, and then, as he felt her breathing gradually slow, he eased her down until she was lying in the circle of his arms.

She was the most astonishing, wonderful female he had ever met, Sam thought, and during the war years, as he had followed the Stars and Bars from one battlefield to the next, he had met quite a few. There were always women in the presence of the army, camp followers mostly, who combined their less-savory careers with that of laundressing, though there had also been the women in the occasional town they occupied and even, once, the bored wife of a colonel. There had been women in Texas, too, after the war, as he strove to wrest a living from the war-torn, tax-burdened land that had once been so prosperous. These had been calico queens like Mercedes LaFleche, who expected nothing besides the coins he gave them, and appreciated the fact that he didn't beat them. He had not allowed himself too near "good" women, for he had had neither the time nor the money to settle down, and knew it was unwise to make himself want something or someone he couldn't have.

He had not thought to find someone like Mercy, who was both good and a naturally passionate partner in lovemaking, but despite his unworthiness, God had granted him the incredible gift of her. He didn't mean to lose that gift, no matter how many Tom Culhanes and Jeremiah Fairweathers tried to come between him and his love.

They were still lying together, his underwear still unbuttoned, her chemise still rolled up around her waist, when the sun suddenly invaded the shadowy soddy, let in by Cookie and Jase, who had finally decided to investigate when it had gotten to be about nine o'clock without any sign of life from within.

"Boss, you all—" called Cookie, his voice breaking off as he caught sight of the sleeping woman's pale, long legs entwined with her husband's, and the splendid perfection of one rose-tipped breast against Sam's chest.

"What the—?" Sam began, confused.

Cookie quickly reversed himself, pushing Jase, who hadn't seen anything yet, back out the door. Sam looked down and saw his wife's naked state and yanked up the blanket.

His sudden motion woke Mercy, who opened her eyes just in time to see the cowboys departing. She glanced downward, and realized what they must have seen.

"Oh, Sam, I didn't even have my *shimmy* on!" she hissed, pulling the blanket up to her neck.

"It was on," he observed with a maddening literalism, grinning as he reached down under the blanket to tug on the garment.

As if she needed reminding that it was all wadded up around her waist, useless as any sort of covering!

"Not properly," she protested, covering her face. "Oh, Sam, what they must be *thinking* of me!"

"They're probably thinking I'm luckier than I have any right to be," he told her, kissing the tip of her nose and grinning down at her. "Don't worry, honey, Cookie didn't see much, and Jase couldn't see anything 'cause Cookie was in the way."

Her expression was disbelieving. Immediately she turned to dressing, putting on the fresh clothing Charity had sent. Then, still keeping her back to him, she combed her hair, rebraided it and mumbled something about going out to help Cookie with breakfast.

Sam was left to dress himself and think about the night as he folded up the blankets.

Congratulations, Sam Houston Devlin, he told himself. You have now made love to your bride twice, once out in the open, and the second time on the dirt floor of a sod house. Mercy deserved better than that—she deserved the finest suite at the biggest hotel west of the Mississippi, in fact, but at the very least she deserved a bridal chamber where rough cowboys didn't come tromping in uninvited.

And how are you going to give it to her? You're nothing but a rough cowpuncher yourself, he reminded himself bitterly. *One who'll be going home with empty pockets.* He hadn't thought much about the lost money before, for he'd been too busy trying to stay alive, but now, after realizing just how hard he'd fallen in love with his wife, its loss rose up to mock him. There was nothing he could do about the sum he'd lost to Earp—that was gambled away fair and square—but he knew Culhane had stolen the rest of his money, and he'd get it back or die trying. It would be bad enough to return home and confess to Garrick, his elder brother, that he hadn't managed to keep a nickel of the profits, but the Devlins would manage to scrape by. But without the money, how could he take a wife back to Texas with him and subject her to a life more full of privation than the one she had now?

"Goin' t' be a fine day," Sam said to the three gathered around the cookfire when he limped out into the sunshine.

Mercy whirled around. "Sam, you shouldn't be up on that leg!" Handing the skillet she had just taken off the fire to Jase, she rushed over to support him.

"Don't cosset me, woman," he said, refusing to take her arm and standing on his own two wobbly legs. He didn't want to admit to anyone how hollow-legged he still felt. "We've already decided I'm not gonna die, so I figure it's high time I was gettin' up an' around. Sooner I get my strength back, the sooner I'll see Texas again. I think I've had about enough of laying around like an invalid. Hell-fire, I think I've had about enough of Kansas, period. Texas is gonna look right fine to us, isn't it, boys?"

Jase and Cookie agreed, though Cookie warned, "Best not t' rush it, Boss. Yore feelin' real strong now, sure 'nuff, but if ya was t' try an' get back on that horse too soon, you'd be headed fer a ree-lapse. Better plan on another day or two o' jest takin' it easy."

Sam just grunted as he accepted the steaming tin cup of coffee Cookie held out. He was just itching to leave, Mercy thought sadly, and he'd said nothing about taking her with him. True, she'd already resolved to set him free, but it had felt better when it had been solely her decision. But Lord, she wasn't ready yet! she cried inwardly. *Just give me another couple of days—two more days to remember all my life!*

"I figure I'll move around a bit today, and see how I feel. Maybe tomorrow I'll feel well enough to ride Buck into Abilene and take care of that little bit of unfinished business," he said, looking at Jase and Cookie rather than Mercy.

He means his revenge against Tom Culhane, Mercy thought, and maybe against Papa, too. Her heart ached. It was all very well for her to forgive Papa, though she would never consent to return to live with him, but she couldn't ask Sam to do so. Sam had nearly died.

He sat on a rough-hewn log bench by the door and sipped his coffee, staring off over the empty prairie, his eyes narrowed against the morning sunlight. Then, when Mercy handed him a plateful of flapjacks and eggs, he attacked his breakfast as if it were Tom Culhane on the plate.

Mercy stared in concern, then met Cookie's knowing eyes. "Don't fret yoreself about him none, ma'am," he said. "Ya kin tell he's gettin' well by how restless he's gettin'. Settin' still never did set well by our Devil, no, ma'am. Jest bite him back iffen he bites at ya."

"Shut up, Cookie. Mercy doesn't need you jawin' nonsense at her this early in the day," Sam retorted. "And stop talkin' about me as if I wasn't there."

Oh, he looked restless, right enough, and illness had etched fine lines of strain about those lean, hard features. She remembered seeing him that first day from the window of Moon's Frontier Store. He was dangerous, she'd thought then, and that was the overwhelming impression he gave now. Dangerous and untamable. Certainly he'd never "set still" long enough to be her husband—even if she loved him so little that she insisted upon it, which was not the case, she reminded herself. No, it was better that she let him go when he would. And perhaps, if she was very lucky, he would leave behind a part of himself in her: a baby that would grow under her heart and look just like his wild, untamed father when he was born—or she. Heavens, she thought, a daughter of Sam's might well make Charity look like a saint in comparison.

She was glad they'd made love last night, *glad,* she told herself defiantly. Sam was obviously none the worse for it, and if she had not already conceived from the first time he'd taken her, perhaps she had last night. And if she had her way, they'd make love again if the opportunity presented itself before he left her forever.

The thought of raising his son—or daughter—without Sam there gave her a pang, but it was surely better than to have nothing left of him at all. She would move to Wichita, or Salina, and hold her head up high. After all, they were married, she thought defiantly. She had nothing to apologize to anyone for.

She noticed Sam playing idly with the knife she'd found in his boot, flinging it into the ground, digging it out and then flinging it again. *Oh, yes, he's restless.*

"Say, Boss, what would you say about Jase an' me goin' into Abilene t' spend the day?" Cookie asked suddenly. "I could leave y'all those leftover venison steaks for yore dinner. Reckon you'd be okay? I figger you an' yore bride could use some privacy, and we'd be back by nightfall."

Mercy, blushing at the implication, started to protest, but Sam was quicker. "Sure, go ahead," he told them. "There isn't anything I can't handle around here, and you two must be bored to tears playing nursemaid. Just leave me a pistol and the rifle."

"But Sam, what about Culhane? Shouldn't someone be on the watch for him here?" Mercy asked, a little alarmed, although the thought of being alone with Sam for hours sounded like a delicious prospect. A bittersweet prospect, she corrected herself. It might be her last full day with him.

She could feel Sam glaring at her. Outraged male pride again. She wouldn't look at him.

"Mercy, I *said* I could handle—" he began.

Jase interrupted him. "Aw, we'll ride herd on that ornery little bastard—beggin' yore pardon, Miz Devlin. He's probably still sleepin' off last night's drinkin', anyway. I doubt if he'd come anywhere near here, in fact. He left Sam fer dead, you recall, and he ain't about to come here lookin' fer his ghost."

Chapter Twenty-Three

He had to get out of town. Tom was damn sick and tired of having Manuel Lopez or Jase Lowry turn up in whatever saloon he had decided to do his drinking and stare at him like a buzzard waiting for a wounded steer to keel over.

For a while he had enjoyed idling in Abilene, a place that was paradise for a cowboy with lots of money in his pocket. He could bed with a whore every night, or twice a night if he chose. He could drink as much and as often as he wanted. He could gamble. But the need to be careful—not to let on how rich he was for a simple cowhand at the end of the trail—was beginning to aggravate him, as was looking up everywhere he went and seeing one of the Devil's Boys there, watching his every move.

He knew why they were there, of course. Devlin hadn't shown up again, and since he was the only one known to have a quarrel with the trail boss, they were waiting for him to tip his hand somehow.

Apparently no one had yet stumbled upon Devlin's corpse in the abandoned soddy. Tom had thought it important to be seen in Abilene for a while after the shooting, acting as if he hadn't a care in the world, so he wouldn't be blamed if the corpse was found while it was still readily identifiable. He'd left nothing on Devlin that would identify him, though, and soon it wouldn't matter if Tom stayed in Abilene or not.

He had half a notion to ride out there and move Devlin's body to somewhere closer to town, just so someone would find it. He'd enjoy the temporary uproar that would ensue, knowing all he had to do was just laze around Abilene, poker-faced, until they gave up and went home to Texas.

With his luck, though, someone would happen upon him hauling the body on his horse and too many questions would be asked. Could he just bluff it through and claim to have found the body? He could make up some story as to how and why he'd found it.

Then he thought of entering the dark, deserted soddy—empty except for Devlin's corpse. What if the stories about ghosts waiting to take revenge upon their murderers were true? What if the ghost of Sam Devlin was just waiting in that soddy for him to come? No sirree, Tom Culhane wasn't going near that haunted soddy.

But he was tired of the Devil's Boys dogging his every step.

"Hey, Lopez—are you smitten with my purty face? Is that why I see you gawkin' at me wherever I go?" he called down the bar to the lounging cowboy. "Cain't a man have a drink in peace?"

The vaquero refused to rise to the bait, though. He just smiled lazily and said, "Nobody ees preventing you from drinking, Culhane. And *sí,* you're very pretty, all right. At least, you weel do until Señorita Mercedes comes downstairs."

"Well, I believe I done allowed you enough lookin' today," Tom growled, plunking a dollar on the polished wooden counter. He strode out of the Alamo, trying to conceal his irritation.

Lopez didn't follow, but Tom knew it was just a temporary respite. No sooner would he get comfortable at some other saloon than Manuel or Jase would turn up, sometimes separately, sometimes together, to continue the vigil that was making him increasingly nervous.

Jase seemed to vanish just before dark. Where was he staying? Cookie and Jase had checked out of the Drover's Cottage, that was all he knew for sure, but they seemed to be lodging nowhere in Abilene. If he could just find out where they were, he'd sure like to sneak up on them when they slept and put a permanent end to their spying.

But he knew he'd never do that, either. There were two of them, after all—three if Manuel was with them. There was too much chance of one of them waking up and getting the drop on him while he was slitting the throat of one of the others. No, he'd let them live, he thought graciously.

It was important not to tip his hand that he was about to leave, though. If the Devil's Boys guessed when he was going to depart Abilene, what was to stop them from ambushing him somewhere on the trail, three against one? Maybe it would be best to sneak out of the Drover's Cottage in the dead of night—and by leaving then, he could also get out of paying his bill.

Well, whatever time he left, he was going to need provisions. Now seemed a good enough time to visit Moon's Frontier Store to start buying them, since no one seemed to be following him.

When he reached the mercantile, though, all thoughts of provisions flew out of his head, for there, peering over the cluttered shelves, was that little blond daughter of the preacher, the one who'd gotten him randy as a goat then refused to cooperate when he tried to lift her skirts. The one who'd started all the trouble he'd had with Devlin.

All the frustration he felt at the Devil's Boys' spying on him sought an outlet, and here was a pretty, vulnerable one. *No woman leads Tom Culhane on like that and gets away with it.*

"Why, good mornin' to you, Miss Charity Fairweather!" he said, sashaying over to where she now stood admiring a bolt of sky blue silk with a stoutly built older woman. "Say, I'd admire to buy you a dress length of that purty cloth—don't you know it'd bring out the purty blue o' yore eyes?"

Charity spun around to face him, dropping the bolt of cloth on the counter with a thud, startling her companion. "You just get away from me, you slimy bucket of hogswill!" she hissed. "The day I let you buy me so much as a hair ribbon they can lock me up for a lunatic!"

"Now, Miss Charity, you oughtn't go on thataway," he said, moving closer, his hands outspread, when all he really wanted to do was carry her off somewhere, rip her clothes off and rape her. That'd wipe that superior smile off her prissy-proud face fast enough! "How am I ever supposed to demonstrate that I've repented of my earlier behavior that got us off to such a bad start, if you won't talk to me?"

Tom could see he wasn't making much headway in budging Charity's resolve, but the other woman was another story. She had looked horrified when Charity started her tirade.

"Charity Fairweather, you're not living up to your name very well," she chided. "Surely you should give this man another chance." The other woman smiled encouragingly at him. "The Good Book says we are to forgive, after all. He may be a lost sheep we can return to the fold, might he not?"

"Mrs. Barnes, you don't know wh—" Charity began, but the woman cut her off.

"It doesn't matter," the older woman said. "He says he wishes to repent, and we must *charitably* give him the chance. I know the perfect opportunity to test his sincerity, my dear. Why not invite him to the supper and prayer meetin' we're having tonight to welcome your father home from his journey?"

"No, I don't think that would be—" Charity started to say, but Tom was too quick.

"What time? I'll be there, Miz Barnes, and I do thank you fer the invite. If Miss Charity will let me share her Bible, I'll pray right along with the best of 'em," he promised. He'd be there, all right. A plan was already forming in his head about what he'd do when he got Charity Fairweather alone.

Mrs. Barnes beamed smugly, obviously satisfied with her part in beginning to set a sinner back on the straight and narrow. "Well, I'll just take myself off. That blueberry cobbler isn't going to get baked for the supper tonight by my standing here chatting."

Charity watched her go before turning back to Tom, and when she did, Tom relished the dismay written all over her face. But then she narrowed her eyes and in a lowered voice said, "You may have fooled Abigail Barnes, but you haven't fooled me. Don't you dare come near our house tonight. I have a beau, and I have absolutely no interest in you, do you understand that?"

Aha, so that was it, Tom thought, staring down at the little blonde's furious face. Charity Fairweather didn't want her beau to have any undesirable competition.

"I think you'll welcome me, lost sheep that I am. You'll welcome me, and you'll even talk yore Papa into welcomin' me if he don't seem so inclined. 'Cause if you don't, I jes' might have to tell him and all the rest o' them holy folks what you was up to with me that night outside o' the Alamo Saloon. Only I won't tell 'em about bein' interrupted afore I got what I wanted..." he said, leering suggestively as his voice trailed off.

"Well, *I'll* sure-to-goodness tell them you didn't," she said, but he could tell his threat had shaken her.

"Yeah, and what will yore beau think of you then, once he hears you sneaked out t' see a crude cowboy like me? Whether I had my way with you or not, he ain't ever gonna think of you as no prim-an'-proper preacher's daughter no more, is he?"

He'd hit that target dead center, all right, he saw with glee. "So you just paste a welcomin' smile on yore face when you see me, and I won't have to ruin yore good name in front of yore papa and his whole church. And maybe after you send yore beau home early, you an' I will get a chance t' talk."

"If lightning doesn't strike you dead the moment you step over the threshold," she snapped, tears standing in her china blue eyes.

He made an elaborate show of checking the weather through the store's dusty windows. "Ain't a cloud in the sky, but by then, who knows?" he said with a smirk.

Watching Mercy cook their simple dinner of corn bread and beans seasoned with cut-up chunks of ham over the open fire, Sam realized some of his earlier restlessness had left him. There was something so peaceful about watching her go about these domestic tasks, as uncomplaining about her rough, crude surroundings as if she were cooking in the kitchen at her father's house. He pictured her at home on the farm in Brazos County, stirring a pot as she helped his mother and his sister prepare the meal. He smiled as his daydream went further, imagining her doing the same task while cradling his child with her free arm, bouncing the baby slightly and singing it to sleep as she worked. That was a mighty pretty image, he decided. Was the child a boy or a girl? It didn't matter to him. He'd be equally happy with a daughter with her green eyes and reddish hair as a son that looked just like his daddy.

He wondered if she was already with child. He hoped so, he realized with a start. For a moment he refused to think about the stolen money, or about what he had to do before he could leave Abilene with his bride. He had another day to think about it, anyway, since he'd agreed to stay an extra day at the soddy.

How wonderful it would be if she was pregnant. They could be home in Texas before she was even showing, and by—he mentally counted off the months—late spring the baby would be delivered! He could just see his mother adoring the new baby in the cradle, and his sister cooing over it. And even bitter Garrick might learn to smile again at the sight of his brother's child.

"You look happy," she said suddenly as she handed him a tin plate piled high with corn bread and beans. "Are you thinking about getting home to Texas?"

"Yes," he said, pleased that she'd guessed half of what he was thinking about, at least. He wondered what she'd say if he told her the other half, that he had pictured her holding his infant son or daughter, and would be happy if she was already in the family way, as he would delicately put it.

Mercy settled herself on the split-log bench beside him. "You have big plans for that farm back in Texas, don't you?" she said. "Getting that stud back in business, raising fine horses?"

He nodded, thinking there had never been a woman easier to talk to than his bride. "It could be everything it was before the war, with the money to buy just a few good mares and one good stallion to start," he told her. "We'd become famous for prime saddle horses in just a few years again—maybe we'd even breed some prizewinning racers.

Why, men used to come clear from New Orleans, even St. Louis and points east, to buy Devlin horses."

"And you could get the stud running that way again."

He looked carefully at her, but there wasn't an ounce of skepticism in her clear green eyes, just a shining belief in him.

Oh, Lord, if only he deserved that unclouded trust, he thought, thinking how impossible it would be to tell her that he'd lost all the money that would start to make his dream—or even a comfortable existence for them this year—possible. He couldn't bear the thought of confessing how he'd gambled part of it away, then tried to regain it by taking on that stupid dare. He couldn't tell her he'd been foolish enough to carry the rest of it with him that morning as he'd gone to claim her, so that it had been child's play for Culhane to steal it while he lay helpless and bleeding.

"We'd sell the extras to the army," he said, afraid she'd guess his thoughts if he allowed himself to dwell on them anymore. "Even the ones that aren't good enough to be Devlin horses would be better than those sorry bags of bones the army gets as remounts."

"You wouldn't mind selling to the federal army? After fighting against them in the war?"

"The war's been over for me for a long time," he told her, and then grinned. "Sure, I wish the South had won, but we didn't, and now I'll get my satisfaction selling the army my cast-off stock."

"It's going to happen, your success, Sam—I'm sure of it," she told him, and when she said it, suddenly he believed it. Just then a bird burst into song from the tree down by the creek.

He didn't think his heart could hold all the love for her he felt at that moment. He would get the money back somehow—at least, most of it. And he'd build the stud up again, just as he'd said, so he could give her everything she deserved.

She continued to smile, but while her lips curved upward, there was a wistful quality to her eyes. Why? Was she already imagining bidding farewell to her father and sister and journeying hundreds of miles from them?

"What's the matter, honey?" he asked her. "You already missin' Charity and your papa?" The smile disappeared, and he wanted to kick himself. There would have been time to talk of all that later.

Mercy bit her lip and looked down at her plate. She'd hardly touched any of the food. "Not Papa, no," she said, her voice a colorless monotone. "How could I miss a man who'd do what he did?"

"Oh, Mercy, honey, don't cry," he said, setting his plate down and putting his arm around her as her shoulders began to shake. "Honey, this'll all get worked out somehow or 'nother. . . ." He'd find a way of getting along with the Reverend Jeremiah Fairweather for Mercy's sake, even if it stuck in his craw to be civil to the preacher.

"I don't want to talk about him!" she cried, turning her face against his shirt just as he pulled her into his arms. The dam broke and he felt her shudders as the tears began to wet his shirt.

He heard her say something like "We have so little time left," but the rest of her words were drowned in sobs. Could she really be feeling sentimental about this dirty old soddy? It was a shabby sort of bridal chamber, but it was all they had, and once they set their horses southward on the Chisholm Trail, they'd have even less privacy.

She raised her head and looked at him, her eyes still brimming with unshed tears. "Sam," she said, "would you please take me inside and make love to me?"

Chapter Twenty-Four

Mercy gave herself up to passion with reckless abandon, giving not only her body but her whole heart to Sam. It would be his to keep, now and forever—even after she let him ride out of her life.

It was heaven, it was hell, making love with Sam, knowing this was not just the first of many such lovemakings that would take place in their married life. The day after tomorrow, if he didn't get too restless to wait even that long, he would be gone. If he lived through "dealing with" Culhane, that is. *Oh, God, how will I go on if he doesn't?*

They slept for a while afterward, and when they woke in each other's arms, the light that came into the soddy window was fading.

"I love you, darlin'," he said suddenly against her hair.

It was the first time he had actually said so. He had called her "love," and he had told her he was going to "love" her, but this was the very first time he had actually said that *he loved her.* It was going to make what she had to do so much harder.

She shifted, propping herself up on her elbow, so that she could see his eyes in the dim light afforded by their window.

"You really do, don't you?" she said. "Oh, Sam, I love you, too. I think I've loved you ever since that day I saw you through the window of Moon's store. Charity saw you first, and she made me look. You didn't see me, but I thought you looked handsome and, umm, fierce and dangerous," she confessed, ducking her head against his shoulder, embarrassed, as she saw him smile.

"Dangerous? Fierce? Me?"

"Yes," she insisted, laughing a little. "But then you laughed at something that cardsharp said to you, and it changed your whole face. That's when I began to love you, I think. Silly, isn't it?"

"No, I don't think so," he told her. "I think I began to fall in love with you the moment you stepped into the Alamo Saloon, lookin' for that sister of yours. You were so beautiful...I just wish I hadn't been eyein' a passel of, uh, soiled doves when you first saw me. I'm not very proud of that now," he said, frowning a little.

"Sshh," she said, putting a finger over his lips. "They *were* pretty exotic looking."

He chuckled. "Especially after just seeing longhorns for hundreds of miles," he said, then grew more serious. "The only thing I've been dangerous to is your good name, darlin'."

She lay back in his arms and sighed. "I'd say knowing me has been a whole lot more dangerous to you than it has to me," she said. "Thanks to my father, you nearly died."

"Now it's my turn to say hush," he admonished her. "That's all past, and anyway, we haven't given your papa a chance to tell us his side of things. Culhane may have just been spoutin' nonsense—"

"I don't think he was," she said tightly. "Why would he make something like that up?"

"Pure cussedness, I expect," Sam said reasonably. "After all, he decided he hated me just for stoppin' him from molestin' a girl who wasn't what he thought she was—in a town full of the sort of women he *was* looking for."

"I don't believe he just mentioned my father's name by accident," she insisted. "After all, he thought you were dying—it didn't matter if you knew the truth. No, Papa had something to do with it, all right. That fact will always be there. And that's why I'll understand when you go back to Texas day after tomorrow."

"You'll understand when *I* go back?" he echoed. "You're talkin' as though you aren't going with me."

"I'm not."

He was still for an endlessly long moment. "You want to tell me why not?" he said at last, his cold voice sending an icy chill through her.

Desperate to make him understand, she raised herself over him, propping herself up on her hands. "Sam, how can I go back to Texas with you as your wife, knowing my father tried to have you killed? And you've said you're going to talk to Papa, and give him a chance to tell you what really happened—how will you feel when you find out it's true, that he *did* pay Culhane to gun you down? Maybe you think it won't matter now, but what about later? I can just imagine you introducing me to your mother. 'This is my wife, Mercy, Mama. What about her people? Oh, her father's back in Abilene. He paid some hired gun to murder me.' How can I live with that?" she asked, her voice husky with unshed tears. She had to make him understand that she was doing the wisest thing, she had to!

He stared up at her. "I don't know what your father's actions have to do with you and me, even if he did every bit of what you think he did. Even if he'd shot me himself—I love *you,* Mercy. Hellfire, woman, you just said you loved me. Once you leave Abilene, what your papa did doesn't amount to a hill of beans—*does it?* I'm not going to let it matter to me."

She was silent, fighting the treacherous urge to give in, so relieved that he apparently wasn't going to seek vengeance against her father, so desperate to believe that it wouldn't matter, because that was what she wanted to believe.

"Maybe you're trying to say it *does* matter," he said at last, his voice a stinging lash. "I guess you've thought better of this little mistake of yours, and decided you didn't like being married to a wild cowboy who'd carry you off to Texas instead of leaving you in the paradise of Abilene, Kansas, with your wonderful father and your sweet, featherheaded sister. Maybe you didn't believe Deacon Paxton is a minister, any more than your self-righteous father did, and you figure you're free to go on just as if none of this ever happened. Maybe you've even got another beau lined up, who'll marry you and save you from the scandal and pretend none o' this ever happened, *is that it?*"

"No, Sam, it's not that!" she protested, her mind spinning at all the things he'd said. "Of course it's not! I didn't lie about loving you and I haven't thought better of what I've done, any of it. But maybe you should wait and see how you feel after you talk to my father. And of course, you're planning on some sort of confrontation with Tom Culhane first."

"That's for dang sure," he said, and she knew he was only responding to the last thing she had said, about Culhane.

"Well, then, maybe you shouldn't distract yourself with all these other plans—"

"Hush," he commanded, taking hold of her arms as she hovered over him. "Even if it comes to a showdown with Culhane, I'm going to be there afterward to claim you. All right, I believe you love me. I'd let you go if I didn't believe that," he told her. "But we've made love, what is it now, three times?" he said. "Do you really think I'm going to just ride out of your life because of your willingness to make some damned noble sacrifice, knowing you could

be carryin' my baby, and that I'd never know? No, Mercy, you're my wife, and I'll marry you every time we find a preacher if it takes that to convince you, but I'm not leaving Abilene without you, you hear that?"

She hung her head, unable to look at him, knowing she would never convince him, knowing that however much she knew that giving him up was the most loving thing she could do, she was too selfish to really want to. For if she'd wanted to, she'd have had to lie to Sam. And she couldn't do that.

"I asked you a question, woman," he said.

She looked up, her tears blurring her view of him. "I hear you, Sam. I—"

But he pulled her down in his arms, then rolled on top of her. "Then you shouldn't be cryin', because we're going to be very happy together all our lives. Maybe you just need more convincin'," he said with a grim smile. "I think you need to realize that now you're a woman—now that you're *my* woman—you'd miss certain things...."

"Miss certain things?" she repeated, feeling her heart begin to pound as she savored his nearness, the feeling of her breasts crushed against his chest and of her hips cradling his.

"I think you'd miss this, first of all," he said, lowering his head and taking her lips with his own, kissing her until she was breathless, and then kissing her some more. "And you'd miss this, too." His hand closed over a breast and he caressed it, circling her nipple until she felt on fire with longing. The flames only burned higher when he lowered his head and took the nipple in his mouth. "Can you imagine doing without that?" he asked a moment later, with a grin that was full of the devil. "Well, can you?"

She couldn't, so she shook her head vigorously.

"And what about this?" he said, his hand leaving her breast to delve between her legs. He began to stroke her, and it was only seconds before her ragged breathing betrayed her arousal.

"And even if you could give up all those, I think this would be the hardest...to give up, I mean," he said, his smile devastating as he started to move suggestively against her and his double meaning became obvious.

"I...I suppose so," she breathed, responding to his infectious grin. "Even if you are the biggest braggart that ever left Texas," she said just before she kissed him back.

Ned Webster hadn't been happy about leaving the Fairweather house without getting a few minutes alone with her afterward, any happier than he'd been to see the bowlegged cowboy show up and pretend to participate in the prayer meeting, Charity realized as she watched from the porch as the blacksmith's son trudged off into the night.

"You plannin' to get hitched to that Ned character?" Culhane said, stepping out of the bushes that shielded the front of the Fairweather house.

"You have your nerve, eavesdropping like that!" Charity hissed, keeping her voice down so Papa wouldn't overhear inside. "I told you I'd be with you just as soon as I saw Ned off—why'd you have to lurk in the bushes and watch? Though I suppose I shouldn't be surprised by anything you do after you had the gall to brazen your way into a prayer meeting like the wolf in sheep's clothing that you are!"

Culhane just smirked. "I don't think I fooled yore papa, though. If looks could kill, this cowboy'd be dead. I'm sure if he knew I hadn't really left when I pretended to, he'd never have let ya come outside with that hayseed."

"Don't call Ned that! And it's none of your concern what I do!" she informed him, her hands on her hips as she spat the words at him. She was so angry she would have liked to slap the smirk right off his face. But then he'd likely retaliate by doing something she'd really regret, and she'd have to scream for Papa. And she didn't want to add to Papa's troubles.

He'd come back from his journey looking so tired and sorrowful. He hadn't found Mercy, so it was likely she and Sam hadn't gone southward as one of his cowboys had told the search parties, Papa had informed her.

It comforted her to know that Mercy was with Sam, and that both of them were safe. She ached to be able to share that fact with her father. But Jase had said she couldn't, not yet, anyway.

"None o' my concern," Culhane parroted. "You're pretty high-an'-mighty for a Kansas cow-town preacher's daughter," he mocked. "I reckon you're too good to give me a little kiss out here in the dark."

"You...you...low-down skunk—you no-account varmint! You're dadblasted right I won't kiss you! Whatever makes you think I'd lower myself that far?" she asked him, her voice scornful, but she was a little afraid all the same. Though he was short and not physically imposing, there was still something about Culhane that frightened her.

"Oh, I think you'd lower yourself that far, all right, 'cause if ya don't, I think I'll march right back into your house and tell yore papa an interestin' tale about you!"

"And that's all it'd be, a tale!" she retorted. "My papa wouldn't believe you if you told him the sun comes up in the east!"

"Well, all right."

He started for the house, and Charity's resolve wavered. "Wait! I don't want you bothering him! He's had a long trip and he's too tired to be putting up with your foolish lies! Very well, just one kiss," she said in a resigned voice, and puckered.

Perhaps it had been foolish to hope that he'd be satisfied with a quick peck, but she wasn't prepared for the brutal, smothering, demanding kiss he gave her. In just a heartbeat he was forcing her mouth open and tonguing the inside of her mouth. At the same time, his hand sought and found her breast and cruelly pinched the nipple.

He just laughed when she wrenched free and slapped him.

"You're horrible! If Sam Devlin was here, he'd teach you a lesson all over again!"

"I notice you don't mention your precious Ned," Culhane jeered. "Well, Devlin ain't here, an' he ain't never gonna stop me from doin' what I want ever again!"

Something in the sureness with which Culhane made his boast set off alarm bells in Charity's head. "You...you're the one who shot him, aren't you? I should have known!"

Culhane's cocky grin faded. "How do you know that? There wasn't no one else there."

She was so pleased at the effect her words had had upon his swaggering confidence that she forgot caution. "I just know, that's all. You didn't kill him, hard as you tried, you snake in the grass. He's getting better, and when he does, you better look out."

"Have you seen him? Where is he?" He stepped closer, his voice menacing.

She shook her head and backed away. "No, I haven't seen him. I don't know where he is. But you better watch out, Tom Culhane!" With that parting shot, she turned and ran through the door, shooting the bolt behind her.

Chapter Twenty-Five

Culhane stood staring at the door for several minutes after Charity Fairweather had dashed inside. So Sam Devlin was alive, was he? His nickname was appropriate, for he had the devil's own luck, damn him!

How had Devlin survived those bleeding wounds, especially the one in his thigh? Tom had been so sure he would bleed to death and that he would never have to face him again! He must have been found by someone not long afterward, someone who'd gotten him to a sawbones.

Maybe that explained the subsequent disappearance of Mercy Fairweather, or should he say Mercy Devlin? Of course—that must be how it had happened. Somehow she'd managed to find that damned vacant soddy he'd left Devlin in to die, and had been nursing him back to health!

And now Devlin was recovering, and the next thing he'd want would be revenge....

Tom's blood ran cold at the thought. He could never have gotten the drop on Devlin if the man had been prepared, he knew that. And now, he knew, it was just a matter of time before Devlin would be coming after him. And this time it would be Devlin who'd have the advantage.

Culhane thought about gathering up his gear and leaving town right now, tonight. With the cover of darkness he could be miles away from Abilene before the dawn broke.

But it was only a fleeting thought. There was no advantage to going back over the Chisholm Trail; it would be too easy for Devlin to catch up to him. And Culhane knew it would be foolish to ride over unfamiliar ground in the dark. He could get hopelessly lost, or worse yet, his horse could put a hoof into a prairie-dog hole in the dark and break his leg, leaving Tom afoot to face retribution. No, it'd be best to wait until it was fully light, though by then he would have to be careful to avoid running into Jase and Manuel.

His eyes narrowed as he thought of the Devil's Boys and their recent habit of loitering around Abilene, watching him. Now that he knew Devlin lived, suddenly it all made sense. They were keeping an eye on him so they could report back to the trail boss!

Judas priest, but he was a stupid fool. He should have left Abilene right after the shooting, maybe gone out into the Territories, or down to Mexico, and gotten himself lost where the law would never find him. But now it was too late for that. Now he had to find a way to put an end to Devlin first.

He'd bet money Devlin was right where he had left him, in that soddy. It had been only four days since he'd shot Devlin, and even though Devlin had survived it, he wouldn't be feeling any too frisky. The odds were he wouldn't have moved from there. If he'd been brought into Abilene, Tom would have heard about it for sure. The soddy's isolated location had been an advantage to Sam. Although crude and dirty, it was the perfect place to hide out and keep the fact of his survival secret until the right time had come.

But how was he to get the advantage over a man he knew to be much better with a Colt than he'd ever hope to be? Culhane had seen Sam Devlin face danger on the trail—from marauding Indians, rustlers and stampedes—and knew he was not only a dead shot but completely cool in the face of danger.

What he needed was a shield, something that would get him close to Sam without endangering himself, close enough to kill him.

All at once he thought of a way to achieve both goals—killing Devlin and teaching Charity Fairweather that he wasn't just some hayseed she could tease.

And he'd enjoy both. Seeing Devlin go down, a bullet through his heart and a surprised look on his face while Mercy screamed in the background, would be infinitely satisfying, but so would his reward afterward. Once Devlin was dead, he was going to take that spiteful little blond bitch somewhere that she would be completely at his mercy—but he wouldn't show her any. And then maybe he'd take her into Texas by way of the Staked Plains, and sell her to the Comancheros. She wouldn't tell any of those rough men no, by God. She wouldn't tell any man no, ever again.

"Charity, you look troubled. Is there anything you want to talk about?" the Reverend Jeremiah Fairweather asked suddenly the next morning, startling the young girl as she stared down at her cup full of coffee.

"No, Papa. Nothing," she said, too quickly. "I mean, I'm still worried about Mercy and all...."

Her father's pale eyes were piercing as he gazed at her across the kitchen table. "Well, of course you are. We both are. It just seemed that there was something additional...weighing you down. I just thought perhaps you had a little...misunderstanding with young Ned Webster last night? I heard raised voices, though I couldn't hear what you were saying, of course, and then you ran in and slammed the door, awfully suddenly, it seemed to me. And

I heard you pacing the floor in your room afterward, daughter."

Charity turned eyes that felt full of grit toward her father. She felt as if she hadn't slept a wink last night, worrying about what she had said to Culhane. Oh, why did she have to have such a quick tongue and temper? She had known as soon as she saw the sudden gleam in his eye that she had been wrong to taunt him with the fact that Sam Devlin was alive. He hadn't known that fact, and now he'd be on his guard—perhaps he'd even go looking for Sam! Did he know where to look? If only she knew where they were, she could somehow warn them. But she didn't, and she could only hope she would encounter Jase or one of the trail boss's other cowboys in Abilene today.

Of course, she must have gotten some sleep, because she'd had a bad dream, a nightmare really, in which Culhane gunned down Sam Devlin, and then turned and ravished her, right in front of Mercy and Papa, who were tied up and unable to help her. "No, Papa. Ned and I didn't have a fight."

Her father lifted an eloquent brow, and she knew he wouldn't be satisfied with what little she had said. She hated lying to her father, but there was no help for it, not right now.

"It...it wasn't a real fight. I—I guess I was just anxious about my sister. Please, you won't say anything to him, will you? We'll get it straightened out, I'm sure we will," she pleaded. All she needed now was for Papa to ask Ned Webster about a quarrel she'd never even had with him! Oh, please Lord—please let this all be settled soon, with Mercy and Sam safe and happy, and everything else back to normal! She'd never tell another lie as long as she lived!

"I...I just want you to know, Charity, that I had a lot of time to think while I was off looking for Mercy. A lot of time to pray. I think it's important for you to know that I love you and your sister very much, and I just want both of you to be safe and happy. I...just pray that nothing's happened to her—" His voice trembled and broke off, and Charity, her eyes firmly trained on her biscuits and coffee to avoid giving away secrets, suddenly heard strange sounds coming from her father's side of the table. She looked up to see her father was weeping!

"Oh, Papa, don't...don't," she said, going around to the other side of the table and putting her arms around her father's shaking shoulders. "Mercy's going to be all right. I—I just know it." Oh, Lord, how she longed to comfort him by telling him that she knew Mercy and Sam were safe! But Jase had said not to—there were people who meant ill toward Sam, he'd said. And though her father's heart seemed to have softened toward Mercy, Charity still didn't know how he felt about Sam.

Her father leaned against her, and she stroked his head and smoothed his hair while he murmured, "Oh, child, I wish I had your faith. I...I just can't bear the thought of harm coming to your sister. First your mother is taken, and now Mercy. Father in Heaven, I can't take it...."

She couldn't bear his weeping. She hadn't seen her father cry since their mother's death, and she couldn't bear to see the man who'd always been strong as a rock sobbing like a child. It sapped her will to keep the secret.

She would keep it until nightfall, she decided. Something might very well happen today so that everything would be resolved, and if it did not, she would at least tell her father that Mercy was safe with Sam, though she could not, of course, tell him where her sister was.

"I'm sorry...for breaking down like that, my dear," her father said at last. "I don't know what came over me, except that I'm not sleeping very well, either. I—I think I'll go back up to my room for a while, and pray about it...."

"Yes, Papa," she said, noticing for the first time how drawn and old he was, how stoop-shouldered he looked now—Papa, who'd always walked proud and straight! "And if you hear me go out, don't worry," she called after him, hating the necessity of lying again. "I'm just going to go to the mercantile and see what Mr. Moon will trade me for some eggs."

She would do no such thing, of course. She had to find Jase or one of the cowboys and pass on her warning, and pray to God she wasn't too late!

The next morning Mercy awoke to the sound of men's low voices outside the soddy. She put out an exploring hand and, just as she had suspected, found that Sam had already dressed and gone outside.

After dressing quickly, she found him at the campfire, holding a cup of coffee, deep in conversation with Jase and Cookie.

"It ain't gonna come to that, Sam, and you know it, so there ain't no use in talkin' about it," Jase was saying.

"I certainly hope not, but if it does—"

"Mornin', Miz Mercy! Did ya sleep well?" Cookie inquired, interrupting Sam a little too heartily.

"Yes, I did. I seem to be interrupting a conversation, gentlemen. Please continue," she said, looking from Sam's face to Cookie's to Jase's. Sam looked uncomfortable, and the other two men refused to even meet her gaze. They soon made excuses to go into Abilene.

While the two approached their hobbled horses and began to saddle and bridle them, she looked back at Sam. Beside him, lying on a cloth on the ground, were two pistols to replace the ones Sam had told her he had left in the safe at the Drover's Cottage. Sam had advised Jase not to try to claim the pistols from Mr. and Mrs. Gore, fearing that the innkeeper and his wife might comment about the fact to others. Obviously Sam had been cleaning the new ones.

She watched as Jase and Cookie galloped off in the direction of town. "They didn't even have breakfast, did they?" she asked, turning back to Sam.

"No, but that's no reason we can't," Sam said with a ghost of a smile. "Cookie left us some biscuits in the pan, and there's bacon and eggs all ready to go. Tell you what, I'll even cook," he offered gallantly with a crooked grin that touched her heart.

"Oh, no, you don't, Sam Devlin. I've seen what happens when you try to cook, and if this is going to be our last 'soddy breakfast,' I'd like it to be edible," she said, her tart tone giving no indication of the uneasiness she had felt when he and his hands had shut up at the sight of her. She felt as if she had interrupted a conference of war.

He went back to cleaning one of the Colts while she cooked, his eyes narrowed in concentration while he hummed a tune she recognized as the Civil War song "Lorena."

She had hoped to make this last day here a special one, but already she saw that it was not to be. His mind was clearly more focused on the preparations for tomorrow than on being with her here today.

She was being childishly selfish, Mercy told herself. After all, if he was ready for what tomorrow might bring, they would have a lifetime of "todays" together. If, instead, he spent the day lazing around with her as if they were two lovers who hadn't a care in the world, all her memories of today would not make up for the endless years she might spend without him.

"What will you do when you get to town? About Culhane, I mean? Are you just going to. . . to have a duel with him?"

"A duel?" He laughed shortly, mirthlessly, but she didn't feel that his laughter was aimed at her. "Lord, Mercy, calling it a duel is surely gussyin' up the truth. No, I'm going to try to avoid a gun battle—I'd rather turn him over to the law, if I have my druthers. But I may not get my druthers, you know, Mercy."

"I...I know," she said, turning away so he would not see the anguish she felt. "He may not give you the chance. You may have to kill him."

"What I *aim* to do," he went on, "is take him by surprise, hog-tie him and take him to the nearest town with a jail, where I'll swear out a complaint for attempted murder. That'd probably be Wichita. The boys'll help me get him there."

"What...about me?" she asked at last. "Am I going along with you while you take Culhane to the nearest law?"

He blinked and looked thoughtful. "No, I don't reckon that'd be wise. There's no tellin' how ugly Culhane might act, especially if he figured he could get under my skin by offendin' you."

"I'm not going back to stay with Papa," she said quickly, then wished she hadn't spoken. She hated to bother him with additional details when he might be facing death at Culhane's hands tomorrow, but she would not spend another minute under her father's roof!

"Then we'll put you up at the Grand Hotel till I get back."

But how would she know? She assumed he would want her to wait here at the soddy until the matter was decided, but would he ride back for her afterward? Or, if the worst happened, would one of the Devil's Boys come to tell her the awful news? But his silence was impenetrable as he pushed the eggs around on the tin plate and pretended to eat. She did not voice her questions.

After breakfast he got up without a word, got some of the empty tin cans that had contained beans and set them up in a row at some distance from the soddy. "Target practice," he explained when he noticed her questioning look. And then, while she washed the dishes, he took out the Colts and began to fire.

The first shot made her jump, for she had been looking down at the plate she was washing and hadn't seen him draw. He missed the first can, and then the second.

"Hellfire, I hate usin' someone else's guns," he growled, already irritable because he still couldn't bring himself to tell her he had no money to pay for her to stay at the hotel, unless he could recover what Culhane had stolen, and who knew what that sidewinder might have done with it in the meantime? Sam would be in the humiliating position of having to borrow from his own cowboys just so he and Mercy would have traveling money, not that Jase or Cookie or Manuel would grudge him the loan. But there was no use borrowing trouble. First things first.

Sam raised the pistol again and fired. This time his aim was true; his shot sent the can flying, as did his next shot and the next. He fired until both pistols were empty, and did not miss again.

Cheered by his rapid improvement, Sam was surprised to look behind him and find Mercy gone. He was disappointed that she had not witnessed his expert shooting, wondering what was so all-fired important in the soddy that she couldn't wait and praise his aim—until he noticed the tin plate that had been just dropped in the dirt instead of into the soapy washwater.

Some instinct warned him to holster his pistols and seek his wife inside the soddy. He found her there, pacing back and forth, tears streaming down her face.

Chapter Twenty-Six

"Was the noise scarin' you, honey?" he asked, going to her and taking her in his arms.

"No," she said shakily, reaching down to wipe her eyes on the hem of her dress. "Yes. It's silly, I know. Anyone who's lived in Abilene for the past year should be more than used to gunfire at all hours. But it wasn't just the noise, it was the sight of you, limping out there to set the cans up—every step hurt you, didn't it? Sam, what if that pain slows you down—just enough? Let's just forget all about Culhane and go back to Texas! Can't we do that, please?"

He struggled for the words to make her understand. "That's runnin' away from trouble, Mercy, and it doesn't ever pay to do that. Trouble just has a way of followin' a man who runs from it. What's to stop Culhane from hearin' I'm alive and settin' up an ambush for us down the trail?" He wanted to admit he was scared, too, not of Culhane but of the very thing she had mentioned, the possibility that the pain might make the critical difference in his speed if it came to a gun battle with Culhane.

"You men and your damned pride!" she raged, wrenching away from him. "You'd rather take a chance on being dead than run from a fight! Well, go ahead, then! Why wait till tomorrow? Go on into Abilene and have it out with him now!"

Sam could see there would be no reasoning with her in her riled-up state, and being around her would just shatter the state of calm concentration he had always tried to achieve during the war before going into a battle. He didn't try to take her in his arms again.

"I think I'll saddle Buck and go for a ride," he said, keeping his voice even as he retrieved some more ammunition from the pouch Jase had left. "I need to get used to bein' on horseback again, too, and maybe I can shoot us some meat for supper. So don't worry if you hear any gunfire."

She whirled around and faced him, her eyes like rain-wet jade. Her mouth moved as if she was trying to speak, but no words came. At last her shoulders sagged and she turned away again, as if to avoid seeing him go.

Tom Culhane couldn't believe his luck as he stood in the passageway between two saloons fastening his saddlebags onto his horse. He was all packed and ready to go, and the Devil's Boys were nowhere in sight. And there, coming down Cedar Street, was the very object of his frustrated lust, Charity Fairweather.

She was wearing a straw bonnet that shielded her face, but there was no doubt it was her. It was way too early for the soiled doves from Texas Street to be up and about, and in any case they would have disdained to wear such a simple gingham dress. And the golden curls he glimpsed underneath her bonnet could belong to none but the preacher's younger daughter.

What was she doing here on Cedar Street, he wondered, among all the saloons and gambling dens? Hadn't she learned her lesson that night she had sought out his company? Could she have yet another cowboy beau to rival her local hayseed? He watched her for a moment as she peeked over a saloon's swinging doors. Evidently she didn't find whoever she was seeking in there, for she stepped back into the street, holding her skirts high above the dust and exposing booted feet.

It was still early enough that there were few people about, and certainly no one who would try to stop him. Backing the horse out of the passageway between the frame buildings to the alleyway that ran behind them, he mounted quickly and rode behind a couple of saloons until he could come out onto Cedar Street behind Charity. The preacher's daughter was still striding purposefully down the street, totally unaware of her danger.

Culhane grinned as he set spurs to his horse, knowing now how the hawk felt as it swooped down on a helpless rabbit. The surprised gelding leapt into a gallop.

She couldn't have failed to hear the pounding hooves behind her. He saw her whirl around, saw her mouth drop open in horrified recognition, and then she started running toward one of the saloon entrances.

He was too quick for her. As his horse thundered toward the girl, Tom dropped the tied reins over the horse's neck and, guiding him with his knees, leaned down and grabbed Charity around her slender waist, hauling her up and across the saddle like a sack of cornmeal.

Her head down, Charity set up a screeching that would have wakened the dead, much less the late-rising soiled doves of Abilene, and thrashed violently against him in an effort to escape.

"Shut up, girl!" he shouted at her, smacking a hand hard on her fanny. She continued to struggle wildly, flailing her feet against the horse's side. "Shut up and don't move or I'll throw ya off, ya hear me?" he yelled down at her.

The threat did not deter her, although even a fool girl had to realize she could very well break bones if he threw her off at such a speed. If he didn't gain control of her, she was going to get them both pitched off.

Out of the corner of his eye he saw someone stepping out of the Alamo Saloon ahead of them.

"Hey, stop, mister, you can't—" he heard the man yell, and then the rest of the shouted words were lost in the thudding of the horse's hooves as they swept past. He glanced back over his shoulder—was that Deacon Paxton? Drat his luck! If he'd had his gun drawn, he'd have sent some bullets to say his farewells to the meddling bartender.

But remembering his pistol gave him an idea. Holding Charity down firmly with one hand, he ignored her ear-splitting shrieks for the time it took to draw his Colt, and then he placed the cold muzzle of the gun directly against her ear.

"Now shut up, Charity, or I'll use this on you, I swear I will."

She was instantly obedient. As the horse continued to gallop along, heading for the edge of town, her skirts blew in the wind, exposing lacy petticoats and pantalets. Her bonnet had come loose and blown off. Here and there townsfolk and visiting cowboys stopped and stared, pointing, but with Charity in that ignominious, head-down position, Culhane doubted anyone could recognize her. They probably figured it was just one of the cowboys up to mischief with one of the saloon girls—who weren't worthy of anyone's protection, anyway.

He waited until they were out on the prairie before pulling his horse to a stop and yanking her up astride the horse.

"What are you gonna do?" she asked, turning her head slightly. He could feel her trembling against him, and he knew she was wondering if he was going to pull her out of the saddle and ravish her right here. The idea amused him and made his groin ache, but he had something more important to do first.

"I'm jes' gonna make it a little easier to travel without any interference from you," he growled against the back of her neck. "No, don't you try nothin', or you won't like what happens. An' there ain't no one out here to screech to, so keep that purty mouth shut, okay?"

She nodded against him.

He reached down and grabbed a length of rope from inside one of his saddlebags and tied her wrists tightly together, then reached behind his neck to unknot his bandanna.

As he brought it out in front of her, and began to twist it, she must have guessed his purpose. "No, don't gag me—I won't scream, I swear it! After all, you said there was no one to scream to, didn't you?"

"Not out here, but there might be where we're going."

"Why? Where are you taking me?" she asked, her eyes round with alarm, just before he forced the gag into her mouth.

"I jes' figured you might like t' pay a visit to yore sister and her new husband," he said, snickering as he saw her startled look. "That's right. I'm damn near certain I know where they are. I jes' thought you might like t' be there—t' comfort her fer a minute or two after I blow that damn bastard Devlin clear t' kingdom come."

He guffawed at his own humor, and laughed all the harder when he saw a tear slide down Charity's pale cheek and disappear into the dark fabric of his bandanna.

"That's right," he said. "You're gonna be my shield so's I can get the drop on Devlin. He ain't gonna shoot at me when I come ridin' up t' that soddy they're stayin' in with you on the saddle in front o' me, no sirree. And he'll have t' drop his guns out where I kin see 'em, or I'll let daylight through you, right in front o' yore sister." He chortled at the thought, and felt her shudder against him.

"Then I'll shoot him down like a dog," Culhane went on, enjoying his captive's terror, "and after he's finished kickin', I'll kill yore sister, too. Ain't no point in leavin' witnesses t' put a noose around my neck, is there? You an me kin go somewhere afterward, somewhere nice an' private like, and celebrate—just like we were about to celebrate before, that night we first met, remember?" He squeezed her breast, just in case she didn't remember.

She tried to talk, the words hopelessly garbled by the bandanna gag, but the hateful expression in her eyes told him clearly enough what she was thinking.

He snorted. "Ya don't like that idea much, do ya? I didn't think ya would. And there won't be no one to stop me then, Charity," he said, allowing his hand to rove over her rigid body as the horse took them farther out over the rolling prairie, where only a wheeling hawk overhead could see what indignities he was inflicting on his captive.

Deacon Paxton set up a pounding on the door of the preacher's house that would have wakened the dead. Even so, it seemed an eternity before he heard footsteps and a rumpled and sleepy-looking Jeremiah Fairweather finally opened the door. Deacon saw him stiffen as he saw who it was.

"What is it? If it's about your serving as deacon—"

"It isn't," Deacon said, interrupting him. "Listen, Reverend, there's trouble, and it's about your daughter. Not five minutes ago I saw a cowboy gallop past the saloon with your daughter over his saddlebow, and she was yellin' like a scalded cat."

"Mercy?" the preacher breathed, his face paling. "He had *Mercy?* What cowboy? Who was it—tell me!"

"No, it wasn't Mercy, it was Charity, the other one."

Jeremiah blinked behind his smudged spectacles. "But that's impossible. Charity said she might just go to Moon's to trade some eggs."

"It was her," Deacon insisted grimly. "Blond curls and all. And the cowboy was that little bowlegged Texan, Culhane, that's been loiterin' around Abilene. He was headin' west outta town when I lost sight o' him."

"He's got *Charity?*" the preacher cried, his face stricken. "Great God in Heaven, we've got to catch him! Why, he could do anything to my poor innocent daughter—!"

Deacon nodded grimly. "But I don't know where he was heading with her. Just 'cause he was heading west doesn't mean he'll keep going that way. We've got to put together search parties, and quick. The longer of a lead he has, the farther he can get with her. Why don't you come on down to the Alamo just as quick as you can saddle your horse and I'll set the girls to roundin' up the cowboys for a posse."

The preacher's face was anxious as he tried to take it all in. "The girls?" he repeated.

"The saloon girls," Deacon repeated impatiently. "Don't worry about that, preacher! Get moving! There's no time to lose!"

Mercy gave a little cry of joy when she heard the approaching hoofbeats. Sam was back already! Maybe he had become worried about how upset she had been when he had loped away from the soddy, or maybe he had just gotten lucky quickly and they would have venison or rabbit or prairie chicken for supper. Either way, she didn't care. She had a desperate need to tell him that she loved him and always would, and that she was sorry she had been so childish when he was clearly doing what a man had to do.

Impatient for him to see her smiling, happy face since all she had shown him earlier was storm clouds and tears, she threw open the door to the soddy without even glancing out the window first.

"Oh, Sam, I'm so glad you're back! I just can't wait to tell you—"

"What cain't you wait to tell him, Miz Devlin? Why, ain't yore husband here now that I've come callin'?" Tom Culhane drawled, a nasty smile on his face, his Colt trained on her while his other arm held her sister in front of him on his horse. Charity was bound and gagged, and her frightened eyes begged Mercy for help.

"What are you doing with my sister, Mr. Culhane? Let her loose! And what did you want with my husband?" Mercy demanded while her mind raced. She had no idea how far away Sam was, and here was the very demon who had nearly killed him, and he had her sister! Her blood turned to icicles in her veins.

"Aw, me and yore sister are jes' gonna have some fun," he said, still with that nasty smile. "What did I want with Sam Devlin? Why, I jes' wanted t' finish what I left undone." The cowboy smirked. "And then I'll be the first t' pay my respects to his widow, of course."

So this was how a rattlesnake must look when it was about to sink its fangs into a cornered mouse, Mercy thought, struggling to remain calm. "Did you know I was here?" she asked, not because it really mattered, but because she was playing for time. It would be much better for Sam to find them outside the soddy talking than for Culhane to have time to prepare an ambush.

"Oh, yeah, thanks to your talkative sister, I shore did," Culhane said with a grin so smug she wanted to wipe it off his face with a doubled-up fist. But she had to keep her temper, had to keep calm.

Charity's eyes closed for a moment, and then she turned her sorrowful gaze back to her sister, obviously asking for forgiveness.

For a moment Mercy was confused. She had asked Jase Lowry to tell her sister she was all right, but they had agreed he wouldn't say where she and Sam were, hadn't they?

She must have looked as puzzled as she felt.

"Oh, I put two and two together," Tom said. "When yore sister let it slip that Devlin was still alive, I figgered you musta been the one t' find him and patch him up, since you was missin', too. An' I figgered he wasn't strong enough t' travel very far, so y'all must still be here, right where I left Sam fer dead. Well, he didn't die when he was supposed to, but he'll die today, all right. And don't you worry about bein' a weepy widow for long, 'cause you're gonna die, too, preacher's daughter."

She froze, unable to look away from the deadly muzzle of his Colt. "But why, Culhane? What did Sam ever do to you that would make you want to kill him? And me? Are you really so angry about that night you tried to take advantage of my sister and he stopped you? You were just making a mistake, that was all...."

When she saw the irrational gleam in his eyes she realized how futile it was to argue with a madman. The gun wavered for a second, then was held steady again.

"Nobody tells Tom Culhane what he cain't do," the cowboy growled between gritted teeth. "An' I finish what I start. I started t' kill that sumbitch Devlin, and I'm gonna, jes' as soon as he comes back here. I started to take yore slut of a sister, here, and I'm shore enough gonna do that, too, jes' as soon as you and Devlin are outta the way, Miz Mercy. And when I've finally had my fill o' havin' her, I'm gonna sell her to the Comancheros out on the Staked Plains. She'll be glad to be dead when she finally gits t' join you."

Mercy heard Charity moan behind her gag. Her sister's eyes were wide with terror, and while she watched, two tears escaped from Charity's brimming eyes.

Mercy looked steadily at her sister, trying to pass a message of hope and encouragement she was far from feeling.

Dear God, what was she going to do? She had to save Charity! Where was Sam? Now, above all, she didn't want him to come! If he stayed away, at least *he* would live! And the longer Culhane waited for him, the more chance there was the young killer would grow bored with the waiting—and grow careless. And she thought Sam had left his boot gun somewhere in the soddy.

"He'll be back any minute now, but I wouldn't count on finishing those 'tasks,' Tom Culhane," she told him with a false confidence. "He's going to have Jase and Cookie and Manuel with him. You'll be hopelessly outgunned. Why don't you forget all about those plans and just leave Charity here with me? Ride off, and I won't even tell Sam the right way you went, I promise." *In a pig's eye I won't,* she thought angrily.

Culhane seemed only momentarily nonplussed by the thought of facing not one but four cowboys. "Well, if we're goin' t' have company I expect we'd better get ready for them," he said, keeping his pistol trained on Mercy as he dismounted. He pulled Charity roughly off the saddle with one arm around her waist. She staggered and nearly fell, and he jerked her upright. "Go on in the soddy, girl," he ordered Charity. "And you, Miz Devlin, you take my horse down to the creek there while I keep my eye on you, and tie him to that tree so he's out o' sight. I wouldn't want Devlin t' spot my horse an' ruin my surprise welcome."

Chapter Twenty-Seven

The saloon-lined street sounded like the middle of an insane asylum, the preacher thought as he rode up to the Alamo Saloon. The saloon girls, dressed in scandalously short, feather-trimmed wrappers in a rainbow of gaudy hues, some shod in matching slippers, others barefoot, were standing in front of the biggest saloons banging pots with spoons yelling, "Come out an' join the posse, boys! We need a posse, right now! Free drinks an' entertainment at the Alamo later for all who ride with the posse!"

Excited by the noise, horses whinnied and plunged at the hitching posts outside the saloons. Cowboys were pouring out of the saloons and thronging the streets, some shooting their guns in the air, others whooping as they loosed their horses from the hitching posts.

He spied Deacon standing outside the Alamo Saloon, holding a very tall, restive black horse. The bartender was talking to a nattily dressed cardsharp and surrounded by a trio of cowboys already on their horses. The Reverend Mr. Fairweather recognized the cowboys as the ones he'd seen around Devlin that morning inside the saloon at his daughter's "wedding" breakfast.

"I don't think—" he began doubtfully, indicating the dozens of cowboys mounting up on all sides.

"Don't think," the cardsharp interrrupted. "There isn't time. You better be especially glad the Devils' Boys, here, heard all the uproar. They know where Devlin and Miss Mercy are—and they think there's a good chance Culhane is makin' his way there with your other daughter. We're going to divide the cowboys into four posses, and each head a different direction, but you'll go with Devlin's cowboys to the place where they were hiding out."

While Fairweather was absorbing all this astonishing information, a woman appeared behind the cardsharp, a redhead arrayed in a shiny satin robe. "You listen to Wyatt, Preacher. You better take all the help you can get. You sure can't summon your sodbusters off their farms as fast as we can put together a posse, can you?"

Fairweather felt as if he were in some kind of waking dream. Surely he must be, since he, an upright and God-fearing minister of the Gospel, was about to agree with a whore. "No, that's true, I can't." He had seen the mayor, Horace Barnes, and the blacksmith, Bob Webster, striding down the street toward the Alamo, but they had been afoot.

"Hey, I don't want to keep you, but there's somethin' else I think it's high time you knew, Preacher, about that new son-in-law of yours," the woman called as Fairweather started to rein his horse in line with the others. "And it's about how this whole mess got started with your daughter and Sam."

"I'm listening, woman."

"My name's Mercedes LaFleche, Preacher," the woman corrected him, giving him a quick, cheeky grin as she did so. "And you might say the whole thing is my fault, in a way. You see, Wyatt here bet Sam Devlin when he came into town—before Sam and I met, that is—that he couldn't, ah, *enjoy my favors*—if you'll excuse the words, Preacher—without him payin' me. Sam took the dare. And then he met your daughter Mercy when she came lookin' for your other daughter one night, and he thought she was me." She twirled a loose curl that lay in color-clashing splendor against the scarlet satin of her robe. "We're both lookers, we both got red hair and our names—Mercy, Mercedes—you see how it could happen? Your son-in-law wasn't tryin' to ruin an innocent like your Mercy. He thought she was—" she cleared her throat "—fair game. And then they fell in love."

Fairweather's mouth fell open as he realized how Culhane had lied to him. Culhane had said Sam had gone after Mercy deliberately, knowing she was an innocent girl. Then Culhane had used his fatherly anger to tempt him into doing something he might not have considered otherwise. He opened his mouth, fully intending to tell Mercedes that what she was saying might well be true, but Deacon had mounted up and it looked as if everyone was ready to go. He'd better be ready to ride if what she was saying was going to matter in the long run.

"I know, you've gotta go," she said. "I just wanted to tell you that, 'cause I've been dealin' with the pretend version of love long enough that I know what the real thing looks like. He loves her, Preacher. And she loves him. So you better be nice to him once you find them, Preacher, or you're going to lose your daughter."

"Thank you, Miss LaFleche," he said, feeling strangely humbled even as he said the ridiculous name that made him squirm with its implications. "I'll think about what you've said." He would have a lot to think about, and much to atone for, if God granted him the chance. He had been wrong, so very wrong, to judge Sam Devlin without really knowing him, just because he was a Texan. And then he had trusted Culhane—another Texan—just because he had offered himself as an instrument of vengeance, without examining Culhane's motives for being willing to achieve that vengeance! What did the Good Book say? "Vengeance is mine; I will repay, saith the Lord.'' Revenge wasn't up to him, it never had been! And now he might lose both daughters because of it! Truly, he had much to repent, though his mistakes had begun out of love for his daughters.

But he had to learn that love did not mean ownership.

''Go with God, Preacher,'' Mercedes said, her eyes gleaming with a perceptive sympathy.

Mercy, her hands and feet bound, a gag in her mouth, watched as Tom Culhane stared out of the soddy. He was careful to peer from the side of the window, so that anyone coming could not see him. But the prairie was evidently empty, and Culhane was getting increasingly restless. He'd stop watching every few minutes to pace across the floor, glaring at her and Charity as if it were somehow their fault he was here. Then he'd go back to his vigil, swearing under his breath.

Her nerves were stretched to the breaking point, but there was nothing she could do. She lay trussed like a chicken on the hard-packed dirt floor, unable to see out herself or plead with their captor.

Charity sat, looking pale and exhausted, across the floor from her. Tom had refused to let them even sit close together, as if bound and gagged they could still somehow pose a threat to him.

If she ever got out of this alive she was going to make Tom Culhane pay for every moment of misery, every indignity he'd visited on her poor sister and herself, Mercy thought angrily for the hundredth time.

''I got an idea,'' Tom said, and they both looked up. ''I think we'll change the plan jes' a little.''

The last time Sam had felt such a prickling on the back of his neck, the herd had stampeded, and that had been on a cloudless clear day at high noon. He had only had a moment to gather up his reins and steady himself in the saddle, and hadn't even had time to shout a warning before the run began. The stampede had happened so suddenly that one cowboy, who had been riding the left flank, had been caught dismounted and checking his mount's hoof for a stone. The herd had turned in his direction, and the cowboy's screams as he'd been trampled had been drowned in the pounding hooves and clicking of colliding horns as the cattle panicked.

Sam had first learned to trust that atavistic warning during the war, and it had never played him false since. He was feeling it now, unmistakably, as he approached the soddy with the wild turkey he had shot slung over the saddle.

"Mercy?" he called, a few yards from the soddy. There was no answer. "Mercy? If you're in there, don't play games with me!" he called, but still no one appeared. Had she gotten so angry she had just walked away from here, back to town, possibly? Had a herd come by, and had some cowboy from it just abducted her? There weren't wild Indians in the area, were there? Hellfire, if she was just sitting inside sulking, he was going to put her over his knee!

But deep inside, he knew Mercy wouldn't play silly games with him. She was distressed about the coming danger, but she was not one for sulking and tantrums. His apprehension rose. "Come look at what I brought us for supper, honey!"

Oh, dear Lord, what if Tom Culhane had suddenly taken a notion to ride out and view his supposedly rotting corpse, and had found Mercy here alone? He drew his .45 and dismounted slowly, listening, and keeping his eye on the small, vacant square they'd laughed to call a window.

A horse nickered from down by the creek, and Buck answered. Whose horse? He was just about to go and see if he recognized the animal when he heard another noise from within the soddy. It sounded like a muffled whimpering...Mercy must be hurt! Throwing caution to the wind, he rushed to the soddy and threw open the door.

There was Mercy, lying against the wall directly in front of the door, bound and gagged, and beside her, similarly tied up and gagged, was her sister, Charity.

Their eyes were wide with alarm. Both of them were shaking their heads vigorously and trying to talk in spite of the gags.

"Mercy! Charity! Who did this to you? Who—"

And then he felt the two jabs of cold steel against his back, and he knew who had done it, even before Tom Culhane snickered behind him and said "*I* done it, Devlin—didn't you guess? I suppose I ain't no Devil's Boy, so I guess maybe that makes me an Avenging Angel, don't it?" He laughed nastily and jabbed Sam in the back again. "And now I reckon you better just reach for the sky."

Sam did as he was told, feeling sick inside. "Sure, Tom. But I reckon it's only fair to warn you that the boys are right behind me," Sam said with a nonchalance he was far from feeling. "Jase and Manuel and Cookie, well, they won't take kindly to seein' you—especially not with you holdin' guns to my back."

Tom chuckled. "You must think I'm dumb as a wagonload a' armadillos," he said, and Sam heard the creak of leather as Culhane holstered one of his guns before reaching to take the one Sam held and the one still in his holster.

Sam heard his guns land with twin *thumps* behind him, far out in the yard.

"You kin see fer miles out here, and I checked to see if you had anyone followin' you afore I snuck around th' side of th' soddy and got the drop on you. I seen your boys in town awhile back. They didn't see me, but they was lookin' mighty comfortable. I don't think they'll be headin' this way any time soon. And you didn't see my horse 'cos I tied him down by the creek." Culhane finished in triumph.

"Real clever, Culhane," Sam retorted. "I guess you learned somethin' on the drive after all. You weren't nearly that bright when you left San Antone."

"Shut up or I'll shoot you in the gut instead of the heart," snarled Culhane, pushing him inside with a booted foot against his backside. "And then I'll let you watch while I rape your wife."

Sam had to grit his teeth to bite back the retort that might have made Culhane do just as he promised. "Sorry—didn't mean to rile your temper," Sam murmured in mock contrition. "Look, Tom, it doesn't have to be this way. You could just take the money and head out for the Territories, you know. You could even get to California—you could live high on the hog in San Francisco on what you stole from me. Or you could cross the border and buy a hell of a rancho with it, as well as a *señorita* for every day of the week. Go ahead and take it, Culhane. I won't send the law after you." He hated having to bargain with the bastard, hated to sound as if he were begging for his life, but if it got Mercy and her sister out of this alive, he didn't care what he had to do.

Sam saw Mercy stare at him quizzically.

Culhane had apparently seen it, too, and correctly interpreted it. "Oh, so he didn't tell you about th' money, did he? Tsk, tsk. Husbands and wives shouldn't keep secrets from one another, ya know. Yeah, he was carryin' twenty-six thousand dollars, Miz Mercy—less what was left after he frittered it away at the gamblin' tables that night y'all met. That was why he took that stupid dare, ya know, about that whore—he was trying t' make up what he'd lost t' that cardsharp Wyatt Earp," he jeered. "Still proud o' yore handsome Texan, Miz Mercy?"

Sam's and Mercy's eyes met, and what he saw there was only a desperate love and adoration, not condemnation. She nodded, her eyes never leaving Sam's.

"Yeah, that's right, Miz Mercy, he was carryin' a handsome sum when I shot him down," Culhane continued, "and now it's all mine, yes sirree, all mine, jes' like yore sister's gonna be all mine—fer as long as I want her, that is—after I kill the both of you. So I guess it won't matter to you folks that I'm gonna have that money, now, will it? I mean, y'all are gonna be angels up in heaven, so you won't begrudge Tom Culhane a few thousand..."

Sam swallowed hard to conquer the fury he felt at Culhane's casually cruel announcements. Fury wouldn't help them get out of this situation. It would only cloud his mind when he needed it to be crystal-clear and sharp. "Take the money, dammit, Culhane," Sam insisted. "Take me out and shoot me, if you have to. Your quarrel's with me, just me. Let the women go. You don't want Charity—she'll only slow you down while you're runnin'. With that kind of money you can have every fancy lady between here and the Pacific Ocean."

"Oh, I don't think I have t' make any compromises with you, Devlin," Culhane drawled. "I'm th' one with th' guns here, I'm th' one who decides, an' I've already decided what I want. An' I want th' both of you dead, so neither one of you can put the noose around my neck. Oh, you're going to be really dead this time, Devlin. I'll make sure."

Sam forced himself to chuckle.

"What's so dang funny?" Culhane demanded.

"Oh, just thinkin' about how I'm gonna haunt you, Culhane," he said. "You won't take an easy step the rest of your life. That's if you kill Mercy, that is. You leave her alone, and I might reconsider...."

Sam wondered if he could make Culhane angry enough to forget caution, wondering if he dared try to wrestle with

Culhane in this enclosed space. No, he decided regretfully, there was too much chance a wild shot might hit one of the women.

It was late afternoon, and Jase and Cookie might return soon, but he couldn't count on it.

"Well, all right, Culhane, have it your way. I guess you can call the shots, so to speak. But you wouldn't deny a man a few last wishes, would you?" He would stall as long as he could. If he could just stall long enough, the Devil's Boys would arrive and there'd be nothing Culhane could do but surrender—or die.

"What are they? I ain't listenin' to anythin' that takes very long. I know you're tryin' t' stall," Culhane said shrewdly.

"No, I wouldn't try your patience that way. I know when I'm licked, and I'd just as soon get it over with and be walkin' those golden streets of heaven with my sweet wife," Sam said with all the resignation he could fake. His back still to Culhane, he caught Mercy's eye with his own and winked at her before going on. She stared back, hope mingling with terror in her green eyes.

"It's just that...well, I've almost died once in here, and once was enough. I have a hankerin' t' die out in the open. That's not too much t' ask, is it?"

"No, I guess not. You can walk outside, as long as it ain't near where I threw the guns. But you said there was more than one wish," Culhane reminded him, his eyes narrowed and suspicious.

"So I did. I was thinkin' it might be real romantic to die with my arms around my wife, and hers around me. Only her arms are tied. Would you let me untie her, so she can put her arms around me one last time? Maybe even let us have a last kiss?"

Tom hooted. "Shee-it. Ain't you the lovebirds? Who'd have ever thought it of Devil Devlin? All right, go ahead and untie her, an' take her gag off. But don't try nothin', Devlin. I'm gonna have my gun on you the whole time, and it would please me just as much to put holes in you in here as out there. I'm just grantin' a condemned man his last wishes out of the kindness o' my heart," Culhane said, guffawing again.

Mercy stared up at the man she loved while he undid her bonds, as calm as if they weren't just about to die.

"I love you, Sam," she whispered after he removed her gag, her voice hoarse from her attempts to scream past the cloth. She hated the fact that Culhane stood so close he could hear everything.

The rope had been so tight that her returning circulation sent pins and needles stinging through her arms and legs. Sam chafed her hands, then tipped up her chin with one finger. His blue eyes were large and luminous in the shadowy light. "And I love you, sweetheart. *Courage,*" Sam whispered back. Just words, but they steadied her trembling limbs as she got to her feet. *Courage.* Sam wanted her to die bravely, she thought, for it would rob Culhane of his victory if they did, and since Sam wanted it, that was what she would do.

She tried to recall some Bible verse that would give her additional fortitude, but the only fragment she could recall just echoed Sam's command: *"Be strong and of a good courage."*

"Put your hands on your heads, both of ya," Culhane ordered. "If I see either one of ya so much as twitch, we ain't waiting fer no last kiss." Wordlessly they complied.

Charity was weeping, her tears coming in great gulping sobs as she watched them go. Her hands were still tied, so she could not wipe them away.

"Don't worry, Charity," Mercy heard Sam murmur to her sister as she went past, and she had to fight the urge to laugh hysterically. *Don't worry? When Charity knows*

Culhane means to violate her just as soon as he kills her sister and Sam Devlin? How can he say such a thing?

They filed out into the yard and from there onto the waving sea of grass that grew high as a man's waist.

"Walk single file, with Miz Mercy in front," Culhane ordered.

As Mercy moved to comply, she had to pass Sam. "When I wink, get mad," he whispered.

What on earth does he mean? What on earth good will that do? Unless her anger was meant to act as a diversion. Suddenly she felt the courage he had asked her to have flowing strongly through her veins. Sam had a plan. He did not mean for them to die, meek as lambs.

The grass rustled as they walked through it, dry from the summer's heat, Mercy first, then Sam, with Culhane following, his guns cocked and aimed at them.

"This is far enough," Culhane called when they had gone perhaps fifty yards from the house. "Go ahead and kiss—how about if I shoot while you're kissin'? Then ya won't ever know what hit ya!" he jeered.

"No, I'd just as soon enjoy the whole kiss," Sam retorted. "Hey, Culhane, hold on a minute. I got another request."

"*Another* one?" Culhane snapped. "Naw, I ain't havin' no more o' yore stallin', Devlin. It's time fer you t' die."

"Aw, Tom, I was just gonna leave you somethin' you expressed some admirin' for, but if you aren't interested..." Sam said with reluctance, and opened his arms to Mercy.

"What is it, then?" Culhane asked. "Make it quick."

"Well, that day I bought these new boots you said how much you liked 'em," Sam said, pointing to the boots he was wearing, with the Lone Star stitched in the side of each. "And I'd always hoped to die with my boots off, in bed, as an old man. Well, it don't look like I'm gonna get the last part of my wish, but if you were to let me take my boots off, I could at least get the first part, and you could have the boots."

Tom snorted. "Well, that's right thoughtful of ya, Devlin. And I know that's all it is, 'cause I found your boot gun among your things in the soddy. I expect if you ain't wearin' 'em when ya die, they ain't as apt t' be all bloody, right?" He laughed his awful laugh again. "Shore, I'd be happy to take your boots. Go ahead and pull 'em off."

Mercy stared at Sam, wondering if fear had sapped his sanity. They were about to die, and he was worried about dying with his boots off and giving their murderer his boots?

Sam sat right down in the tall grass as if there was an easy chair beneath him. "Wife?" he drawled, turning away from Culhane, "I believe this is your job?" And then he winked.

"My job?" she gasped, her voice full of all the indignation she could muster. It wasn't hard to come up with indignation, either, as angry as she was at Culhane for the terror he had put them all through. "You have your nerve, Sam Devlin, ordering me around when it's your fault we're about to die! And as for you, you—you *ghoul,*" she said, glaring at Culhane as she picked up the proffered boot at the heel and began to pull it toward her, "if you have enough gall to wear my dead husband's boots, I hope you choke to death the minute you put them on, you, you sidewinder—"

"Now, wait jes' a gol' durned minute, woman," Culhane snarled. "I'll be danged if I'm gonna listen to your chin-waggin' while I'm nice enough t' let ya have these last few moments!" He leveled one of the Colts directly at her head and cocked it. "Think I'll jes' show ya what I think o' women who don't know their place—"

Suddenly the boot came free in her hand, and something metallic gleamed as it fell free. There was a blur of motion as Sam dived for his boot knife and threw it.

Chapter Twenty-Eight

"Hey, wha—"

Culhane never got to finish his question because the knife, embedded in his chest, stopped his heart before he could. Mercy saw him clutch at the knife hilt, desperately trying to pull it out, but it was too late. He went down heavily in the tall grass, a look of horrible surprise on his face.

Sam reached her side and threw his arms around her, shielding her from the sight of Culhane's twitching body until he was still.

"Oh, darlin', thank God you're safe. I love you so much," he breathed into her hair while she sobbed her relief against his chest. "You were so fine and brave."

"Oh, no, I wasn't, Sam Devlin," she cried, "I was scared to death! I thought we were going to die and that you just didn't want us to give him the satisfaction of begging."

"It was a near thing, too damned near," he admitted, punctuating the admission with a kiss to her forehead. She could feel the truth in the way his arms trembled as they held her.

"That knife throw was miraculous," she said, gazing up at him, marveling that she would be alive to look at him just this way for many years to come. "How did you know he would let you take your boots off, and that you'd be able to throw that knife in time?"

"I didn't," he confessed, rubbing his upper thigh as if it hurt. "Damn, but that bullet wound is achin' now. I didn't feel it at all when I grabbed for the knife. I did a lifetime of prayin' these last few minutes, Mercy. I was gonna try throwin' myself at him at the last possible second if this hadn't worked—"

"But you would have been killed! He would have shot you!" she cried, horror-struck.

"Maybe not. Culhane never was too great a shot," he said with a grin that wasn't entirely convincing. "But the important thing is I didn't have to try it, 'cause you did exactly what I wanted you to, Mercy, my wonderful, brave woman," he told her just before his lips descended on hers.

The kiss was tender and sweet, a homecoming, a promise of forever together.

All at once Mercy remembered, and jerked away from him. "Oh, heavens, Sam—Charity! She doesn't know what happened!" she said, wheeling and running back in the direction of the soddy. Behind her, Sam started running, too.

But Charity, whose feet had not been tied, had struggled to the door and was watching them come. Mercy and Sam arrived at the same instant, and as soon as they had removed her gag and untied her wrists, all three embraced, laughing and crying at the same time.

"You didn't—" Mercy began, hoping her sister had not seen the horrible moment when Sam had killed Culhane.

"No," Charity said, guessing what her sister couldn't bring herself to put into words. "Culhane was already down when I came out. Oh, Mercy, those were the longest few minutes of my life! I knew I ought to try and make a break for it, but I hated the thought of trying to escape while he was k-killing you, and I figured I couldn't get very far anyway, with my hands tied! I thought any second I would hear gunfire, and it would probably mean you were dead." She paused for a moment and wiped away a tear. "I couldn't move. It was as if I was paralyzed. But then when I heard nothing, I finally made myself come to the door."

Mercy drew a long breath. "It's a miracle we're alive."

"Amen," Sam murmured, an arm around each of them. "And now, maybe we ought to see about gettin' your sister back to town, Mercy. Your papa's bound to be worried sick about her. Maybe he'll manage to forgive me for takin' one of his daughters if I bring back the other one," he said with the ghost of a smile.

Mercy's smile faded. She had forgotten all about Papa and the conflict that still rose like a brick wall between them.

"I can't—" she began, her eyes raised to his.

"Looks like you're not going to have to take me to him," Charity interrupted, looking beyond them out over the prairie. "Look yonder."

As she turned, the sound of galloping horses penetrated her consciousness, and she saw a dozen horsemen riding over the prairie, heading straight for the soddy.

"It's Jase and Cookie and Manuel," Sam said, shading his narrowed eyes to watch them come. "And...it looks like Deacon Paxton, and half a dozen cowboys I've never seen before—and your papa."

But Mercy had already focused on the oldest man among the dozen, the one riding the chestnut gelding that normally only pulled her father's buggy when he had a pastoral call beyond Abilene. Conflicting emotions warred in her breast as she watched him come, knowing he had paid Culhane to kill Sam, but remembering that moment in the soddy when she had been fighting to save Sam's life and that still, small voice that had told her to forgive. But how could she forgive such a thing?

You must forgive. It's your father. You promised you would.

The party had to pass Culhane's body before reaching the soddy, and Mercy saw Sam's friends stop and dismount there. Then she focused on her approaching father.

Jeremiah Fairweather jumped off the chestnut, heedless of the fact that his only horse started to trot away and Deacon Paxton had to catch its reins. He ran to Charity first, throwing his arms around her and exclaiming, "Oh, thank God! You're all right, daughter?"

Charity hugged him back. "Yes, Papa," she said through her tears. "I was so afraid when Culhane captured me—right off the street! But Sam saved us all."

Fairweather turned to Sam. "I owe you a debt of gratitude, Sam Devlin—for both my daughter's lives," he said, his face solemn.

Sam's face was wary, his eyes guarded. "Y-you're welcome, sir."

Then her father turned to her. "Mercy, I'm so glad to see you. I've been so worried. Are you all right, too?" he asked, his hand visibly trembling as he reached for her.

"Yes, I'm fine... P-Papa," she said through lips that seemed strangely numb. Her heart hammered in her breast. "But I have to know right now, *why did you pay Culhane to kill my husband?*"

She felt everyone's eyes on her, but she kept hers trained on her father. He flinched as if she had struck him, and it seemed as if every drop of blood drained from his face.

"Mercy, I never asked Culhane to *kill* your...to kill Sam Devlin, and I never gave him so much as a penny," he said, his voice quavering but his gaze steady. "I swear it on your mother's grave."

"But he said—"

"Daughter, I have been guilty of great foolishness, for I trusted that despicable scoundrel, but I beg you to believe me when I say I did not desire Sam's death. Foolish as it sounds, I know, I believed Culhane would merely...remove Sam from here, from Abilene and from your life... somehow. He told me he wouldn't harm him, and I was a fool to believe him. And now I must beg your pardon and Sam's."

Mercy stared at him, openmouthed. "You thought you could just... *separate us* and that would be the end of it?"

Her father hung his head, and his shoulders sagged. His eyes, when he raised his head at last, were red rimmed and brimming with unshed tears.

"Yes, and I was wrong. I am aware now that my stubbornness and my ill-considered trust almost caused Sam's death. I would not want any man's death on my conscience, but especially not that of a man my daughter loves. All I can say is how deeply sorry I am, Mercy—and Sam. And I...I am prepared to accept now that you love this man...and that you wish to be his wife."

"I *am* his wife already, Papa. In every way," she said stiffly.

Sam stepped forward. "Sir, I reckon we could let bygones be bygones," he said, and extended his hand to her father.

Fairweather took it, but instead of leaving it at a simple handshake, he embraced Sam, smiling through his tears. "Welcome to the family, Sam."

The sight, and her father's words, crumbled the wall around Mercy's heart. She tried to blink back her own tears and failed.

She murmured, "Papa?" so softly and hesitantly that it didn't seem possible he could have heard it, but he did. He took a step away from Sam and opened his arms.

Mercy flew into them, crying, "Oh, Papa!" Nothing in this world—except for Sam's embrace, of course—felt as good as her father's arms around her, and knowing that he hadn't tried to hire Culhane to kill Sam. She kissed his wet, lined cheek, realizing that before today her father had never ever admitted to being wrong about anything. "Papa, I love you," she said, and they smiled at each other.

"And I you, daughter. If...if you still want me to, I'd be honored to marry you and Sam, or I'll accept that Deacon is a minister and you're already married, if you prefer," he added with a nod toward the bartender-minister, who was standing several yards away with the cowboys. "I've finally realized what a good man he is, however he earns his bread."

Before she could speak, however, Jase, Cookie and Manuel came over to them.

"Uh, boss, we found something on Culhane you might like to have," Jase said, holding out a small leather pouch to Sam. "It's that money that sidewinder took from you. We've been counting it while y'all were jawin'. Looks like Culhane spent some of it, but most of it's still there. Guess you won't leave Abilene poorer than when you came, after all," he said, grinning as he slapped Sam on the back.

"Thank the Lord," Sam said as he took it, to which Mercy's father said, "Amen!" and everyone laughed.

Sam put an arm around Mercy. "I can think of two things we're going to buy with it right away," Sam said, his smile infectious as he gazed down at her. "Supper for everyone and a night at the Grand Hotel for me and my bride—that is, if you can bear to leave your 'mansion on the prairie' here," he said, nodding wryly toward the soddy.

"Yes, I think I can bring myself to do so, if you'll throw in a hot bath," she said, grinning back.

"It's a deal," he told her, the warmth in his eyes hinting that he'd be happy to wash her back and anything else she wanted him to.

It took only a few minutes to gather up their belongings. When Sam emerged from the soddy carrying a bundle of clothing, he found Deacon Paxton waiting beside the same tall black stallion he had seen in the livery.

Sam held out his hand. "Deacon, I'm mighty obliged to you. My new father-in-law tells me you organized search parties to help find us."

"You're more than welcome, Sam," Deacon said, shaking his hand heartily. "I'm just glad everything turned out so well. I, uh . . ."

The bartender-minister's gaze seemed oddly intense to Sam. Not knowing what to make of that, Sam said, "Deacon, if you'd ever be interested in sellin' that black horse of yours—" he nodded toward the tall stallion whose reins Deacon was holding "—I'd sure be proud to buy him. I've been admirin' him in the livery, not knowin' who owned him. It's impossible, of course, but he sure looks like an older version of Goliad, the stallion my brother rode away to the war on. I've been plannin' to start my family's horse farm back up, and—"

"It's not impossible, Sam. It *is* Goliad."

Sam stared at the man. *"What are you saying?"*

Deacon Paxton smiled, and the grin lit his scarred face. The eye that wasn't patched twinkled. "I'm saying that this black stallion *is* the same horse I rode away to war on when you were just eighteen and mad as a rained-on rooster 'cause Mama was tryin' to keep you from marchin' away with the army just as Garrick and I had."

Sam felt his mouth drop open. "You're *Cal? The brother I thought was dead?*" Beside him, he heard Mercy's sharp intake of breath.

Cal nodded.

"It *is* you, isn't it?" Sam breathed, realizing why little things about the man—the shape of his eye, the way he smiled—had seemed faintly familiar each time they had met at the Alamo. All at once he realized the implications of his discovery and he was furious with the smiling man standing before him. "Then where the hell have you *been?*" snapped Sam. "When they told us you were missing, Mama kept hopin', even after the rest of us had given you up for dead. Her hair was black as coal when you left, remember? Hellfire, it's completely white now, and she looks like an old woman. She's worn black since the middle of the war, dammit! Couldn't you have written her, at least, and told her you were still alive?" he demanded bitterly.

"Sam," Mercy began reproachfully.

Caleb's smile faded somewhat. "I don't blame you for being angry, little brother. But I can explain. When that shell burst right next to me, blinding me in this eye," he said, pointing to the patch, "and knocking me half out, Goliad must have carried me off the field. The next thing I knew I was lying in some widow woman's farmyard with Goliad standing over me. I didn't have any idea who I was or where I was. Wouldn't have known I was a soldier if it hadn't been for the blue uniform. Lizabeth, the widow, patched me up and persuaded me not to go back to the army—not that that took much persuading, I admit. I still didn't remember anything, and by that time it was obvious that the Confederacy was going to lose. I decided to stay on the farm and help Lizabeth. We were married, but in the last days of the war she died in childbirth. The baby died, too."

Sam could only stare, astonished at what he was hearing. He was vaguely aware of the others standing around, their faces mirroring his own shock.

"I was so miserable I just left the farm without even bothering to sell it. I just took off," Cal went on. "I drifted for a while, roaming from town to town, figuring maybe I'd run into someone who could tell me who I was. I wasn't sure I'd ever had my own church and congregation, but I knew the Good Book pretty well, and I was just sure I was a preacher. Eventually I ended up in Abilene, and when the

Alamo opened I began tending bar. And then you came—"

"But didn't you recognize *me?*" Sam interrupted. "It's hardly surprising that *I* didn't put two and two together, with that patch and all, but didn't you know *me,* your own brother?"

Cal shook his head. "Not right away, but there was something about you, something familiar. And the feeling that I should know you, that I *did* know you, got stronger each time I saw you. That morning after the wedding breakfast, you said I reminded you of your brother who was a minister, remember? Well, that remark made me just about certain we were related, that *maybe* I was your missing brother. I told you to come talk to me before you and Mercy left town, and then I spent all night thinking and praying about it. By dawn my memory had all come back to me, but then you disappeared. I thought maybe I never would get the chance to tell you that we're brothers. But thank the Lord, here we are—*brother.*"

"Brother," Sam repeated numbly. It was too good to be true, but it was true. Caleb Devlin had returned from the dead. *Cal was alive!*

He grabbed his brother in an exuberant hug. Laughing, slapping each other on the back and even shedding a few tears, the two brothers embraced, and then Mercy was included in the joyous reunion.

"Mercy, I'm so glad you married my rascal of a baby brother. It was obvious from the first moment he darkened the door of the saloon he needed the right lady to tame him," Cal told her, grinning.

Mercy grinned back. "I'm not sure any woman could actually *tame* Sam Devlin. But maybe with you there to look over his shoulder, I can just sit back and enjoy being his wife."

Sam saw that Mercy's father wanted to say something to Cal. "Papa Fairweather—*may* I call you that, sir? I'd like to present my brother Caleb. Before the war he was the rector of the Brazos County Episcopal Church. 'Course, he ain't a Baptist, but I can now swear to the fact that he *is* a minister without a doubt."

"Always good to meet another man of the cloth, Deac—ahem, Caleb!" Jeremiah Fairweather said. "I...I have much to apologize to you for. And I hope you will believe I intended to do this even before your startling revelation to Sam. I've realized I was wrong to shun the folks who work in the saloons and the, ah, *other* businesses that cater to the cowboys. The church should welcome everyone, not just stuffy, self-righteous fools like me." There was a wry twist to his mouth. "You once offered to be my deacon, Caleb. Instead, I would like to very humbly beg you to become my copastor at the First Baptist Church of Abilene. The town's growing, you know, and before long we'll have to have a real church building."

As Sam watched, Cal smiled at the preacher regretfully. "I'm real honored, sir, and I know that your work in Abilene's really going to be blessed now."

"But?" the preacher asked.

"But now that I've found my brother, and remembered where I belong, I've got a hankerin' to see Texas and my family again."

"But you could just go down there and visit, and then return to Abilene, Cal. I need you here. *Abilene* needs you," Fairweather added persuasively. "You have a real gift for dealing with people—"

"You'll do fine without me, sir, now that you've figured out who your sheep really are," Cal insisted with a gentle smile. "I don't know if my church back in Brazos County still needs me, but I've got a family who does—and I've got the stud for our reborn Devlin stud farm, right, Sam? Old

Goliad here is getting long in the tooth, but I reckon he's got a few more great colts in him."

Sam, who'd been stroking the big black stallion's neck, laughed out loud. "The last of the Devlin line, and you're bringing him back home to Texas!" Sam let out a whoop, which made Goliad toss his head, but having been trained by the war, the horse stood steadily.

"Mercy, do you hear that? In a few years there won't be a horse who can catch up with any of Goliad's colts or fillies! I can't wait to see Mama's face, and Garrick's, and Annie's—there's a telegraph station in town, isn't there? Let's get back to Abilene. If I get any happier, I think I'll burst!"

That evening the party lingered over the remains of dinner in the main dining room of Abilene's Grand Hotel—Sam and Mercy, Cal, Jeremiah Fairweather and Charity, as well as the dozen cowboys who had formed the search party. The cook had outdone herself providing a feast on short notice—ham, chicken and roast beef, mashed potatoes and fresh-baked biscuits, and even a freshly made chocolate cake that would have to serve as a "wedding cake," though the roughly clad diners looked to the grumpy cook as if they had forgotten to wear their Sunday best for the occasion. Ah, well, this was Abilene, after all, the roughest town in Kansas. Just after the cake had been cut by a blushing Mercy, and the bride and groom had fed each other a piece, Wyatt Earp strolled through the door, with Mercedes LaFleche on his arm, and headed straight for the wedding party.

"You're just in time for cake," Sam called, welcoming them. Mercy glanced uneasily at her father, but he just smiled and moved over so that the newcomers could sit together by Sam and her.

The smiling Mercedes was resplendent in a gown of apple green silk taffeta that made her emerald eyes even greener. It had a high, lace-edged neck, but when the woman let a matching lacy shawl slip, Mercy could see a heart-shaped cutout over the bodice that did much to hint at the charms it covered. Wyatt, too, was nattily attired in a brocade waistcoat and gold watch chain under his black frock coat.

"Thanks, but we can't stay," Wyatt drawled. "We just wanted to drop by this wedding present." He handed an ornately carved wooden box to Mercy. "Careful, it's heavy."

It *was* heavy, so heavy she nearly dropped it. Inside lay what appeared to be hundreds of dollars in twenty-dollar gold pieces. "Oh, but we can't accept this," she breathed, looking to Sam for confirmation. "It's too much—you shouldn't have...."

"Oh, but he insists, don't you, Wyatt?" purred Mercedes.

Wyatt grinned and patted his companion's arm. "Yep, that I do. It's really Sam's money to begin with, Mrs. Devlin. I won it from him that first night he was here, and the loss of it probably led him to take a dare he would have had too much sense to otherwise," he said with a wink. "I just thought it'd be nice to give it back as a wedding present."

Sam stood and shook the cardsharp's hand. "I'm real grateful, Wyatt. I'm not takin' any more dares, but any time you want another card game, or a good horse, you just come on down to Texas, you hear?"

Mercy, stunned, added her thanks.

"It's a deal," Earp agreed. "And now, if you'll excuse us, Miss LaFleche has consented to spend the *evening* with me."

Mercy saw Wyatt Earp wink again at Sam, but this time the meaning of the wink was lost on her. She saw Sam's grin widen, however, and he winked back.

As the pair began to walk away, she turned to Sam and whispered, "Now, just what did you two mean by those winks? What's going on now, Mr. Sam Houston Devlin?"

Sam held up a finger to his lips and nodded toward her father, who had apparently been unaware of the byplay going on over his head. He was now pursuing Wyatt and Mercedes to the door, and Mercy heard him say, "Wyatt, Miss Mercedes, I'd like to invite you to come for services on Sunday."

Mercy smiled. "It'd almost be worth waiting around Abilene to see if they come. I can just picture Abigail Barnes's face, can't you, Charity?"

Her sister nodded, laughing, too.

Then, when Charity had turned back to hear something Jase Lowry was saying, Mercy turned to Sam. "Don't you think to distract me, Sam—why were you and Wyatt winking because he was spending the evening with Mercedes?"

"Because his evening looks like it's going to go on till morning," he whispered back. "Looks like Wyatt won, just like I did in the end." He gave her that smile that always made her all hot inside. "Now, isn't it time we tell our guests good-night?" he added with a meaningful nod toward the hotel stairway. "I think it's time we collected *our* winnings, also, Mrs. Devlin."

Epilogue

"Are you sure we can't persuade you to come with us right now?" Sam asked his brother. "The Alamo Saloon will get a new bartender soon enough, even if you did leave with us today! It seems awful to be sayin' goodbye to you, even for a little while, after just findin' you again, Cal."

Cal smiled up at Sam, already mounted on his buckskin gelding. "Aw, I couldn't leave the owner of the saloon flat like that, Sam—he's been awfully good to me, giving me a job and a place to live when I didn't even know who I was. I'll probably be just a few days behind you—maybe I'll even catch up to y'all on the trail. Besides, this way you can arrive just enough ahead of me to prepare Mama for my, umm, changed apppearance."

Sam sobered at that. "I will. But she'll just be glad that you're alive, Cal. We'll kill the fatted calf when you get there," Sam promised. "Lord, it'll be good to have you back home. With me bringin' home a bride and your being alive, we'll sure enough get Garrick to learn how to smile again! And there's a whole new crop of unmarried girls who'll sigh an' swoon about the bachelor preacher, just like they did before the war. Don't worry, they'll probably think that eye patch is romantic!" Sam laughed, and then he caught himself as he saw the cloud pass over his brother's face. "I'm sorry, Cal. I plumb forgot about you losin' your wife."

"That's all right, Sam," Cal said. "I've had time to accept losing Lizabeth, though I don't suppose one ever really gets over such a loss. And there *is* a girl back in Brazos County that I was thinking about last night—she's probably already married, though."

"Who is it, one of the Goodwin twins? They're both married and have five children between them," Sam teased.

"No, not one of the Goodwin twins," Cal said, but when Sam tried to josh him into revealing who he was thinking about, Cal became smilingly evasive.

Already mounted on the pretty pinto mare Sam had purchased for her, Mercy gazed fondly at her father and Charity. She had already hugged and kissed them goodbye. Since Papa now fully accepted that Caleb Devlin was a genuine minister, he had only asked to say a prayer of blessing over the newlyweds this morning before they rode out of Abilene to start on their journey to Texas.

He'd agreed to come soon for a visit, but she hadn't yet persuaded him to pull up stakes and move himself and Charity to Brazos County, Texas, to be with them. She suspected he was too enthused over his new plan to save the souls of the soiled doves and bartenders of Abilene's saloons and have them attend his church services.

"Oh, Mercy, I'm going to miss you so much!" Charity said, going over to clasp her sister's hand one more time. "You will write often, won't you?"

"Of course I will, and you'd better write back," Mercy commanded in her best older-sister tone. "You ought to come with us. I'm sure Sam would wait while you packed! Just think, Charity," she said, leaning down and lowering her voice so that only her sister could hear, "there'd be days and days to talk to Jase Lowry. I know you think he's good-looking."

Charity darted a glance at the cowboy, who was checking his cinch before mounting, and gave Mercy a wistful smile. "Yes, but what about Ned Webster? He's sweet on me, and he's ever so nice... and I like him, too. But if I marry him we'll probably never leave Abilene—Ned likes it just fine here! I'm so confused, Mercy," she said with a sigh.

Mercy reached down and ruffled her sister's blond curls affectionately. "There's no need to hurry and decide, Charity. You're only fifteen, after all. Besides, I'll bet Jase Lowry will be back again next summer, with another Devlin herd, or with some other outfit. Well, it looks like Sam is ready to head out. Be good, little sister, and look after Papa, won't you? Don't let him forget to eat."

"You know I'll take good care of him, though I hope I can learn to cook as good as you do! Mercy, I'm so glad you and Sam love each other."

"Me, too," Mercy said, blushing as she remembered just how *thoroughly* she'd been loved by her handsome Texan last night in their room in the Grand Hotel. "And to think we might never have met if *you* hadn't been staring at the cowboys through Moon's store window!"

* * * * *

Author Note

Abilene's first church building, a Baptist church, was erected later that same year of 1868.

Many of the places in Abilene mentioned in *Devil's Dare* actually existed. The Alamo Saloon was the premier establishment that catered to the Texas cowboys, and it was situated at the corner of Texas and Cedar streets. The Tw[illegible] Barns were but one of the many liveries in Abilene and we[illegible] located north of the railroad tracks that brought the cattle boom to Abilene. Moon's Frontier Store may have been the first mercantile, and many a Kansas sodbuster's wife or daughter spent precious hours in there, dreaming over the yard goods and dress patterns. The Drover's Cottage was located right next to the stockyards, and "Colonel" and Mrs. Gore were its host and hostess.

As anyone who has seen the Kevin Costner movie *Wyatt Earp* will attest, Wyatt Earp had a checkered career before becoming the famous lawman who cleaned up Tombstone, Arizona. *Texas: An Informal Biography,* by Owen White, the book that first began my thinking of how a Texas hell-raiser and a preacher's daughter might come to fall in love, mentions Wyatt Earp being a cardsharp in Abilene in its early boom days.

Abilene was only a rip-roaring cattle town for a few years. In 1867 the Kansas Pacific Railroad brought both prosperity and a culture clash to the infant town. It was not until 1870 that serious attempts were made to control the Texans' wild behavior. The first few sheriffs did not last long, but when Wild Bill Hickok accepted the job, law and order began to settle in Abilene for good. By 1872, however, the railroad had moved farther west, and the cattle trade became divided up between the cities of Newton, Ellsworth and Wichita. The boom in Abilene was over, and many of the saloon girls and cardsharps left, leaving Abilene perhaps duller but a decidedly safer place.